T0312294

THE WAVE

THE WAVE

A Novel

Christopher Hyde

DOUBLEDAY & COMPANY, INC.
GARDEN CITY, NEW YORK
1979

PUBLISHED BY DOUBLEDAY
a division of Random House, Inc.

All characters in this book are fictitious,
and any resemblance to actual persons,
living or dead, is purely coincidental.

A hardcover edition of this book was
published in 1979 by Doubleday

Copyright © 1979 by Christopher Hyde
All rights reserved. No part of this book may be reproduced or transmitted
in any form or by any means, electronic or mechanical, including
photocopying, recording, or by any information storage and retrieval system,
without written permission from the publisher.
For information, address Doubleday, a division of Random House, Inc.

DOUBLEDAY and the portrayal of an anchor with
a dolphin are registered trademarks of Doubleday,
a division of Random House, Inc.

Original Jacket Design by Lewis Friedman

The Library of Congress has cataloged the
hardcover edition as:

Card Number 78-22328

First paperback edition published 2003
Hardcover Edition: ISBN: 0-385-14762-7
Paperback Edition: 0-385-51301-1

AUTHOR'S NOTE

The technical material contained in this book is accurate. The Mica Dam exists as and where I describe it. The geological studies made for the Mica Dam have never been released, nor has any of the studies made to assess the possibility of a major slide into the Mica Reservoir. The same is true of studies and tests done for the new High Revelstoke Dam, currently under construction. The press has frequently requested that this material be made public, but the British Columbia Hydro Authority has refused. Members of the British Columbia engineering fraternity have also consistently refused to comment on the possibility of a slide at the Mica or at the new High Revelstoke Dam. Information contained in this book relating to the other dams on the Columbia system is also accurate, as is all the information on dam disasters in the past, both in North America and elsewhere.

During the closed congressional hearings into the Teton Dam disaster of 1976 the question of multiple dam collapses was brought up, but no hard information was provided by the director of the Bureau of Reclamation. This man has since retired.

The hearings revealed that the Teton collapse, a result of poor site planning and geological studies, was far from an isolated incident. There are at least eight such dam sites in the United States, and at least that many nuclear facilities located on or close to major geological fault areas. There is at least one such situation in Canada, as well as a reactor that is located directly below a containment structure that is more than fifty years old. This reactor was also the site of the first major accident at a nuclear facility.

During the course of the Teton hearings it was also disclosed that there have been more than seventy dam failures in the United States since 1935 and three major reactor failures since 1950, including a potentially disastrous one at the Enrico Fermi Reactor located just outside the city of Detroit.

In 1978 it was revealed that a gigantic radiation accident had occurred in the Soviet Union in the early fifties—an accident that killed at least four thousand people and was caused by poor siting of fissionable materials at a radioactive waste dump much like the one at Richland, Washington.

The Richland material in this book is founded in fact, although the Richland fast breeder is still under construction. All information concerning accidents at the Richland Nuclear Reservation is true.

There is no such organization as the Office of Environmental Safety and Inspection. In fact, there is no government body in the United States responsible for the regular inspection of dams. Nor is there an Emergency Planning Council, such as the one I have described, in the United States or Canada.

The last major flood on the Columbia River occurred in 1948, and despite the supposed flood-control valve of the various dams on the river, many lives were lost and millions of dollars worth of damage was done.

Design criteria for the Mica Dam were based on only fifteen years of flood-level fluctuation data, although it is well known that many rivers have a maximum flood cycle as long as a hundred years; in other words, no one can accurately say when the next major flood on the Columbia will occur or how large it will be.

At the time of writing there is no disaster-warning system for any of the dams on the Columbia River, or on any other river in North America.

While the bulk of the material on this book is based on fact, the characters and events are fictional, and any resemblance to persons living or dead is entirely coincidental.

CHRISTOPHER HYDE

THE WAVE

PROLOGUE

The Lear jet split the gathering dusk, its tail burnished gold by the setting sun. Alone, in the rear of the plane's dimly lit passenger compartment, two men sat in high-backed swivel chairs. The only sound was the roar of the jet engines, muffled by the thick acoustic insulation under the compartment's dark wood paneling.

The man facing the rear of the aircraft was slim and white haired. He was dressed in an impeccably tailored gray suit. He stared out the thick oval window, watching as a final shard of sun flamed on a snow-capped peak of the Canadian Rockies, ten thousand feet below. The man seated opposite him appeared to be a few years younger. His close-cropped military-style haircut was only just beginning to lose its dark color. He was a bulky man, wide shouldered and barrel chested. He looked uncomfortable in the dark blue, off-the-rack suit he was wearing, as though his thick body was unaccustomed to civilian clothes.

As the last of the sun fled behind them the man in the gray suit turned away from the window and spoke. His voice was soft, but held an underlying vein of tension.

"I presume we can take it for granted that the Canadian figures are accurate?" he said.

The other man nodded. His tongue was dry against the roof of his mouth. He desperately wanted a drink, but he knew from the trip west the previous day that the jet carried nothing but mineral water. He swallowed and then cleared his throat noisily, running his tongue across his thick lips.

"The figures are accurate," he mumbled nervously. "Better than ours. But then they knew about the problem right from the beginning."

"They didn't seem to be unduly upset," said the man in the gray suit.

The other man gave a short, barking laugh. "They were upset. They just didn't know what to do about the situation. They're bureaucrats, not engineers. They're worrying more about the political implications than the geological problem."

"One begets the other," said the man in the gray suit with a thin, humorless smile. He stroked his eyebrow with one manicured finger. "A public disclosure this close to the new Columbia Treaty signing could be ruinous for them, and for the federal government."

"Ruinous for us, too," said the heavy man, shifting uncomfortably in his chair. "The only openhanded way of dealing with this thing is to drain the entire Mica Reservoir. That's a multimillion-dollar problem."

"More than that," said the man in the gray suit. "We're talking about more than a simple, short-term loss of power. Any tampering with the Columbia flow rate is going to effect all the industries that use the river's power, not to mention the fact that it would throw the treaty negotiations into a cocked hat." The man paused and looked out the window again. Outside the night had fallen completely and he could see nothing but the distorted, ghostly reflection of his own face. "We're talking about one-third the hydroelectric power for the United States," he said, almost to himself. "We're talking about billions of dollars, not millions." He turned and looked at the other man, his face blank and expressionless. "The Teton disaster in 1976 did enough damage to us, General, and the Teton was a flyspeck in comparison to the Mica. And there is no way we can deny our own culpability in this affair. We pressured for that site from the beginning. The Canadian plan, the one that we refused to accept, had no diversions that high on the Columbia. We knew about the geological problem, and we knew about the quality of the fill that was used. As ye sow, so shall ye reap."

"Pardon?" said the other man.

"The chickens are coming home to roost, General," said the man in the gray suit, a sour note in his voice.

"So what do we do?" asked the general.

"Our course of action depends on a number of things." The other man paused. Finally, he held up his left hand and began ticking off points on his fingers, one by one. "First, how sure are we that the slide will come down? Second, what is the time frame for such an occurrence? Third, is there any way we can expose the Canadian error without implicating ourselves and precipitating a full-scale investigation?" He looked at the other man, his eyes suddenly cold. "A full-scale investigation of both our organizations, General. I think we both understand what that would mean." The man in the gray suit now held up only his little finger. Its base was encircled by a narrow silver ring, the delicately carved skull-and-crossbone design it bore barely discernible. "Fourth, we stand to lose much more than the Canadians if the maximum damage projection is accurate. Their problem begets ours, but we will be the ones in the most trouble. Given that, and if the Canadians are not willing to act, what kinds of intervention should we be considering, and how should they be implemented?"

The general pursed his lips thoughtfully, considering. "I'm not quite sure what you mean by 'interventions,' but the rest of it is pretty straightforward. The slide will come down. It's just a matter of time. That survey they ran leaves no doubt. The computer says it'll be sometime after full pool, which is normally in the first week of July. We may get lucky, though. Our people say the pack is still solid. Melt's about two weeks late already. If it stays cool and dry, we may be able to get through the end of July before things start to happen. If we put some pressure on the Canadians between now and then, maybe we can get them to carry the ball."

"I don't think we can take that chance," said the man in the gray suit softly, his fingers drumming on the curved sill of the window. The other man watched the rapidly moving fingers and the flashing silver ring and felt a cold shiver of fear run up his spine. The man in the gray suit looked out and down at the night-shrouded earth. The mountains were almost invisible now, their hulking forms merely shadows in the darkness. "All we can do for now is hope it doesn't rain," he said.

Two miles below, a pebble no larger than a thimble dislodged itself from the earth and began to roll. It skittered down the steeply canted slope, bouncing and rattling over projections and ricocheting off larger boulders. It struck the exposed root of a recently toppled juniper bush and arced into the air. It spun down through the darkness, finally striking the placid surface of the reservoir with a muted plop. The tiny ripples began to fan away from the base of the mile-high slope, fading into the darkness as they moved inexorably toward the upstream face of the gigantic dam, 850 feet high, that held back the massive lake. By the time the ripples traveled the seven and a half miles to the dam, they would cause nothing more than a microscopic shifting of molecules. But they would reach the dam, and their message would be acknowledged.

It had begun.

PART ONE:
CREEP

PART ONE

Chapter One

JUNE 13

Jonathan Kane lay in bed and listened to the water trying to hammer its way through the roof of his house. Thirty-four straight days of it, a continuous dissonant symphony of drumming, sprinkling, tapping, gurgling, and dripping. If it doesn't stop soon, thought Kane, the entire city of Seattle is going to wrinkle up like a prune and float out into Puget Sound.

He pulled the covers up over his head, but the sound of the rain was still there, and with it the knowledge that he would have to endure one more day of thumping windshields, lethal umbrellas, and the all-encompassing gray shroud of mist that seemed to have covered the city forever.

It wasn't that he minded rain, at least not in its proper place. Kane had grown accustomed to the endless drizzle of the West Coast winter and to the endless smart-ass cracks that at least he didn't have to shovel it. More than an inch of rain a day between November and March was a fact of life in the Pacific Northwest, but this was mid-June. It wasn't fair, thought Kane, curling his toes in the cozy warmth beneath the blankets, wondering if he'd somehow managed to sleep through the summer and that it was November again.

Another sound began to filter through the other damp noises

and into his waking brain—the regular swishing of tires on wet pavement. Kane sighed. The day had begun. With a jerking motion he hauled himself out of the seductive warmth of the bed.

"Jesus!" he groaned, weaving slightly. He gazed at the framed MIT diploma on the far wall above his chest of drawers. A blur. He turned, rummaging in the litter on his bedside table until he found the case for his contact lenses. He took the case and shuffled out of the bedroom and into the hall. As he negotiated the obstacle course of stacked books, he made a mental note to get some shelves. He'd made the same mental note every morning for a month, but so far he hadn't built or bought anything to hold the welter of hardcovers and paperbacks. He really would have to do something about it, he thought as he reached the bathroom. After all, he'd been living in the house for almost six months. He shook his head blearily. Had it really been that long? It could have been yesterday. He felt a brief contraction in his stomach as he remembered the scene before Ruth had walked out on him and gone back to her goddamn Social Register family in Boston. He looked around the bathroom. If Ruth's mother could see this place, it would confirm all her worst suspicions.

The bathroom was in worse shape than the hall, if that was possible. There were four dirty shirts soaking in a foul scum of detergent in the tub and a couple of half-clean ones sagging from the shower curtain rail. The floor was a litter of towels and the soap dish on the sink held an uncapped stick of deodorant that had long since given up the ghost.

He peered into the open medicine chest. It was empty except for his lens-cleaning solution, a disposable razor that had seen better days, and a mangled tube of toothpaste. What would they say at the office? By day, a compulsively tidy engineer-geologist, filling his waking hours with the meticulous analysis of computer printouts and stratigraphic analysis charts. And at night? Shazam! Superslob! He groped for the lens solution and began his morning toilet, wondering if there was any way he could convince Chuck to pitch in and repair the damage. He seriously doubted it.

Twenty minutes later, vision restored, he struggled into one of the three identical seersucker suits that made up his entire summer wardrobe and went downstairs to the kitchen.

He brewed himself a pot of espresso and drank two quick cups standing by the stove. He took a third cup into the living room and pushed back the curtains, wondering as usual what could have possessed him to rent a house that looked out on the parking lot of a fast-food outlet.

HERFY'S, said the sign, its logo a black bull on a yellow ground. Home of the Herfyburger. Once, after a hard day of meetings with representatives from the Bureau of Reclamation and the Army Corps of Engineers, Kane had actually been stupid enough to try a Herfy Combo. It had been a fittingly revolting end to a rotten day and he'd never repeated the experience. Ever since, just looking at the sign made him slightly queasy.

Kane searched through the jumble of cups, ashtrays, and old newspapers on the coffee table and found a battered package of Camels. He lit one and turned back to the window.

Rain. Puddles of it in the Herfy's lot, rivers of it in the gutters. Cedar shingles wet with it on the roofs of the faded pastel houses beyond. The leaves of the magnolia tree in front of his window dripping with it. Vague sheets of it drifting down from the dull pewter sky. As he watched, sipping his now-lukewarm coffee, a puddle of water grew behind a lip of soil at the edge of his garden. The puddle was slowly climbing the lip and threatening to flow down the shallow slope to the edge of the Herfy's parking lot. Then a small section of topsoil at one side of the puddle slipped into the pool. Its ripples were enough to send the first trickles over the lip. Within a few seconds the lip had crumbled away and the water flowed freely downhill, forming a grimy puddle in the parking lot. Given sufficient time and water, the stream would deposit enough soil to provide a flowerbed. The idea of a flowerbed at a Herfy's was ridiculous, but the implication of the small stream scouring the soil wasn't funny at all.

Kane's responsibilities as regional director of the Office of Environmental Safety and Inspection took in all the American dams on the Columbia River from the Grand Coulee to the Bonneville, as well as a dozen or more major industrial sites including the massive Richland Nuclear Reservation and Radioactive Waste Storage Depository that spanned the Columbia just above the

twin cities of Pasco and Richland. A rain like this, coupled with
the heavy, late-melting snowpack in the Canadian Rockies, was
raising water levels in the reservoirs of all the dams. The Canadian dams on the Columbia were out of his jurisdiction, and consequently he had no hard information on the situation north of
the border, but he was sure that it wasn't good.

There were three Canadian Columbia dams: the Hugh Keenleyside Dam at the foot of the Arrow Lakes, just above the international border; the High Revelstoke Dam a hundred miles or
so farther upriver, five miles north of the mountain city of Revelstoke, British Columbia; and the largest of the three, eighty-five
miles north of the High Revelstoke—the Mica, the largest dam
of its kind in the world, the headwater dam of the Columbia
power system. With its 135-mile-long reservoir, the Mica was the
key to one third of the hydroelectricity in the United States.

The American dams were concrete; the Canadian dams were
earthfill—little more than gigantic, scientifically designed piles of
dirt. Kane had never liked earthfill dams. He sipped his coffee
and stared out at the puddled surface of the Herfy's lot. Give
him concrete any day of the week. Not that it mattered much
any more. He seriously doubted that he'd ever be involved in the
building of another dam. He took another sip of his coffee. The
large salary offered by the OESI had wooed him away from real
engineering work, and he knew that the nice fat paycheck he got
every two weeks would be a hard habit to break. He had hoped
one day to set up his own engineering firm. He'd certainly had
enough experience. A geology degree from CalTech. Three years
with a big New York survey company, two and a half years with
the Corps of Engineers in Vietnam, and then his engineering degree from MIT. Yes, he could have done it easily. Ruth's family
would have put up the money to keep him afloat. He could have
made it big eventually. That was the problem. Ruth's family. He
couldn't have stood that. So when the job at OESI had come up,
he'd jumped at it, and Ruth even went along with it for a while.
But eventually Seattle and the life of a petty bureaucrat's wife
got to her, and she went running back to papa's big bucks.

Kane sighed. What the hell, it was over now. There was no
sense going over and over it. The divorce would be through in a

month, or even less, and that would be that. He had more important things to think about. Like the rain.

He butted his cigarette and swallowed the remains of his cold coffee. Picking his raincoat up off the floor, he went outside. He was wet by the time he reached the battered convertible he called the Garbage Can, and by the time he reached the Fiftieth Street freeway ramp, he was wetter still, courtesy of a steady trickle down his neck from an invisible leak in the canvas roof.

"You're wet," said Gladys as he entered the ninth-floor offices of OESI. Gladys Petrick was the office manager, which was almost a contradiction in terms, considering that there was almost no office to manage. Other than Kane and Gladys there were only two secretaries, neither of whom was at her desk.

"Soaking wet," Gladys elaborated. She took his coat from him and put it neatly on a hanger, clucking and wagging her head mournfully. Gladys was about twenty-five years into childless widowhood. She had one of the most incredible hairdos Kane had ever seen—a complex twisting of combs, swirls, and rolls. In blonde. After a number of surreptitious investigations Kane had discovered it was her natural color.

To Gladys, Kane was both the husband she had lost and the child she never had. At first Kane had balked at the role, but finally he had given in, gracefully. Gladys was not someone you argued with.

He picked up the day's mail from the reception desk. Gladys looked pointedly at the IBM clock on the outer office wall. It was nine-thirty.

Kane followed her glance. "Traffic," he said, explaining.

"Uh-huh." Gladys was not convinced.

"Where are the girls?" asked Kane, more to change the subject than because he wanted to know.

Gladys snorted. "Karen is taking her public administration course and Leslie phoned in sick."

"Oh," said Kane. He took the mail into his own office and sat down at the round table that served as his desk. A moment later Gladys followed, a mug of steaming instant coffee in her hand. Decaffeinated. For the first few months Kane had tried to convert Gladys to the joys of espresso, but once again Gladys had been firm. It was caffeine, she said, that had been her late husband's downfall, and she wasn't going to lose her boss as well.

She handed the mug to him and he took it. He sipped and winced. It was god-awful, just like the weather.

"Great," he said, gesturing with the mug, and forcing a smile.

"Better than that sulphuric acid you like," she muttered, tight lipped.

Kane wondered if Harry had died of caffeine or an overdose of Gladys. He put down the coffee and lit a cigarette, ignoring Gladys's look of disgust.

"What's on tap for today?" he asked, blowing a cloud of smoke at her. Gladys cleared her throat pointedly and began rattling off his schedule. With her around, Casanova wouldn't have needed a datebook.

"Kellog from the Bonneville Power Authority at ten. Lunch with Johnson from Techtron at eleven. Nothing for lunch. The only thing for this afternoon is that Strand person about his effluent problem."

"Wonderful," sighed Kane. "Anything else?"

"Yes. Washington turned down your request for more time on the computer, and Benson called to say that the last report from Richland was next to useless because of the security blackouts."

"Kellerman again," grunted Kane. "You'd think they were still working on the first A-bomb out there."

Gladys, frowning, continued. "You have the dam inventory material in front of you and you had a call from a woman."

"A woman?" said Kane, feigning disbelief.

Gladys's frown deepened. "She said her name was Chuck and that you'd know who it was."

"I do," said Kane, trying to keep a straight face.

Gladys added a steeply arched eyebrow to her frown. "Chuck!" she hissed under her breath. She turned on her heel and marched out of the office. Kane reached for the phone and dialed. His call was answered on the first ring by a voice like a croupy foghorn.

"*Post!* Bullpen! Brooks!" Kane had called Chuck at the *Post Intelligencer* often enough to know what the man was talking about. According to Chuck, Brooks was the best man in the city room. Kane had his doubts. The man sounded as though he'd be more suited to a hog-calling contest.

"Charlene Daly, please," Kane asked and held the phone away, knowing what was coming next. Even with the receiver six inches from his ear, Brooks's voice was deafening.

"Hey, Chuck!" he bellowed. Kane moved the phone back and waited, wondering when Chuck was going to get a private line. A few moments later she came on the phone, breathing hard.

"Charlene Daly," she said, puffing.

"It's Jon," said Kane.

Chuck's voice brightened. "Hi there! Long time no see!"

"Since last night."

"That's long enough," said Chuck, getting her breath. "So what's happening?"

"I don't know, you phoned me. Remember?"

"Oh yeah, right," said Chuck. "Things are a bit crazy here. Some clown jumped off the space needle and it turns out he was the mayor's brother-in-law or something. Quite the scandal."

"Who am I to compete with the mayor's brother-in-law?" said Kane.

"I bet you play a better game of pool than he ever did. Anyway, funny man, that's why I phoned. I just wondered if we were on for a game tonight."

"You bet," said Kane. "A glass of wine, a cue ball, and thou."

"Yeah, but in what order?" asked Chuck.

"First the cue ball, then the wine, then the thou."

"That sounds pretty good," said Chuck. "Eight?"

"Eight. I'll be in the basement fondling the rosin."

"Ugh!" groaned Chuck, and hung up.

Kane leaned back in his chair, trying to imagine his exwife and Chuck in the same room. After a few seconds he gave up. They had absolutely nothing in common. And as far as Kane was concerned, that was just perfect.

He had met Chuck entirely by accident. Kane had been looking at pool tables in a downtown billiard outfitters and Chuck had walked in. The house he had rented had a table in the basement, but for years Kane had wanted a full-size Brunswick, something Ruth would never have allowed. He'd played the game a lot as a kid, and honed his skills at CalTech and in Vietnam. Chuck's experience had been much more direct; her father owned a chain of pool halls in Pittsburgh.

Chuck later admitted that she'd set her sights on him as soon as she saw him in the store. According to her the sight of Kane's six-foot-one frame and curly blond hair had been overwhelming. Kane told her it was probably his technique with bridge shots. They'd played a few test games on a table Kane thought he might buy, and her short slim body, bright oval face, and tousled thatch of short russet hair had played hell with his game. So he had summoned up his courage and demanded a rematch in his basement. To his surprise, she accepted on the spot and asked him if dinner came with the replay.

The rest of the afternoon seemed to fly by. Kane found himself keeping up with Chuck's hectic pace as she roared from one errand to the next in the big old Mercedes Benz she handled like a stock-car driver. As night fell they slowed down, to Kane's relief, and traded biographies over dinner. By the time they finally reached Kane's house and began playing it was as though they had known each other for years, not hours.

They played eight games. Chuck took him six to two. At midnight she set her cue abruptly down on the table. She walked over to him, reached up, pulled his face down to hers and gave him a long, lingering kiss, her tongue weaving around his in a way that would never have occurred to Ruth. Then she stood back, looking up at him.

"Good," she whispered.

Kane just stood there, his mouth hanging open.

"Good what?" he managed at last.

Chuck smiled. "I knew we had something on the first break," she said. "I was just making sure."

"Oh," said Kane. It came out as a grunt.

Chuck took him by the hand and began leading him away from the table toward the basement stairs.

"C'mon, Johnny-boy, let's go fuck each others' brains out."

They did just that. That night, and during the nights that followed they made love passionately and often, Kane slowly but surely sloughing off the gray depression that had shrouded him since splitting up with Ruth.

Kane sat forward in his chair again and wondered momentarily if he was falling in love with Chuck. He banished the thought quickly. He wasn't ready for that. He reached behind him and pulled the thick Dam Inventory file out of his "Urgent" box. The big boys in Washington were depending on him to complete the inventory before they got into the preliminary negotiations on the treaty, and he was their leading expert on the Columbia and its dams. He opened the file, frowning, still annoyed that he had been refused more time on the computer. How the hell was he supposed to do a half-decent job if he couldn't get at the information? He lit another cigarette and began to write. Outside, the rain was still streaming down.

Max Rudnick, chief of security for the Richland Nuclear Reservation, snorted blasphemously as the red mud oozed up over his shoes and stained the sharply creased cuffs of his trousers.

A hundred yards away, across the almost flat expanse that was Storage A, the five-man radiation detection squad trudged abreast in line. As they walked slowly forward, the ground mist from the steady drizzle swirled around the baggy legs of their bulky radiation suits and condensed on the blank-faced helmets they wore. Against the lifeless thousand-acre plain of the storage area, they looked like actors in a science-fiction movie.

Rudnick swore again, peering at the men as they moved closer. At least their suits were keeping them dry. Meanwhile he had to stand out here in the rain up to his keister in mud just to make sure they did their job right. If the goddamn rain hadn't washed out the service road, he would have been able to stay in the car. As it was, he'd had to walk the last few hundred feet to the edge of the site.

He watched as the squad veered off to investigate a new area. He wished to hell they'd hurry it up. A thousand feet beyond them, barely visible though the curtain of rain, Rudnick could make out the steel-gray ribbon of the Columbia River. He squinted, trying to see how high the water had risen since yesterday. He shook his head and frowned, his thick lips pulling down into a tense grimace. If it rained much longer, they'd have to start sandbagging the whole perimeter.

He stuffed his hands deeper into the pockets of his poplin raincoat and gritted his teeth. The pains were getting worse. The

clawed stub of his right fist throbbed dully, and the fire in his
gut was almost enough to make him double over. He remained
where he was, stiff and motionless, the rain running down his
face. He wasn't about to give the men on the rad squad anything
to laugh at. He decided to wait another couple of minutes to see
if they found the leak and then he'd go back to the car. He
blinked the rain from his eyes and continued watching.

He'd had days like this back on the force in Chicago. Worse
even, but he'd been younger then, a lot younger. Once he'd
stayed out in January for three days, dressed like a wino, staking
out a drug meet. It had been worth it. He'd made the bust, and
when a pusher fought him, he'd broken the punk's arm. But
what the hell was he doing standing in a mud puddle in the middle of Washington State? There probably wasn't even a leak.
Just those goddamn EPA types complaining about dead fish
again.

There was a sudden flurry of activity among the white-coated
figures of the rad squad. The man on the right-hand end of the
line had stopped and was bent low over his Tracerlab detector.
Then he stood up and waved a gauntleted hand. The other four
men closed in on him in tight formation. They'd found something.

"Shit," Rudnick said under his breath. There was a leak. He
could see his whole guard schedule going out the window. He'd
have to assign a whole detail to the area, and the roster was
stretched to the breaking point already.

As he watched the eerie figures outlining the perimeter of the
leak, another pain tore through his stomach. He shuddered.

"Screw it," he grunted. He turned on his heel and slogged his
way back to the car.

Once inside the black government-issue station wagon, the
pain in his stomach eased somewhat and he began to feel a little
better. He pulled the package of cheap Coronas off the dashboard and lit one, savoring the harsh taste of the tobacco. He
dragged on the cigar for a few moments, waiting for his stomach
to return to normal. He belched loudly and grimaced. Goddamn
gas. Outside, the steady rain hammered on the roof of the car and
fogged the windshield in front of him. Kellerman and his lousy

budgets, dumb turkeys like Haberman his assistant, and all the rest of the crap. And now the rain. And a leak.

He turned on the ignition, battered the car into gear, and slued away from the storage site, spewing a rooster tail of mud.

As he reached the gates leading into the reactor compound he slowed, easing the car through the maze of buildings, most of them empty since the cold war boom in atomic weapons had eased off in the late sixties. He maneuvered the car between the megalithic remains of the old Hanford One Reactor where the active ingredients for the bombs dropped on Hiroshima and Nagasaki had been produced. As he headed south toward the administration complex on the far side of the reservation, Rudnick snorted loudly around the wet stump of his cigar. This was one place they didn't include on the guided tour. It looked too much as though they'd lost the war, somehow.

He didn't give a good goddamn. Maybe if they'd dropped a few more of those bombs. On Moscow or Peking. Then he wouldn't have to be beating his ass into hamburger trying to guard this pile of junk. He rolled down the window and spat the remains of his cigar out into the rain. Maybe Richland had been a big deal once, but now it was nothing. Just a headache for people like him. Except for the new experimental fast breeder, the only work done at Richland was storing waste. Rudnick reached for another cigar. A night watchman in a garbage dump, that's what he was.

He pulled into the administration parking lot and parked as close as he could to the water-stained cinder-block building. He went into the building. It was noon, and most people were in the main-floor cafeteria. He banged open the fire doors to the basement stairwell and clattered down. His office was located at the administration end of the service tunnel that connected the building with the fast breeder site, a quarter of a mile to the south.

Rudnick's office said nothing about the man who worked in it. Ten by ten, the walls peeling government green, twotone. The only furniture was a vintage government desk, bracketed by a matched pair of scarred surplus filing cabinets, and two chairs, one for the desk and one for Rudnick's infrequent visitors. The left-hand wall, beside the door, held a large-scale plan of the entire reservation, while the wall to the right contained the guard roster blackboard.

Rudnick eased his heavyset frame through the narrow doorway. He slid out of his wet raincoat, wincing as his hand caught on the sleeve, and draped the garment over the visitor's chair. Then he closed and locked the door and sat down at his desk.

He held out the scarred talon of his right hand. It hurt. The thumb was almost twice the size of the one on his other hand, and turned in toward the palm. The two middle fingers and the index finger were welded together by angry red bands of scar tissue, and the fingers themselves were shriveled and bent, the bones so badly broken that they were pulled down into a permanent crook. The little finger was missing completely, sliced off at the knuckle. He flexed the hand experimentally and gritted his teeth as a shrieking pain tore up his arm. Six months and the pain will be gone, the doctor had said. That had been more than ten years ago.

With his left hand he pulled open the center drawer of his desk and took out a pill bottle and a container of Maalox tablets. He shook four of the capsules from the pill bottle onto the desk and added half a dozen of the thick ulcer tablets. He took a key from his jacket pocket, unlocked the side file drawer, took out a half-empty pint of rye, unscrewed the cap, and took a long pull. Then he began taking the pills, washing each one down with the whisky. When he was finished with the pills, he leaned back in his chair and closed his eyes, his hand still wrapped around the bottle of rye. For the thousandth time he told himself that he should see the reservation doctor about the pain in his stomach. But the hand was bad enough. If Kellerman thought he had an ulcer, he'd use it as an excuse to get rid of him. Rudnick hated his job, but he knew that these days there wasn't a hell of a lot else available for a crippled excop. No. He'd keep on with the pills until they stopped working and then . . . well, he'd see. Anyway, the pain would be gone soon, for now anyway.

Paula St. George slipped quietly out of the noise and smoke-filled office of the Greentree Association, hoping that Ron hadn't seen her go. The last thing she wanted was for him to come rushing out, like a mother hen, and ask her why she was leaving.

She walked down the narrow stairway and let herself out of the scarred door of the small decrepit building in Vancouver's water-front district. The light drizzle and relatively fresh air of Hastings Street were a relief after the meeting. She crossed Hastings and went up Howe Street toward the parking lot where she'd left the MG. The staccato clacking of her boot heels on the wet pavement hammered out her frustration and her anger.

She was furious. She'd thought the whole thing out carefully, leaving almost nothing to chance. She'd spent hours rehearsing how she'd present the idea to the Greentree Executive, but when she finally did it, they had ignored her. They had tossed the idea aside as though it had been an idle flight of fancy on her part. And Ron! The guy she lived with, and he hadn't even had the guts to back her up. That great, round, embarrassed baby face of his. As though he was ashamed that he even knew her.

She frowned, the lines on her forehead marring the almost flawless beauty of her face, the rain plastering trails of long black hair to her smooth cheeks. She nodded to herself. It was time. She and Ronald Bateman, high and mighty chairman of the Greentree Association, were going to have it out once and for all. If he wanted to live in his fantasy world of bullshit sixties peace and love, he was welcome to, but he'd have to do it without her. That kind of thing was all over. If you wanted to change the world, you had to fight.

She reached the parking lot and tucked her long legs into the small canary-yellow car. She turned on the ignition and sat waiting for the engine to warm up, her long, buff-colored nails tapping angrily on the wooden steering wheel.

Fuck the Association, she thought. Automatically, she adjusted the choke control and the idle slowed. The plan was a good one. No one else had come up with anything to match it—for publicity, anyway. There were a dozen environmental action groups all fighting for the limelight these days—at least three others in Vancouver alone. Greentree was going down for the third time. Even Ron was willing to admit that. Their last grant application had been turned down, and if they didn't get some new funding pretty soon, that would be it. Curtains. Greentree could fold its tent and fade into the night like a thousand other half-assed groups before it.

Maybe that's what they deserve, she thought. The great cru-
saders. In two years they'd done almost nothing beyond picket-
ing a mercury reduction plant and doing five different studies on
sex hormones in beef. Jesus!

Biting her lip thoughtfully, she wondered about Ron. They'd
gotten together right at the start of Greentree, and in the beginning it had been good. But things had changed. She didn't find
him as exciting as she once had, and the appeal of his insurance
annuity and his professor's post at the university had worn off
long ago. It was nice living in a good apartment, and some of the
faculty parties had been all right, but when you got right down to
it, they lived a pretty boring life. They talked about doing
things, but they never actually pulled much off. Maybe it was
time to split up.

She slammed the shift into reverse and wheeled the car
around. She paid the parking attendant and then, with a deafening roar, shot out into the heavy midafternoon traffic. She drove
aggressively, running through the gears as she wove in and out
of gaps in the traffic flow, heading toward the Burrard Bridge
and the apartment in Kitsilano, across False Creek.

On impulse she swung the car across three lanes and turned
into the high-rise canyons of the West End. The plan had been
weak on details about actually getting into the place. If she
could somehow convince Ron that it was possible then maybe
he'd go along with it. She'd have to talk to Vince first. If anyone
could pull it off, Vince Snyder was the man.

She stopped the car outside a rundown apartment building
and rang one of the bells. Then she ran up the stairs and pushed
her way in one of the doors on the second floor.

Vincent Laidlaw Snyder read through the thin sheaf of paper,
one hand gently massaging the thick mat of straw-colored hair
on his chest. He sat on the mattress that was both bed and couch
in the tiny bachelor apartment, while Paula sat in the only chair.
Snyder's hair was still wet from the shower, and Paula tried not
to look on the damp patches on his skin-tight jeans. It wasn't
easy. The only two pieces of decoration in the apartment were a
Dayglo poster of Jimi Hendrix and an ordnance map of South Vietnam. She didn't like Hendrix, and the map was covered with a

fine web of lines, joined here and there with heavy red dots. She didn't know what the lines and the jots meant.

Finally she looked across the room at Vince. He seemed totally absorbed. As he read, she watched the movement of his hand over his thickly muscled chest, and then, unable to resist, she let her eyes fall on the taut bulge of his crotch. She looked away quickly, but not quickly enough. He smiled and put the papers down on the floor.

"It's good," he said, his thin lips smiling. He leaned back against the wall, his legs spread aggressively.

"You think so?" she asked. His physical presence was upsetting her.

"I wouldn't say I thought it was good if I didn't think so," answered Snyder in his slow California drawl. Even after six years in Canada the accent was still strong. Snyder had deserted from the infamous Black Beret Tactical Group, an offshoot of the Special Forces Green Berets, and had been in Canada ever since. No one was quite sure why he deserted, but he'd hung around on the fringes of the radical groups ever since his arrival across the border. Ron was almost positive that he was a CIA infiltrator, but Paula thought that was just paranoia. She preferred to believe Vince's version of events—that he'd deserted for ideological reasons.

"But is it technically possible?" asked Paula, leaning forward in her chair. Snyder shrugged. He stood up and brought the papers over to her. He handed them over and their fingers touched as she took them. She pulled away with a jerk and the pages slipped to the floor. Snyder grinned and bent down to retrieve them. He stood up again and gave them to her.

"You nervous or something?" he asked, returning to the mattress.

"A bit."

Snyder laughed, a sharp, unpleasant sound at odds with the almost angelic face under the thatch of honey-colored hair. "So you should be," he said. "It's not every day you work up a plan to knock over a nuclear reactor."

"I don't want to knock it over," Paula sounded offended. "I want to occupy it. A political act."

"Occupy, knock over. Same thing," he said. "First, you have to get inside."

"Is it possible?"

"Sure." He paused, grinning. "Anything's possible if you've got enough money. And time."

"Money?" asked Paula.

"Yeah, money." He looked at her thoughtfully. "You really serious about this thing?"

"You're damn right I am. It's what Greentree needs. Jesus!" she said, her eyes flashing. "Can you imagine the press we'd get!"

"Yeah. I can imagine," said Snyder, his voice cool. "I can also imagine what the judge would say when it was over with."

Paula shook her head vehemently. "No way," she said. "Public mischief. And anyway, we'd be Canadians. At most we'd get a suspended sentence, or just a *persona non grata* and a quick ride to the border. No sweat."

"Maybe you're right." Snyder looked up at the ceiling for a moment, then back at her. "And the money?"

"For what?" she asked.

"Research. Some equipment. I've seen Richland. It's not exactly like opening up a piggy bank."

"I can get the money," she said.

"From Bateman?" asked Snyder. "Don't kid yourself. He doesn't have the guts for this kind of thing."

"You leave that to me, Vince. I think I can convince him. The question is, If I can get him interested, would you want to be a part of it?"

"Maybe," said Snyder. He stood up and Paula followed suit. They went to the door and Snyder opened it. Paula stood beside him uncertainly, waiting.

"You'll think about it?" she asked finally.

"I'll think about it. Let me know if you can get the money from Ronnie-boy. There's no point in getting into it until I know if the money's there."

"Don't worry," said Paula firmly.

"I don't," Snyder smiled. He reached out with one hand and put it behind her neck, pulling her toward him, his fingers cold and hard on her skin. She tried to pull away but his fingers tightened, bringing her forward. Then his mouth was on hers and she felt the expert touch of his tongue as it speared deeply into her mouth, burning into her body, taking her breath away. He reached down with his other hand, slipping it between her thighs, reaching up for the tight flesh of her buttocks, his forearm like an iron bar pushing hard into her groin, lifting her an inch off the floor. Then abruptly he let her go and pushed her gently out into the hall. She stared at him blankly.

"Just so we understand each other," said Snyder, his mouth smiling but his eyes gray and cold. He shut the door slowly, and Paula was alone in the harshly lit hallway of the apartment building.

She stood there for a long moment, staring at the door. Then she turned and walked unsteadily toward the elevators.

Night fell on the mountains, and the only sound that rose above the pattering rain was the spectral whispering of a thousand streams, water flowing from the melting snow and the glaciers of the Monashee and the Selkirks as it had each spring and summer for a million years. The water slipped down the steep tree-covered slopes, joining into streams until the broader courses came at last to the river.

The river itself had flowed unhindered for as long as the streams. Its giant current had carved the narrow canyon down through the thick layers of granite and the thin flaky strata of mica, the water always moving downward, searching blindly for its final destination, the sea, a thousand miles away.

But now the way was blocked.

The dam sat like a massive wedge, almost a thousand feet high, a Gargantuan tourniquet squeezing the river into submission. It held back the total drainage of ten thousand square miles of mountain, creating a lake 135 miles long, and in places 700 feet deep.

The seemingly impenetrable mountains groaned beneath the burden that had been inflicted upon them by the hand of man, and now, after almost three weeks of incessant rain, the earth was beginning to move.

Chapter Two

JUNE 14

Kane lay in the darkened bedroom, his head propped up on his pillow. It was past midnight, and the glow of their lovemaking had faded long ago. In its place had come the gnawing worry that had been invading his thoughts for the past few days. He looked down at the sleeping form beside him.

Chuck. It seemed a harsh sort of name for the woman it belonged to. It was hardly descriptive, he thought. Sometimes the name suited her; when she was dressed in her business clothes, the super journalist in leather and jeans. But now, as she lay naked, the smooth curving lines of her thighs melting into the larger forms of her dimpled back, the delicate neck and tousled cap of russet hair against the pillow, the name seemed out of place.

He watched as she moved slightly in her sleep, turning on her side, her small breasts coming into view, the circles of her nipples barely visible in the darkness. Kane smiled to himself, bemused. He knew what he saw in her, but he was damned if he could figure out why she was interested in him, beyond the fact that they were both addicted to pool. He frowned. To hell with that. He had enough on his mind without worrying about her feelings for him. It was enough that she was there at all.

The dams. Always the dams. Ever since he had begun work on the safety inventory of dams on the Columbia the worry had been there. What about the Canadian dams?

Kane shook a Camel from the pack on the bedside table and lit it, trying to ignore the foul taste in his mouth from the half-dozen other cigarettes he'd smoked in the past hour. For what seemed like the thousandth time he tried to put it together in his mind. There had to be a logical, obvious reason for the lack of information on the state of the Canadian structures.

The American dams had been easy. Ask a question, get an answer. For one thing, most of what he wanted was on the central library computer tapes at the OISE headquarters in Washington. Anything that wasn't on the tapes was readily available from the Bureau of Reclamation or the Army Corps of Engineers. No problem at all. But even the most basic questions concerning the status or even the background of the Canadian dams came up double zero. The computer either spat out a "not available" or a "utilize secondary source" answerback, and phone calls to the Bureau or the Corps met with a solid cold shoulder. "Sorry, outside our jurisdiction" was the reply he got most often.

And that was what worried him. The situation was not only ridiculous, it was dangerous. The Columbia River's dams and reservoirs worked in such a way that each one depended on the other. The headwaters of the Columbia were in Canada, and the three Canadian dams were key components in the system. If there was a problem in Canada, it was going to be reflected in the United States, in Kane's jurisdiction. He spat a bit of loose tobacco from his tongue. Sure, the Columbia River Treaty was up for renewal, but the politics of it didn't interest him at all. He was a geologist and an engineer, and to do his job he needed both geological and engineering information about those dams. At first, he'd been sure that some information exchange must have been set up between British Columbia Hydro, the authority controlling the Canadian dams, and the United States, but so far he hadn't found it. At first the lack of information had been merely annoying, his research a needless waste of energy. But now it seemed that what he had was all he was going to get, and he didn't like it. B. C. Hydro, the Bureau, and the Corps all knew that the entire Pacific Northwest had been undergoing extreme and unusual weather conditions. Water levels in all the American Columbia reservoirs were up an average of three feet over the norm for this time of year. On that basis alone there was cause for alarm. But apparently they couldn't care less.

"It stinks," he said out loud. Chuck, beside him, grunted.

"Damn right it does," she mumbled sleepily. "It smells like you've been having an all-night poker party or something."

Kane turned and looked down, angry with himself for having disturbed her.

"Sorry if I woke you up," he said. He reached out a hand and ran his fingers through her hair.

She shook off his hand and sat up. "You didn't," she said. "I've been lying here for an hour listening to you think. What the hell is bothering you anyway?"

"Nothing," said Kane. "Problem at work. Why don't you go back to sleep?"

"Because I don't want to go back to sleep. I want a cigarette. I also want you to tell me what's on your mind." She took one of her low-tar-and-nicotine cigarettes out of the package on her bedside table, lit it, and crossed her legs.

"Okay, shoot," she said crisply. Kane laughed.

"What is this, an interview?" he asked.

"You got it, Johnny-boy. Spill it."

"I told you, it's nothing. Just a work problem. I need some information and I can't get it, that's all." Kane lay back, closing his eyes.

"What kind of information?" asked Chuck. "Maybe I can get it for you." She assumed a thick German accent. "Vee investigative reporters haf our vays, you know."

"How about the baseline geological studies done for the High Revelstoke, the Keenleyside and the Mica dams in British Columbia?" asked Kane, a note of bitterness in his voice.

"What do you want that kind of thing for?" asked Chuck. "Why do you care about Canadian dams? This is America, right?"

"Yeah. Outside my jurisdiction," said Kane. "That's what they keep telling me."

"So?" Chuck shrugged. "Forget it."

"How the hell can I forget it? Jurisdiction or no jurisdiction, it's part of my job. Those Canadian dams are part of the Columbia system, an important part. If they won't tell me what's going on up there, how am I supposed to make any recommendations in the U.S.?"

"So what's wrong with the Canadian dams?" asked Chuck.

"That's the point." Kane lit another Camel off the butt of the last. "Nothing, probably. But I don't know, and I don't like not knowing things like that. We've been having a lot of rain, and . . . well, rain and earthfill dams don't mix very well."

"You think they're going to fall down or something?" asked Chuck, a tinge of professional excitement creeping into her voice.

The civil servant in Kane began shouting warnings, and he backed off. "Now hold on. I didn't say that. Sometimes I don't like my job much, but it's the only one I've got, so stop sniffing for a story. The last thing I need is some wild news article about Canadian dams about to collapse."

"It wouldn't be a wild story, Mr. Kane. I don't write things unless I have facts to back them up, so screw off." Chuck mashed her cigarette angrily into the ashtray on Kane's chest.

"Sorry," said Kane. "I'm a little uptight."

"Okay, okay," said Chuck. "I was just trying to help, that's all."

Kane reached out and touched her gently on the leg. "I said I was sorry," he whispered.

There was a long silence.

"Cover-up? Someone scared?" said Chuck at last.

"There you go again!" Kane laughed. "No, I don't think anyone's trying to hide anything. I think there's a lot of red tape in my way, and I also think that everyone's worried about the new agreement. The Canadians started bitching five minutes after they signed the original one, so I guess the powers that be figure it'd be bad PR to have someone like me snooping around at this point, that's all. No cover-ups, sweetie pie."

"But you still want the information, right?"

Kane sighed. "Yes, I still want the information."

"So maybe I can help, just like I said."

"How?" asked Kane, exasperated. "What the hell do you know about dams?"

"Nothing." Chuck's voice was dangerously sweet. "But I know people. One in particular. A guy named Halleran."

"Halleran? Never heard of him."

"You wouldn't have," said Chuck. "He's a reporter. Canadian. Environmental specialist, and if I remember right, he's got the hots about the Columbia River. I've met him a few times. I could get in touch with him if you wanted."

"Sure," said Kane. "And five minutes after you hung up, he'd be working on a story. No thanks."

"If you think reporters are such an untrustworthy breed, why do you hang around with me?" snapped Chuck. "Shit! I just thought that maybe he might know something, that's all!"

"Oh, God, sorry again," muttered Kane. He tried to suppress a yawn and failed. "I appreciate the thought, but . . ."

"Okay, okay," Chuck lay back on her pillows. "Message received. But if you want me to get in touch, just let me know, okay?"

"Okay." Suddenly, Kane smiled. They looked at each other for a few seconds and then he reached out a tentative hand, brushing his fingers lightly over her breasts and stomach. She shivered and moved into his arms.

"Peace?" whispered Kane into her ear.

"Peace," she murmured. She put her arms around his neck and drew him down on top of her, her thighs opening in quiet invitation. She took him with his first thrusting movement, the flaming patch of her loins rising to meet him, her legs locking around the small of his back in a shuddering embrace that pulled the worry from him like the first rushing wind of a rising summer storm.

Rudnick sat in the worn armchair, a tall glass of rye and ginger ale in his right hand. Beside him on a small table sat a chrome ashtray and the cold remains of a cigar.

He stared blankly at the window in front of him. Outside, the first four letters of the large Richland Motor Inn sign flooded his dim bachelor quarters with alternate green and yellow.

Apart from the chair he sat in, there were only two pieces of furniture in the room—a hide-a-bed along the right-hand wall and a Formica table on the left, beside the arch that led to his kitchen and bathroom. On the table lay Rudnick's past. In a leather folder standing at the back of the table were two photographs—his police academy graduation picture and a faded snapshot of a much younger Rudnick, his hairy arm protectively wrapped around some forgotten girl on a beach. In front of the folder, neatly arranged in a line, lay Rudnick's bronze detective badge, the Purple Heart he'd been given for the piece of Korean shrapnel in his thigh, and a gold-plated Kennedy half dollar. They'd given him that when he retired.

Retired. Rudnick looked at the bleak array on the table and laughed. The room turned green, turned yellow, and it was 1968 again, June, the Conrad Hilton Hotel.

They'd known it was going to be bad right from the start. At least Rudnick had known. For one thing it was hot, and heat in Chicago always meant trouble. The news people had made it even worse. The upcoming Democratic Convention would be a kind of battle they said, trailing their cameras and mikes lovingly across the assembling warriors, the hippies, yippies, and other assorted freaks who were drifting into the city from all over.

At first, before the convention actually began, there was a carnival atmosphere about the whole thing; the yippies preening for the TV cameras, Jerry Rubin demonstrating his best karate moves, and all the while Chicago's finest standing around playing the straight man.

The day before the convention Rudnick took a walk through the park across from the hotel, threading his way through the knots of young people with their sleeping bags, their women, and their hair. Even in plain clothes they'd recognized him for what he was, and somehow that pleased him. He was cop all the way through, and he was glad it showed. Most of the kids kept out of his way as he walked. One didn't. Hair down to his shoulders, skinny as a rail, the kid had blocked his path.

"Excuse me," said Rudnick, smiling.

"Shit," said the kid. "You're shit."

"Right," said Rudnick. "Now move out of the way."

"Fuck you, pig." The kid's eyes were like small black pebbles. A crowd began to gather, watching.

"Come on now, out of my way," Rudnick said, his voice almost breaking with the effort to keep his tone polite.

The crowd around them had grown larger and the boy played

to his audience. He raised one hand to his cheek, tilting his head coyly and rolling his eyes. "Oh dear! Plump wittle piggie-wiggie's getting all upset!" he crooned in a stage falsetto.

Rudnick's patience snapped. He leaned forward and grabbed the boy around the throat, bringing his beefy face to within inches of his adversary's.

"Not yet," he hissed. "But when the time comes I'm going to find you and run your pimply ass into the ground, and then I'm going to take you by those scrawny balls of yours and I'm going to shove them down your fucking throat. Understand?" He pushed the boy backward and walked away, going back the way he had come, barely containing his rage. The jeering laughter of the crowd followed him.

At roll call the next morning he volunteered for convention duty before the duty captain even asked. If there was going to be a showdown, he wanted to be there.

During the riots Rudnick stayed in the thick of it. It was almost as if he could metabolize the acrid tear-gas fumes, reveling as he dragged boys and girls alike into the waiting paddy wagons. It was an almost religious experience: the sweeping power of it throbbing in his genitals as he beat and hammered his way through flesh and bone—like, he told himself, an avenging angel. Then he spotted the kid from the park. The kid saw him, and saw too the blood that splattered Rudnick's white shirt. The kid turned and ran.

John Wayne, thought Rudnick, as he surged after the running figure. He was the Duke and the punk was a bull to be cut from the herd, and once cut, thrown and branded. He was looking forward to that part of it.

He threaded his way through the ebb and flow of the riot, straight-arming anyone who got in his way. The kid turned down an alley. Rudnick knew the alley. It was blind, full of garbage cans. He grinned and slowed to a walk.

"Alone at last," crooned Rudnick. The punk retreated behind a garbage can, fear blossoming in his eyes, chest heaving as he fought to catch his breath.

"I told you, faggot," said Rudnick gently. "I told you how it would be." He stopped a few feet away from the terrified boy and waited. The punk feinted left and then made a break to the right. Rudnick's arm lashed out like an iron bar. The kid made a noise somewhere between a cough and a gurgle and fell to his knees, gagging. Rudnick stepped around in front of him and kicked him hard in the stomach and he went down all the way, moaning. Rudnick took a deep breath and then kicked the boy as hard as he could between the legs. The punk screamed, lips pulling back and tongue writhing like a snake within his mouth.

"Quiet!" scolded Rudnick, grinning at the wreckage at his feet. He took another look and then turned to go back onto the street.

Five figures stood at the head of the alley, outlined starkly in the light from the searchlights.

"We saw, pig," said a voice. Rudnick thought he saw a gleam of light on metal in one of the hands and instinctively reached inside his jacket for his gun. Before he could draw, the middle figure of the five took three quick steps forward and launched himself into a flying kick that took Rudnick in the temple and sent him to the ground beside the kid from the park. He tried to rise but the others were on him like a snarling pack of jackals, tearing and ripping. He felt a heavy-booted foot smash into his lower chest and distinctly heard one of his ribs go. He squirmed under the weight of the five, but he couldn't break free. Finally they pinned him, two of them holding down his left arm. He heard a soft click and then the sound of a voice, high, almost a girl's.

"Oh yes, oh yes," said the voice softly. Suddenly Rudnick felt a sharp pain in the little finger of his left hand. He tried to wrench the hand free but it was firmly clamped.

"Sharp. Much too sharp for you, pig," said the voice. "For you it should be dull, real dull." Again the pain in the finger. Red waves of agony tore at Rudnick as the blade sawed into the flesh at the base of his little finger and began to go through bone. The voice grunted and the tempo of the sawing increased. Rudnick fainted. He never felt the final cut as his finger came away, or the crunching sounds as the heavy boot hammered at the maimed hand, breaking every bone within it until there was nothing left at the end of his wrist but a flattened, oozing flipper.

Rudnick came awake with a jump. His face was shiny with

sweat. His hand throbbed and he lifted it gently from the faded fabric of the chair arm. He shook his head blearily.

They hadn't wanted a crippled cop. Having him around with that hand was bad PR. They retired him on full pension. At first he lived off the insurance money from the hand, and when that ran out, he left Chicago. Without the force there was no reason to stay. No wife, no kids, no house. He'd never needed any of that before. He'd had the job.

There had been no trouble getting work. A good cop could always get a good security job. Though he wasn't sure how good a job being security officer at Richland was. Right from the start he'd had his doubts about it, and his relationship with Kellerman had never been the best; but the money was good, and anyway, he was reaching the age where he didn't have much choice. That had been five years ago. He'd kept the job, but Richland had never become his home, and his only friends were drinking buddies.

He stared out the window at the blinking sign, wondering where that kid was today. Would he remember? Probably not. Rudnick took the bottle by the neck and hurled it across the room. It shattered against the far wall with a splintering crash.

"We have a problem?" asked the man in the gray suit.

Outside, dusk was falling, but the office lights had not yet been turned on. The half-darkness made the man in uniform uncomfortable. "Two. We checked the most recent run on the satellite. The entire slope is beginning to creep."

"How big?"

"Base of about three thousand feet, up about fifteen hundred. No way of telling how deep it is."

"Do any of your people know?"

The man in uniform shook his head. "No. You couldn't tell anything unless you checked the scan on the last run and compared the two. The movement only shows up on computer analysis."

"That's something, at least." The man in the gray suit stroked his eyebrow with the forefinger of his right hand. "How fast is it moving?"

"About a centimeter a day, maybe less."

"Dangerous?"

"Yes. It's a highly unstable formation, and it's getting worse."

"How long?"

The man in uniform shrugged. "Five weeks at the outside. Could be less if it doesn't stop raining."

"The first week in July, then, for . . . remedial action."

"At the latest," said the uniformed man.

The man in the gray suit drummed his fingers lightly on the surface of his desk, thinking.

"And the other problem?" he asked finally.

"Yes. Someone in the OESI has been asking questions," said the man in uniform.

The man in the gray suit nodded. "Kane. I know. We've had questions, too. Disturbing."

"Is there anything we can do about it?"

The man in the gray suit frowned. Then he rose abruptly to his feet. "Yes. Leave it with me. From now on I think we should see each other only on official business and in the company of others."

"I understand," said the man in uniform, standing.

"I don't think you do."

The man in uniform waited awkwardly for a moment, wondering if he should shake the other man's hand. Then he decided against it, turned, and left the office. As the door closed, the man in the gray suit reached for his telephone and began to dial a number in Langley, Virginia.

"Where the hell have you been?" asked Ronald Bateman. He stared owlishly up at Paula St. George as she came into the bedroom. Bateman, a worn yellow terrycloth robe draped over his narrow shoulders, was sitting up in bed, a well-thumbed copy of Rachel Carson's *Silent Spring* on his knees and a pencil in his hand. The bed around him was scattered with notebooks and papers. Paula yawned and went to the dressing table on the far side of the room. She sat down, watching Bateman in the mirror for a moment, then picked up a brush and began stabbing at the wet tangles of her hair.

"I asked you where you'd been," said Bateman.

"Out," she said, her voice cool. "Driving around. Nothing to get all steamed up about."

"I was worried," said Bateman. "It's almost two o'clock in the morning."

"I'm aware of the time, Ron," said Paula. She stood up and began taking off her clothes. She looked for a reaction from Bateman. There was none. It would turn Vince on, for sure. She closed her eyes for a moment and felt his touch again. A shiver went through her at the memory.

"See?" said Bateman, solicitous. "You've got a chill."

"For Christ's sake!" said Paula. "You sound like my mother!" She sat down again, naked, and began going over her face, searching for blemishes.

"I'm concerned, Paula, that's all. There's no need to bite my head off. You weren't there when the meeting ended, and when I went to the parking lot the car was gone. That was almost eight hours ago. Don't you think I have a right to be worried?"

"Sure, sure," groaned Paula. "Really worried. Maybe I was out getting my rocks off with some stud at the Crown. God knows why you'd care if I was, though. It's not as if you've ever shown much interest in that kind of thing."

"That's cruel and unnecessary," Bateman's face had turned scarlet.

Paula shrugged. "It's true, though." She began scrubbing the makeup off her face.

"Life is not a continuous orgasm, you know, Paula," said Bateman, his voice brittle. "I've been working, and hard."

"On what?" asked Paula jeeringly. "Another paper on how nasty the pulp and paper industry is. Resource depletion?"

"Something like that," replied Bateman. "You object?"

Paula threw the wad of gauze down onto the dressing table and whirled around.

"Damn right!" she shouted. "We're getting nowhere with that kind of thing, and you know it! What we need is some definite action!"

"I suppose you're referring to the plan you presented to the executive this afternoon," said Bateman, sighing.

"Yes! That's exactly the kind of thing I'm referring to!"

"You were turned down, Paula. Democratically."

"Horseshit! If you'd given me even the slightest support they might have listened. But did you? You sat there like some kind of caterpillar on a mushroom!"

"Don't be absurd," said Bateman. "The idea of taking over an American nuclear installation is not only ludicrous, it is also highly dangerous. And what purpose would it serve?"

"It would get us press. Clout, Ronald Bateman. In case you hadn't noticed, that's the name of the game. No one listens to you if you screw around writing letters and setting up steering committees."

"We are environmentalists, not terrorists. The idea is utterly ludicrous," said Bateman emphatically.

"Some people don't think so," Paula's voice was tight.

Bateman looked up sharply, frowning. "What's that supposed to mean?"

"Vince thinks it's got possibilities," she replied, a smile curling her lips.

Bateman put aside his book without taking his eyes from her. "Vince Snyder? When did you see him?"

"This afternoon," said Paula. "I told him about the plan. He thought the idea had possibilities. We're going to get together later to talk about it."

"Is that where you've been all night?" asked Bateman, the words coming out haltingly.

Paula drew out the moment, savoring it, then shook her head. "Don't worry. I was only there for about half an hour."

"Oh," said Bateman, not believing her.

Paula let out a long, theatrical groan. "Oh God, Ron! Vince didn't lay a hand on me," she lied.

"I don't want you to see him again," snapped Bateman, trying to stop his voice rising. "The man is dangerous."

"Why?" asked Paula icily. "Because he's got the balls to know a good thing when he sees it? That doesn't make him dangerous, that makes him smart."

"Just keep away from him," said Bateman. "I don't trust him."

"With me?" laughed Paula. "You afraid he's going to take me away from you? Really, Ron. Wasn't it you who once told me that jealousy was a mark of immaturity?"

"I'm not jealous. I'm just looking out for your well-being."

"Christ!" muttered Paula. "Now you sound like my father!"

"Turn off the light and come to bed," said Bateman.

Later, in the darkness, she felt his hands moving clumsily over her body, like two blind animals. As he rolled over on top of her and fumbled his way between her legs, Paula wondered if it was the thought of Vince doing this to her that had aroused him. She tried to imagine what it would be like; to feel Vince's hard legs against her, the ramrod strength of his cock burning into her. Almost before the fantasy had a chance to evolve in her mind, Bateman moaned loudly and came within her. A few moments later he was snoring loudly.

She waited until she was sure he was asleep. Then, with her own fingers, she conjured Vince's presence and with his phantom body riding hers she brought herself to a shattering climax, her moans of pleasure muffled in the pillow.

As the sky began to lighten over the Monashee, the first signs of movement were becoming apparent. Small trees and bushes along the reservoir bank were beginning to lean slightly toward the water, and here and there beneath the trees the fantail patterns of minute slides trailed downward.

But no alarm was given. There were no slope indicators, tiltmeters, or any other kind of monitoring instruments more than four miles back from the dam. The warning systems stopped three miles short of the huge sheet of slowly creeping earth at the confluence of the Canoe and Columbia rivers.

As the first wraiths of morning mist began to weave their dawn patterns between the trees, water at the mountain's base shivered slightly. But the still, blue morning was silent, except for the angry screeching of a bald eagle, a thousand feet above.

Chapter Three

JUNE 27

As the DC-9 banked steeply and began its final approach to Vancouver's Sea Island airport, Jonathan Kane's stomach began to churn again. For the 2700th time, once for each second of the forty-five-minute flight from Seattle to Vancouver, Kane cursed himself for finally following Chuck's advice and visiting Halleran. It was none of his business, after all. There was almost nothing in the world that Kane hated more than flying.

Nothing, that is, except being given the kind of runaround he had been getting for the past two weeks. Every conceivable method of extracting information about the Columbia dams had ended in a brick wall of bureaucracy. The problem had been compounded by the limited time he was able to give it. Although the question of the Canadian dams gnawed at him, the terms of his job said that the Safety Inventory took priority. That, at least, was complete.

But not complete enough for Kane. It seemed obvious that the exclusion of the Canadian dams was inexcusable in any meaningful inventory. But after two weeks it seemed as though he was the only one who thought that way.

As the days passed, Kane's frustration and his suspicions increased. His first assumption—that the various agencies involved were worried about prejudicing the upcoming negotiations on the Columbia Treaty renewal—just didn't make sense any more. Chuck had done some investigating on her own, and she had discovered from Halleran that there had been a long history of secrecy about the geological siting of the Canadian dams. Halleran had sent down a collection of newspaper clippings going back to the beginning of construction of the Mica. Early reports that the location for the dam was unsafe were denied by the British Columbia government at the time, and the geological studies were never made public. The story died for a number of years, but was revived when B.C. Hydro began work on the High Revelstoke. There was another flurry of press activity about poor locations, and then the story faded once again. As far as Kane could tell, none of the questions posed by the newspaper stories had ever been adequately answered.

He decided to act. He completed the dam inventory, told Gladys he was taking a week's holiday, and went home, taking all the information with him. It was in the litter of his living room, as he leafed through the logs of fruitless telephone conversations and piles of correspondence, that he realized what he was doing. He wasn't compiling information; he was gathering evidence, although evidence of what he wasn't sure. The only thing he did know was that something was going on, and too many people were trying to keep the lid on.

A part of him realized that for his own sake it was probably best simply to shelve the whole thing and get on with his regular work. After all, the rain had stopped and any danger was probably past. For the last ten days there had been nothing but sunshine and seasonable temperatures, and in a few weeks the water tables would return to normal. But another part of him— the stubborn part of him that had taken him through graduate school, the Vietnam War, MIT, and in the end, Ruth—refused to back off. The danger was probably over for now, but what about the next time? The stubborn part of him won out, and Chuck had phoned Halleran and set up an appointment for Monday. The reporter was Kane's last hope.

Some masochistic urge forced Kane to look out the window of the Canadian Pacific jet as they came in over the waters of Sturgeon Bank. It looked as though they were no more than ten feet above the ocean. Abruptly the water changed to grass, and then to asphalt. A knuckle-whitening lurch and then they were down. Fifteen minutes later, Kane was in a taxi and heading over the Knight Street Bridge into Greater Vancouver.

The Canadian Broadcasting Corporation's regional head-quarters are located in a giant truncated ziggurat of concrete and smoked glass in the downtown core. Kane wasn't expecting it to be so big, and it took him almost twenty minutes to locate Halleran's office in the rabbit warren of the public affairs section, on the third floor. When he finally reached it, the door was firmly closed.

Kane knocked.

"Go away!" came a rasping voice from inside. It was the voice of a man who either smoked too much or ate barbed wire. Kane stood outside the door.

"It's Jon Kane. From Seattle," he said finally. There was silence from inside the office.

"So what?" said the voice after a moment.

"I've got an appointment to see you. Charlene Daly set it up." There was another brief silence, then the voice croaked, "All right. C'mon in."

Kane opened the door.

The office made Kane's house look almost tidy. There were tables along three walls, each of them piled high with back copies of the Vancouver *Sun* and the *Province*. Here and there among the newspapers were what looked like file folders, their contents spilling out everywhere. Beside the door was a bank of battered green filing cabinets oozing paper from every drawer. The room was dominated by a huge, fuzzy blowup of an old and incredibly sway-backed horse. Below it, cowboy-booted feet up on a table, sat Halleran. He looked up, tipping back the brim of his sweat-stained stetson, revealing a round, bespectacled face topped by a high forehead that swept back hairlessly to a bald skull. He was wearing tight-legged jeans crusted with filth, and a checked shirt bound at the collar with a bandanna that could have doubled as a dishcloth.

"It's all right, I'm eccentric." Halleran grinned, revealing a gleaming gold cap on his front tooth. "C'mon in. Have a seat."

Kane looked around. There were no other chairs in the office.

"Where?" he asked.

Halleran hooked a pile of newspapers with the toe of his boot and pulled. The pile slipped down to the floor, leaving a bare spot on the table.

"There," said Halleran.

Kane sat.

Halleran peered at him. "You're from OISE?"

"That's right," said Kane, shifting himself on his uncomfortable perch.

"And you want to know all about the Columbia dams."

"The Mica in particular."

"You're sure?"

"Yes," said Kane.

Halleran laughed.

"Then you're as crazy as I am."

Kane stared. "Why do you say that?" he asked.

Halleran grunted. "Because, Mr. Kane, it would take you a year just to get through the political crud around the treaty dams, another year to figure out just what the hell went on when they were building them, and then about five years trying to make head or tail out of all the stuff you read. A fool's errand, Mr. Kane, no doubt about that. No doubt at all."

"According to Charlene you know all about them," said Kane.

Halleran laughed again, a sour note in his voice. "Well, I wouldn't say I knew *all* about them. I probably knew more than anyone outside of Hydro, or you folks in the States, that's all." He gestured around the office. "I only know what I read in the papers. And anyway, you can never really know what the dams are all about till you've seen them."

"I intend to," said Kane. "I was going to rent a car and drive up to Revelstoke and the Mica tomorrow."

"Why don't you come up with me?" asked Halleran. "I could use some fresh air. Been stuck in here all week. We could leave this afternoon. Right now, as a matter of fact. Sooner the better. Talk on the way. Have you on top of the Mica by four o'clock."

"You must be a hell of a driver. I thought the Mica was about five hundred miles from Vancouver."

"It is. I'm not a hell of a driver, I'm a hell of a flyer. Got a beat-up old Twin Otter I keep down in Coal Harbour. You'll love it," said Halleran.

"I'm sure," said Kane.

The weather-beaten '72 Chevrolet sat in a McDonald's parking lot on the outskirts of Washington, D.C. The tall, heavyset man with thinning hair who sat behind the wheel bit hungrily into a Big Mac, washing it down with long pulls at his chocolate shake. The man in the gray suit, the car's other occupant, was not eating.

"Let's get it straight right now," said the man behind the wheel. "The Company is willing to work this out, but remember, you're getting the fat end of the deal." He took another bite of his hamburger, the thick sauce dribbling out of one side.

"I agree," said the man in the gray suit. "But your agency does benefit." He watched the other man eat, mildly revolted as the last of the hamburger disappeared. The other man belched and lit a cigarette.

"Bullshit," he said succinctly, flicking the match out the window. "We get a blind for some funding, that's all. We've already got a hundred deals like that going. Listen, this is strictly a favor. I am lending you resources which I control. That's all. You know damn well why I'm doing this for you." He looked pointedly down at the small silver ring on his finger and let his thumb rub gently across the discreetly engraved design. The man in the gray suit looked nervously down at his own ring. The two were identical.

"I'm not bringing the fraternity into this," he said quickly, a slight nervous edge in his voice. "In no way am I doing that. I want that clearly understood."

The other man laughed quietly. "So why else are we here? Of course you are. That's what it's for. Informal co-operation, as it were. You are what you are today because of it. So am I. So are a dozen other major forces in this city and a few hundred scattered around the country. There's no way you could avoid bringing the fraternity into it."

"You make it sound like some kind of conspiracy," said the man in the gray suit, frowning.

The man behind the wheel nodded. "It is. It's a conspiracy of co-operative power, and it's been in existence for a long time."

"I'm aware of its history," snapped the man in the gray suit. "We were pledged the same year, remember. We had the same sponsor."

"I remember."

"Let's not discuss it any more," said the man in the gray suit.

The other man smiled, briefly. "All right. Business, then. You still require our, ah, informal co-operation? There has been no change?"

The man in the gray suit shook his head, stroking his eyebrow with the forefinger of his right hand. "The situation has deteriorated, if anything. The action has become a necessity."

"You mean because of Kane?"

"Yes. He is far too close. He's now in a position to do a great deal of damage."

"I realize that," said the other man dryly. "Perhaps we'll have to deal with him as well. We've had quite a bit of experience with that kind of thing, you know."

"I'd rather we didn't talk about it," said the man in the gray suit.

"Squeamish?" said the man behind the wheel. "I mean, really, he should be the least of your worries."

"No. I'm not squeamish. I just don't think it's a good idea for me to know too much about your plans."

"You've got a point. All right. Is there anything else?"

"Yes. The date for the incident. I would like to know that much," said the man in the gray suit.

The other man raised an eyebrow. "Thinking of going on vacation?" he said, the faint smile returning to his face.

"Of course not. It's just that certain . . . contingencies must be provided for," he said.

"I see. Of course. We've set it for July fourth."

The man in the gray suit frowned. "I was hoping it might be earlier. As I said, the situation is deteriorating rapidly."

"You gave me a deadline of the second week of July," said the other man.

"I know. It still holds. I just hoped it could be done earlier."

"We could do it tomorrow," said the other man, "but we'd like to have the Oswald set up properly before we start things."

"The Oswald?" The man in the gray suit looked puzzled.

"Don't ask."

Dennis Penpraze was twenty-eight years old, five foot eight, brown haired, and blue eyed. He had a mild but persistent case of acne and was not, on the whole, attractive to women.

He had enlisted in the United States Army at the age of eighteen and within ten months he was shipping out to Vietnam. While on his first tour of duty there Private First Class Penpraze showed a definite talent for the use of demolition devices; consequently, he spent the next two years blowing up sniper emplacements, bridges, and rice paddies from Saigon to the DMZ. When his term of duty was up, he returned to the United States for a week; after a short but discouraging job search, he re-enlisted. He was given the rank of corporal and was almost immediately returned to Vietnam. Testing on re-enlistment showed Penpraze to be within the physical and mental limits that classified him as normal in the eyes of the military, although the recruiting office psychiatrist noted that he did have marked paranoid tendencies. This was not uncommon in a soldier who had spent time in Vietnam, however, and Penpraze was returned to his old unit. During his second term Penpraze developed an interest in military history, and seemed especially drawn to biographies of great generals. His favorite was Douglas MacArthur. At the same time, and somewhat contrarily, he also developed an interest in the works of Henry David Thoreau and could recite at length from *Walden* to anyone who cared to listen. Few did.

As he came to the end of his second term, his superior officers noticed that he increasingly tended to withdraw from group activities. On three occasions attempts to cajole him into recreational pursuits ended in violence. One of these occasions, during which Penpraze became involved in a brawl, resulted in his demotion to private first class again. It was also during this period that Penpraze ceased his already rare visits to the Toc Do whorehouse district in Saigon because of a continuing difficulty in maintaining an erection. Two weeks before his demobilization Penpraze became involved in another fight, culminating this time in the death of a black private in his platoon. Penpraze was not held responsible for the death and was not court-martialed, but a further enlistment was ruled out. He returned to the United States.

Once again his attempts to obtain work were fruitless. To avoid going on welfare, he enrolled in UCLA under the GI Bill and began taking out a long series of student loans. He maintained a steady C average and joined as many clubs on the campus as he could, and even set up one of his own—The Democracy Society. The society dissolved before its first meeting. Two days later he received a telephone call asking if he would be interested in a government job. Penpraze said he would be extremely interested. The following afternoon he was visited by two men who showed him security passes that identified them as agents of the National Security Agency in Washington, D.C.

They told him that they knew of his financial problem and assured him that if he decided to join their agency his student loans would be paid for. They told him that he would be working as a roving agent for the agency, a group, they explained, involved in highly secret intelligence work. The idea of being a spy appealed to Penpraze and he accepted on the spot. Within three days he had dropped out of UCLA and taken an apartment in the South Gate area.

Over the next few years Penpraze worked for the agency a total of seven times, always in what his anonymous superiors referred to as a "monitoring" role. On each of these occasions Penpraze was required to follow a well-known political or industrial figure and report by telephone on recurring faces among those who met or were near the figures he had under surveillance. Penpraze was given a camera to facilitate his work and an address in Washington to which he was to send the exposed film. On two occasions he was sent out of the country—once to Mexico, the second time to Korea.

Except for his initial recruitment Penpraze had no direct contact with the people he thought he worked for. He was always paid in cash, both for salary and expenses, and he always reported by telephone. The number he used was never the same twice. The address in Washington was a post office box, which was emptied on average once every four months. The film removed from the box was opened, exposed to sunlight, and thrown into the nearest refuse receptacle.

At no time during his period of employment did Dennis Penpraze ever question the orders he was given, or the money he received. He never became aware of the fact that the agency he supposedly worked for did not, in fact, exist.

On the afternoon of July second Dennis Penpraze, acting on orders, boarded a Greyhound bus en route to Seattle with connections to Vancouver and Revelstoke, British Columbia.

Jonathan Kane kept his nose buried in the file of material Halleran had given him. He was trying to ignore the fact that he was flying in a very old and very noisy airplane down a very narrow river valley. A few hundred feet below, the Thompson River boiled westward, like a stream of rapidly flowing muddy lava.

Beside Kane, Halleran kept up a monotonous whistle in competition with the shaking, rattling, and roaring of the airplane's twin propellers. He handled the controls easily and smoothly as he turned and banked, following the sinuous contours of the river.

Kane had been reading steadily for three hours, since the moment Halleran had yanked the Twin Otter from the crowded waters of Vancouver's Coal Harbour. His terror of a sudden engine failure or a collision with any one of a thousand different obstacles made concentration difficult, but despite himself he had managed to take in a considerable amount of information on the Mica Dam.

It was a frightening compendium of fact and theory. The more Kane read the more anxious he became. What had at first been a vague worry was now becoming a terrifying possibility. Halleran's file exposed a web of inconsistencies, poor judgment, corporate finagling, and, from the looks of it, a few outright lies. The file went back to 1967, and as Kane read unbelievingly through it, he saw that the basic problem—the thing that had started the whole ball rolling—was money. Specifically, the lack of it.

It was clear that a gravity dam, or a high-arch dam, would have been the most suitable for the site, but the costs of bringing materials to the site had been prohibitive, so an earthfill design was chosen. Even with the earthfill dam there were financial difficulties. Because of the dam's isolated location, even the transportation of fill and shot rock had posed a problem. Fill and gravel located in deposits close to the dam were tested and found to be extremely moisture sensitive—2 to 3 per cent below the optimum for a dam such as the one proposed for Mica. The material became scattered at this point in the file, but it seemed that somehow the poor grade of fill had been deemed acceptable for construction. It looked pretty innocuous on paper, but Kane knew what that kind of moisture sensitivity could lead to. If at any time the dam began to leak through undiscovered faults, or new faults opened up because of seismic activity, the dam would soak up the water as if it were blotting paper. The entire specific gravity of the structure might change, eventually causing a collapse. This potentially disastrous compromise had been compounded by the building of the High Revelstoke Dam eighty miles downstream. If its reservoir backed up to the downstream face of the Mica, the moisture-sensitive fill in the dam would once again act as a gigantic paper towel, and, like a sodden paper towel, would shred and disintegrate. Kane presumed that the dam engineers had taken all of this into consideration in their design, but it still worried him, especially after the heavy rains of the past month.

As he neared the end of the thick file he came across what appeared to be a script outline for a documentary entitled simply *Mica*. He looked across at Halleran and held up the outline. The broadcaster-pilot nodded.

"Would have been one hell of a show!" he yelled over the roar of the engines.

"Never produced?"

Halleran shook his head, the corners of his mouth turning down sourly. "Naw!" he replied. "You wouldn't have believed the crap I had to go through with that thing."

"Like what?" prodded Kane.

Halleran shrugged. "Well, I heard a few rumors about slides in the area, you know, from old-timers. So I decided to check it out. I asked Hydro if they had any geological reports and they gave me the runaround. Then I went to some professors at UBC. None of them would talk. Figures. Even the profs make a lot of consulting dollars from Hydro. Anyway, I couldn't get any background, you know, scientific stuff, so I had to drop the whole thing."

"I understand how you feel." Kane turned back in his seat to look out the windscreen and found himself staring at a jagged rock wall less than a hundred yards away. He raised an arm reflexively as they careered toward it. At the last moment, Halleran banged the rudder pedal and they sheered away, the giant slab of granite seeming almost to touch their portside wing tip. Then they were in an even narrower pass between two massifs. A wedge of blue sky beckoned a few miles ahead.

"What the hell was that?" asked Kane, his voice shaking, trying to regain control of his stomach.

"A mountain." Halleran laughed. "Area's full of them, you know."

"Cute," said Kane. Halleran looked over at him and grinned broadly. Kane looked around. On either side mountains blocked out his vision, the speed of the airplane making the tree-covered slopes a green blur. Ahead, the slice of blue at the end of the valley was growing. "Just where are we?" he asked.

"Clemina Creek Pass," said Halleran. "The Malton Range." He waved an arm at the mountains on either side. "We've been traveling parallel to the Canoe River. That's where we're headed now, other side of these buggers."

"Canoe River. That's the Mica reservoir?"

Halleran bobbed his head. "Uh-huh. They called it McNaughton Lake. It covers the old riverbed. We'll come into it about halfway down. The dam's back about forty miles. I could have cut across sooner, but I wanted you to see the reservoir."

A few minutes later they burst out of the pass and turned sharply to the right. Below, the flashing water of the lake patched with cat's-paws of rock, stretched away as far as he could see in either direction between the giant shoulders of the mountains.

"This it?" he asked.

Halleran nodded. He jockeyed with the yoke again and the plane dropped. They began flying down the hundred-and-thirty-five-mile-long lake, toward the dam. Swallowing the vertigo that had been threatening drastic action since the beginning of the flight, Kane focused his attention on the land and water below.

At that point the lake was almost five miles wide, the banks on either side stripped of trees for a hundred feet above the water. He knew that the area underwater would look the same, the ground cleared of trees to lessen the amount of "trash" in the lakes. It gave the reservoir a bald, artificial look. Above the cleared line the trees began again, covering the mountains that surged up on either bank in a thick green shroud, above which the stark peaks of the mountains reared like teeth. Kane felt a growing sense of agoraphobia. He really was in the middle of nowhere, the airplane a flyspeck in a sea of brooding mountains. He shivered as he thought of the forces that had torn these incredible monuments from under the surface of the earth, forces and energies that were still there, stored, waiting.

They flew on for half an hour, low, the shadow of the small plane racing on the faintly rippled surface. It was almost hypnotic, the metal water beneath them, the fleeing curtains of trees on either side, the steady hammering drone of the engines. As he watched, Kane felt his senses dull and thicken.

A nudge from Halleran woke him abruptly. He sat up, and realized that the file had fallen to his feet. Amazed that he could have slept, he looked fuzzily through the windscreen. Ahead, the valley was narrowing, the tree-covered slopes moving in, casting long shadows across the lake. Halleran pointed down toward the water.

"Silt runoff!" he shouted, gesturing toward a tall mountain on their left and the band of ochre-colored water that ringed its base. Kane nodded sleepily, barely noticing. He yawned.

"How far to the dam?" he asked. He yawned again.

"Dead ahead," said Halleran, squinting forward. Kane looked. Several miles distant he could see a faintly darker line that ran across the water.

"That it?" he asked.

Halleran nodded. "Water's high, too. Looks like it's right up to the crest."

As they continued their low-level approach, Kane began picking out details. The six-story-high inlet tower, rising like a windowless apartment building on the left abutment of the dam, the lower structure on the opposite side that was the penstock building, controlling the flow to the turbines, and finally the dark line of the access road that ran across the crest of the dam itself. Halleran was right. The water was high. As they swept across the dam he saw that the reservoir was within ten or twelve feet of the top. Kane could pick out individual boulders on the upstream face. A split second later they were over the crest, and Kane found himself staring down into a gorge almost a thousand feet deep. His stomach heaved.

"Hang onto your cookies," yelled Halleran. "I'm going to peel around so you can have a better look!" He nosed the plane into a steep dive and the floor of the gorge raced toward Kane at breakneck speed. Then Halleran was pulling out, the windscreen abruptly filling with a view of open sky. Halleran twisted the plane into a tight banking curve, the pontoons almost brushing the tops of the trees that covered the precipitous slope. A moment of weightlessness as they arced over the top of the climb, and then they were roaring back the way they had come, north toward the downstream face of the dam. Kane's mouth was filled with the taste of bile. He swallowed hard and forced himself to look forward. Halleran pointed.

"The Mica!" he boomed.

In front of Kane's eyes loomed the largest dam in the world.

It rose out of the bedrock in a gravel wall, climbing 850 feet into the clear midafternoon sky, a giant gray wedge sealing the narrow canyon. To the right of the dam the giant spillway, almost two thousand feet long, curved down the valley wall, looking like some monstrous children's slide. Kane stared. The spillway was dry.

"They must be out of their minds!" he shouted, the rolling of his stomach forgotten. "They should have had the spillway gates open long ago!"

Halleran grimaced and pulled the yoke back into his lap. The plane's nose jerked and began to climb towards the crest.

"Every cubic foot that goes over that spillway is water that they can't turn into electricity," he said, with venom. He edged the yoke back, and the gray face of the dam flashed past below. Then they were over the crest, now, McNaughton Lake huge, apparently endless in front and below. Kane looked back over the blue water at the receding line of the dam, shaking his head.

"Anything else you want to see?" asked Halleran.

Kane turned around and peered upstream. Something Halleran had said a few minutes before was nagging at him.

"Yes," he said. "There is something."

After the racket of the cabin, the silence was almost overpowering. The Otter bobbed lightly on its pontoons fifty yards from the base of Mount Dainard, five miles back from the dam. Little waves lapped hollowly at the aluminum floats as Kane opened his door and looked at the water directly below the fuselage. It had a faint brownish tinge.

"Oh, Christ," said Kane.

"What's wrong?" Halleran was craning his neck to see.

"I'll tell you in a second." Kane unfastened his seat belt and edged his legs gingerly out the door, feeling for the pontoon with his feet. He slid clumsily out of the door, holding onto one of the struts. The plane rocked violently. Facing him, the trees on the lower slopes of Mount Dainard stood mutely, somehow disapproving. He stuck his head back into the cockpit, frowning.

"Do you have a cup or something?" he asked.

The pilot shook his head. "What's up?"

Kane looked irritated. "I said I'd tell you later. In a second. I need a cup," he said.

"How about my hat?" Halleran pulled the battered stetson from his head and offered it to Kane.

"I guess it'll have to do," muttered Kane. He took it and disappeared again. A moment later he was back, the hat, now full of water, held in his hands.

"Here, take it," he said curtly. Halleran reached out and took it, soaking his trousers as water leaked out through the porous felt. Kane clambered into the plane again and took the hat from Halleran. He held it out of the door until all the water had leaked through, then brought it inside again. He trailed his finger inside the brim and held it up for Halleran to see. The finger was covered with fine granular mud.

Halleran shrugged. "So?" he frowned. "Silt runoff, just like I said before."

Kane shook his head. He rubbed the mud between his thumb and forefinger and then peered out the open door of the airplane at the mountain rising out of the water beside them. "It's not topsoil." Kane sounded worried. "It's alluvial till. Subsidence. It's another Vaiont."

"Vaiont?"

Kane nodded, looking up at the thrusting bulk of the mountain. His face was paler than usual. "Yes, Vaiont," he said. "It was a dam in northern Italy."

"*Was* a dam?"

Kane nodded grimly and explained. "They finished building it in 1963. The geography was pretty much like it is here. Narrow canyon mouth and a fairly broad, steep-sloped reservoir behind it. Bottleneck dam building."

"Earth dam?"

Kane shook his head. "High arch. Biggest in the world at the time."

"So what happened?"

Kane was still peering through the windscreen at the cliff-like mountain slope a few hundred feet away. "It fell down," he said simply. "They'd had a lot of rainfall and the reservoir was extremely high. A whole mountainside let go. Seven hundred million tons of rock and topsoil."

"Son of a bitch!" said Halleran, following Kane's glance. "Now I remember. There was a town below the dam, wasn't there?"

"Yeah. Longaronne. The wave created by the slide topped the dam by about seven hundred feet. There wasn't a single survivor. It took them months to dig the bodies out. And the engineers knew that they were in trouble long before it happened. They'd noticed a lot of fractional creep in the soil around the reservoir but they didn't do anything. They didn't even warn the people in the town. Three thousand people. Bang, just like that."

"And here?" asked Halleran. Suddenly the mountain looked higher and steeper and he felt a strong urge to gun the motor and get the hell out.

Kane fingered the slick of mud inside the battered hat. "I'm not sure," he said quietly. "Maybe. From the look of it the slope has been badly eroded below the water level. Thank God the rain stopped."

"You mean it might have gone as far as it's going?"

"Maybe, maybe not. To know for sure I'd have to get an idea

of just how bad the erosion under the slope was. If it's as bad as it looks from that discoloring, almost anything could set a slide off now. More rain, a slide somewhere else on the mountain. Just about any frigging thing. Christ! This is why they've been blocking me! They knew about this! This kind of soil condition would show up in even the most basic geology report."

"Why would that bother your people?" Halleran looked as though he knew the answer already.

"Lots of reasons," he said. "They were the ones who demanded this site, for one thing. They pressured for it, that much I know. They might even have done the original geological studies, for that matter."

"So what happens now?" asked Halleran. "I'm going to have to do a story on this, you know."

"And get us both fired? Forget it. I'm not absolutely sure of anything, except that there's a problem here. There's no way of saying how bad it is until a full survey is done."

"That sounds chickenshit to me, Mr. Kane," said Halleran coldly. "You sound as though you're trying to cover your ass. I don't buy it."

"I'm not asking you to buy anything," said Kane. "You want to write a story, write it. But quote me and I'll deny it. I don't want to go off half-cocked."

"So?" said Halleran.

"So I'll go back to Seattle and get in touch with my superiors in Washington. If I don't get some kind of response, and if some kind of action isn't taken—*then* you can write your story, all right?"

"Fair enough." Halleran still didn't look happy. "But what kind of action do you expect them to take?"

"They'll have to drain the reservoir, at least below the slide erosion level. From the looks of that slope the slide area's about three times the size of the one at Vaiont."

"You've got to be kidding! You really think they're going to drain McNaughton Lake? Jesus! You're asking them to throw away a million bucks' worth of electricity."

"That's irrelevant," said Kane. "They have to drain it. And fast."

"I'll believe it when I see it," snorted Halleran. "Not only are you asking them to throw away money, you're also telling them that they're going to have to air all their dirty laundry, and the B.C. government's as well. They start draining the reservoir and the shit is really going to hit the fan."

Kane grunted and buckled his seat belt. "The faster you get me back to Vancouver, the faster we can start throwing it," he said. He closed his eyes. The Otter roared, planed 200 yards on its floats, and lifted steeply into the air.

"What I can't understand is how they got themselves into this position in the first place," said Kane, gripping the sides of his seat as Halleran banked steeply and pulled the nose round to the westward. "Surely to God they didn't do it on purpose!"

"Ah, Christ, it was the wild West back then," said Halleran. "The whole Columbia thing was put together when W. A. C. Bennett was running the province. Wacky didn't give a buffalo chip about the Columbia Project, mainly because it wasn't going to give B.C. any hydro power, or not for a lot of years anyway. He didn't want to wait, and he had his own power system in the works, the Peace River Project, up north. But you Americans were offering a lot of money for the Columbia, and Wacky wasn't the type to walk away from a dollar. That, and he had the province pretty nearly stony broke by then anyway. Juggling budgets, shifting appropriations, you name it.

"Anyhow, to cut it short, Wacky took the money and signed the treaty. A few years later the chickens came home to roost and he actually had to build the dams. Bingo. No bucks left. Not a cent. Most of it sunk into the Peace River Project. But he was getting a lot of pressure from the Americans, so he had to come up with some kind of solution. He took money from a lot of the other departments, highways, education, that kind of thing, and hid them in the main estimates. That raised a lot of hell a few years back, I'll tell you, when they finally figured it out! So, with the money he skimmed he began building the dams. On top of everything else, he hadn't thought about inflation. By the time he finished the dams, they'd cost four times what he'd been paid for them, way back when."

"You really think the U.S. government was pressuring him that hard?"

"Sure," replied Halleran. "They had promises to keep, too,

you know. The Mica alone stores twenty million acre feet—that generates a hell of a lot of power, and it had already been sold. Lot of big industrial concerns on the Columbia."

"I know."

They fell silent. Kane could hardly believe what Halleran had told him. But then, he reflected, it would not be the first time it had happened. The Vaiont catastrophe was a case in point, and so was the Teton collapse in 1976. Kane had read the transcripts of the closed hearings into that billion-dollar fiasco, and it had read like a litany of all the things you should not do when building a dam. They seemed to have gotten just about everything wrong, starting with choosing a site without adequate geological surveys and carrying it all down the line. The only Cassandra had been a nineteen-year-old geology student who had been working on the dam over the summer. She had warned the head of construction that the dam would collapse if they filled the reservoir. The head of construction had fired her and gone ahead with the flooding procedures, and at twice the normal rate. The dam had collapsed, killing half a dozen people and doing more than a billion dollars' worth of damage to six counties in two states.

Dusk was darkening the coastal plain as the Otter roared out of the mountain pass and into the delta area of the Fraser River. By the time they set down in the clutter of Air West seaplanes and floating gas stations in Coal Harbour, they were agreed on a plan of action.

Kane would return to Seattle and contact the OISE director general in Washington after the weekend. Then he would sit down on Saturday and Sunday and organize his presentation of the facts. If the OISE chief refused to contact the Canadian authorities and inform them of the potential danger, Halleran would break the story in the Vancouver press and Kane would leak it to Chuck. With the story circulating openly in both the United States and Canada, they were sure that B.C. Hydro would be forced to lower the reservoir to a safe level. Halleran had wanted to forget about the OISE chief, but Kane's civil service reflexes had rebelled and eventually the journalist had agreed to give the bureaucrats one last chance.

"You want a ride to the airport?" said Halleran.

"No, that's okay," said Kane. He'd had enough of Halleran's driving for one day, and besides, he needed time to think. The two men shook hands and parted. Kane flagged down a taxi on Georgia Street and told the driver to take the long way to the terminal. The driver needed no persuading.

As the taxi took him along beside the waters of Burrard Inlet and Spanish Banks, Kane turned the problem over in his mind.

There could be no doubt that someone had known about the fragile condition of the reservoir slope. Only the most cursory geological survey would have overlooked it. But if government officials had known about it, why hadn't they done something about it? Why had they gone ahead and built the dam?

He supposed there was a possibility that they hadn't considered the problem a serious one at the time. The slope might not have been in such bad shape before construction and flooding of the reservoir. Still, the engineers should have known what nearly ten years of high water would have done. They would have known, for sure. And that meant that someone was deliberately ignoring something somewhere. Which meant worse than incompetence. Something much worse.

Kane lit a cigarette and looked out the taxi window as they climbed the high bluffs above Wreck Beach and began arcing around the UBC campus. Ahead and to his right he could see the last of the sun dipping behind the mountains of Vancouver Island thirty miles away across the Georgia Strait and sending fiery tendrils of light across the water to filter through the tall cedars that lined the road. The smoke tasted harsh in his mouth, and suddenly he realized that he was frightened—and not just by the idea that the slide might come down. There were other factors at work here, factors more complicated than a mass of till and vegetation preparing to obey the laws of gravity: factors that were, in their own way, just as powerful.

As the taxi sped across the Knight Street Bridge and toward the airport, Kane could hardly believe what he'd done. His hand was sweaty on the briefcase handle. All hell was going to break loose when the story came out. There was one satisfaction, though, even if they tossed him out on his butt. He was right, and he knew it.

They arrived at the terminal and Kane paid the driver. He

went to the C.P. Air desk and discovered that the next flight for
Seattle didn't leave for an hour. He bought his ticket, and then
went to the upper observation deck and the pay phones. He dug
around in his pockets for some change and called Chuck. The
phone in her apartment rang seven times, and Kane was about to
hang up when there was an answering click.

"Yes?"

"It's me," said Kane.

Her voice softened. "Hi! Catch me in the tub, would you? I
was just about ready to bite—" She caught herself. "Hey! What
are you doing calling? I thought you were supposed to be in
Vancouver."

"I am. I'm at the airport."

"What about Halleran? You see him?"

"Yes. And the Mica Dam. He flew me up there this afternoon."

"And?"

"Bad."

"How bad?"

"It couldn't be much worse," said Kane wearily. As he stood
there in the huge expanse of the terminal he had an overpowering desire to be with Chuck. He realized that he was very,
very tired. "Look," he said finally, "I'm coming back. Tonight.
How would you like to place your soothing hands upon my
brow?"

Chuck laughed. "I'll do better than your brow," she said. "Why
don't I pick you up at the airport?"

"No. I'm a wreck. Give me some time to clean up first. The
flight gets in around eleven. Would midnight be too late? If it's
not too much trouble."

"What's all this 'if it's not too much trouble' stuff? Of course
I'll be there," she scolded.

Kane hesitated. "Chuck," he began. He paused again. It
wasn't the time he thought, or the place.

"What?" she asked.

"Nothing," he said. "I'm just glad you're coming over, that's
all."

"I think I know what you're trying to say," she said gently.
"Me too. I'll see you around midnight."

Chapter Four

JUNE 27

Snyder unrolled the large diagram on the kitchen table in Ronald Bateman's apartment and weighted it with a couple of coffee mugs.

"All right," he said. "We go over it one last time to make sure of the details, okay?" He glanced up at Bateman and Paula St. George. Paula smiled eagerly. Bateman was scowling.

"I still think the whole thing is too dangerous," said Bateman. His eyes, fixed on Snyder's pale, narrow face, were hostile. "I don't like being bulldozed into things."

"Nobody's pushing you, Bateman," said Snyder. He began to roll up the diagram again. Paula reached out and stopped him.

"Relax, Vince. Ron's just a bit jittery. We all are. Ron's in it, don't worry."

"I just don't want to waste my time," snapped Snyder.

"How about my money?" said Bateman sourly. "You've been going through it fast enough in the past few days."

Snyder snorted. "You think I'm ripping you off for a few hundred lousy bucks?"

"No," said Bateman, coloring. "Oh no, Vince, I'm sure you're not ripping me off, but I just hope you know what you're doing. The only reason I'm in on this thing at all is because I know damn well that Paula would go ahead on her own anyway. I don't want to see her hurt."

"Very chivalrous." Paula glowered. "Look, Ron, I can take care of myself. If you want out, just say so. Vince and I can handle it ourselves."

"I'm sure." Bateman took a deep breath. "No. I'm in, come what may."

Snyder looked up, tapping his fingers on the table. "You all finished? I'd like to get through this."

"We're finished," said Paula, looking pointedly at Bateman. "Go on."

Snyder nodded and pulled a wide-tip felt pen out of his jean jacket pocket. He pointed at a thick blue line running down the center of the diagram.

"The Columbia," he said. "The perimeter fence around the nuclear reservation is about fifteen miles above the town of Richland. That's where we'll be heading on the first. We'll book into a motel and take a closer look then. For now all we have is this map, courtesy of the Energy Research and Development Administration."

"I still can't believe it," said Paula. "You write away to these people and they send you back a detailed plan of the place and a pamphlet about guided tours. What are they, crazy?"

"Maybe they think they have nothing to worry about," said Bateman, smiling for the first time that evening.

Snyder cleared his throat ostentatiously. "You people all done now?" he asked.

Bateman held up his hands. "Sorry," he said. "No more interruptions."

Snyder nodded curtly and picked up where he had left off. "Okay. Like I was saying, the fence is on three sides. The fourth side is the river, but since that's the obvious point of access it's probably pretty heavily patrolled. We can forget that. Over here," he said, pointing with his pen, "we've got what they call Storage A. There's also a B, C, D, and E."

"The nuclear waste," said Paula, slightly breathless.

Snyder ignored her. "That's probably the best way in. You can see that the storage area butts up to the perimeter fence of the reactor section, right there by the railway tracks. We get in by going over the storage area from the river, and then under the fence where the rail line goes through. We'll have to cross the whole reactor area, but according to the map most of it's abandoned, so it probably won't have any heavy patrols. So we cross through the old reactor section, head around the administration building here, and then hit the new reactor. It's right by the southern perimeter wire."

"I still don't understand why we don't go in through there." Bateman sounded plaintive, and Paula's nostrils flared a little. "Why expose ourselves to more risks by crossing the whole reactor installation?"

Snyder sighed. "Look," he said. "Take it from me. The breeder is brand-new. It'll have the heaviest security. They always work it that way. In Nam they put about five hundred guards around a new shipment of maraschino cherries and leave a fleet of F1-11s all on their lonesome. They like to protect the newest toy in the playroom. Take it from me, the long way's the best way. Okay? Now. Once we get to the new reactor, we've got to get ourselves inside. I'll have a better idea about that after the tour. After that it's up to you. Once we're inside my job's over. Except for the dummy bombs."

"Have you got them together yet?" asked Bateman.

Snyder shook his head. "No. There's a chance the car might get searched somewhere along the way, so I'm going to leave them unassembled until we get to the hotel in Richland."

"You're sure they'll look all right?" asked Paula. "The place is going to have all sorts of closed-circuit cameras, and they won't take us seriously unless they really think we've got real bombs in there."

Snyder smiled, and something about it sent a shiver down Bateman's spine. "Don't worry," said the fair-haired man. "*Plastique* and Plasticine look pretty much the same. They'll think the bombs are real all right." He gave a short barking laugh. "In fact I guarantee it," he said.

Max Rudnick cruised slowly through the old section of the reactor compound, occasionally flicking on the powerful beam of the portable searchlight he kept beside him on the seat. He drove the car at only slightly more than a walking pace. Touring the

old end of the compound was a waste of time—he knew that. He
didn't care. He had a lot of it to waste. He wasn't sleeping much
now with the pain in his stomach. He was taking more and more
of the pills every day, too, and that worried him. The pains were
getting worse. He'd need something stronger soon if he wanted
to keep working.

When he reached the railway trunk line he noticed that the
arc lights on the perimeter wire beside it were blown out, leaving the gateway in darkness. He turned on the searchlight and
aimed it out the window. Nothing. The wire, and behind it the
desert. As usual. He turned down toward the river and let the
light play over the twin rails a few feet away. It would have
been better back in the forties, he thought, when the place had
really meant something. The rail line had carried important
things then; the flatcars bringing in strange and secret equipment and rolling out bearing squat, tarpaulin-shrouded bombs to
Alamogordo. Now all they carried was garbage: radioactive
sludge in shielded tank cars, old fuel rods, useless but still lethal,
cladding, contaminated clothing, all the "hot" refuse from other
reactor facilities.

He let the beam from the searchlight ride up over the rails and
through the perimeter wire, illuminating a puddle of ground in
the Storage A area. He yawned. Still nothing. Except the invisible patch of ground out there somewhere that held the leak. He
grunted softly and lit a cigar. At least that problem was solved,
as far as he was concerned anyway. He had managed to convince the director that the security forces had enough to contend
with guarding the new reactor on the other side of the compound. Who was going to steal a goddamn radiation leak? So
they had posted the area with a ring of Caution – Extreme Radiation Hazard signs. If any trespasser fool enough to walk onto
the reservation couldn't read the signs, well, that was his tough
luck.

Rudnick braked the car and looked out into the darkness of
the storage area, wondering why everyone seemed so upset by
this particular "excursion" as they called it. There had been
other leaks in the past, three since he'd been at the facility. The
last one had dumped a couple of hundred thousand gallons of
hot waste into the ground, and they hadn't gotten too upset then.

But this time they were running around like ants in a barrel. He'd even seen the director out there in a lead-lined suit, and the rad squads had been at it twelve hours a day, testing and taking deep-core samples.

Rudnick nodded to himself. They seemed plenty worried. When he'd filled out the security section in last week's log for the OIA people in Seattle, he hadn't seen any mention of the leak. Whatever had come out of the tank buried out there, it was pretty dangerous. He turned off the searchlight. It was none of his business. He drove back again, down by the maze of disused cooling towers and blockhouses by the river, and wound his way toward the administration building. Time for another pill. As he drove he made a note to himself to get the lights by the railway gate fixed.

The man from Langley stood at the edge of the abandoned runway, smoking a cigarette and waiting. He shivered slightly in the cool desert air. Running parallel with the runway was an old service road, barely visible in the moonlight. There was a line of stakes on each side of the road, every tenth stake marked with a red tag. The two lines were precisely 111 feet apart. They looked like survey lines left by a highway crew.

The man dragged on his cigarette and shivered again. He pressed a stud on his watch and the LED crystals flared blood red—10:20. He wondered how the Seattle people were doing. There hadn't been much time after they had intercepted Kane's call from Vancouver. He shook his head. He didn't like to rush things. It made him nervous and it wasn't professional. Then he heard the whistle. He let his finger rest on the lower stud of his watch and waited. The whistle came again, and he pressed. The seconds began to flow by on the watch.

A hundred and fifty yards down the road four men appeared. The man could barely make them out, but he knew their equipment down to the last toothpick. They were dressed entirely in black, with black ski masks covering their faces. Each man carried a large knapsack on his back and held a modified version of an Ashley core punch bar in his hands. The punch bars looked like outsized hypodermic needles—two tubes of titanium steel, one slotted into the other. The outer tube was four feet long, the one fitting into it six. There were handles on both tubes, a T-bar on the inner and a pair of molded grips on the outer.

The four men arranged themselves in a line at right angles to the far line of stakes, standing four feet apart. They dropped the outer tubes to the ground and then fitted the inner one with a screw-on compressed-air cartridge. Then they held the punch bars upright, grasped the outer tube hand grips, and depressed the firing triggers. There was a brief cracking sound as all four air cartridges fired and the inner steel rods rammed downward, the T-bars thudding into the padded stops above the hand grips. The four men pulled up on the T-bars and the inner rods slid out of the ground, leaving neat two-inch-diameter holes. They then moved toward the line of stakes and repeated the operation. They did it six times. When they had finished, a line of twenty-four holes stretched from one line of stakes to the other.

The men laid down their punch bars and shrugged off their knapsacks. Each of them proceeded to load six holes with Du-Pont Gelex-2 high detonation pressure explosive. They placed two of the foot-long cartridges into each hole, crimping the cartridges together with quarry cord before lowering them in. Then a small timing initiator was forced into the blunt end of the top cartridge in each hole and soil replaced above it. The holes that had been cut through the asphalt of the roadway were left uncovered, but the end of the cartridge and the timing mechanism were daubed with a mixture of lampblack and dental cement. The HPD explosive was particularly dense, each cartridge weighing 5 pounds. The four men set a total of 240 pounds of the material.

When they finished loading and tamping the holes, the four men retrieved their gear and melted into the darkness. The man from Langley looked at his watch and waited. Another minute passed, and then he covered his ears. The explosion was incredibly powerful. It knocked him to his knees and he was 450 feet away. The ground shook violently beneath him and the thundering roar slammed painfully into his eardrums. Ears ringing, he clambered to his feet as debris began to sift down from the night sky, pattering on the runway. He pressed the button on his watch, coughing as the acrid fumes caught his throat. He looked down. The whole procedure had taken twenty-one minutes and ten seconds.

The four men appeared out of the roiling cloud of smoke and dust, this time minus their equipment. One of them tied a rope around his partner's waist and lowered him into the trench, while the other two measured its width with a fifty-foot tape. A few moments later the man in the ditch reappeared. The four men conferred for a few seconds and then one of them jogged across to the man from Langley.

"It's right on." The voice was slightly muffled by the wool of the mask. "Sixteen feet deep minimum and eighteen feet wide. It's a bit deeper where the road used to be—asphalt must have forced the blast down."

"Excellent," said the man from Langley. "That should be more than enough. I'll see you again on the third."

"Right," said the man in black. He threw a casual salute and jogged back to the other men. They faded back into the darkness again. A minute later the man from Langley heard a truck engine spring to life and fade into the distance. There were no headlights.

The man lit another cigarette and walked over to the hole where only a few minutes ago there had been only the road and the baked clay of the desert. He smiled and went back to the runway. Five minutes later he heard the sound of a light plane in the sky above him and checked his watch again. It was midnight. The pickup was right on time.

Kane slid his key into the lock and stepped wearily into the darkened living room of his house. He gave a gaping yawn, closed the door behind him, and fumbled for the light switch. Something slammed agonizingly into the back of his neck. As he fell, he reeled into the telephone table across the hall, the bell on the phone clanging as it bounced off the floor.

A foot landed in his ribs, and Kane instinctively grabbed at the ankle and twisted. He heaved and the intruder fell away, crashing onto the newel post at the bottom of the stairs.

Kane struggled upright, gasping for air. His chest and side were on fire. A shadow passed in front of him and he ducked as a high, lashing kick grazed his shoulder. Kane, groggy from the

blow on the neck, flailed his arms hysterically in the dark, trying
to beat back his ghostly attacker. A dim figure rose up in front of
him, and he jerked his knee upward. More by luck than judgment he made contact, catching the man in the groin. The attacker gave a surprised grunt and fell back. Kane rolled away,
through the living-room door, moaning with new pain as his already bruised ribs hit the leg of the coffee table. There was a
dim, flickering light in the room. Just above him he could hear a
dull hissing, and he was sure he could smell kerosene. He tried
to climb to his feet, the sounds of the man by the stairs urging
him on. He reached for the table, searching for a handhold, and
yelped as his fingers grasped something burning hot. He managed to sit up and see what had burned him. There was an old-
fashioned canister blowtorch on the coffee table, a dull blue
flame licking out of its nozzle.

He felt rather than saw his attacker lunge at him. Without
thinking, Kane grabbed the blowtorch and turned the control
knob. Instantly a two-foot-long tongue of flame whooshed out of
the nozzle, lighting the room in a hellish dance of light and
flickering shadow. Kane had a brief glimpse of a black face and
then the man reared back, the flames from the blowtorch licking
at his leather-jacketed shoulder. Kane struggled to his feet. He
felt the vibration of footsteps behind him and whirled, the flame
from the blowtorch roaring in a wide arc. The second attacker
came in low, bowling Kane off his feet again. The blowtorch
spun out of his hand and landed underneath the big picture window, the yellow flame licking at the curtains and running up toward the rail.

Kane was fit and wiry, but it took all he had to get to his feet.
He stood swaying for a moment, and then the second man was
on him, squeezing him in a crushing bear hug. Kane clawed for
the eyes, and the pressure began to slacken. Then something
moved behind him and exploded in Kane's head and he fell. He
felt the coffee table collapse beneath him, then the doors of consciousness slammed shut and there was only blackness.

Ten feet away from his still body, the flames from the burning
curtains licked hungrily at the wall.

The small fissures widened imperceptibly in the night. The

mountain, silent and peaceful for ten million years, was waking from its long sleep. The entire face of the slide was now webbed with a lacy filigree of cracks, and birds and small animals fled, disturbed by the shivering of the earth. A dozen pebbles skittered down the slope. A puff of dust rose in the moonless night. Small trees bowed to a nonexistent wind.

It was almost time.

Chapter Five

JULY 1

Dennis Penpraze sat on a stool in the crowded coffee shop of the McGregor Motor Hotel and brooded. After three days in Revelstoke he had come to the conclusion that it was a royal pain in the ass. The most exciting thing the small, mountain-ringed town had to offer was the Magic Fingers vibrating unit built into his bed.

Five thousand people lived in Revelstoke, and it seemed as though all of them worked either in the Canadian Pacific freight yards or at the sawmill down by the river. As far as Penpraze could see there wasn't any night life at all. He picked his teeth with the corner of a book of matches. The mountains were really bothering him. During the day they seemed to press down on him, hulking shapes thousands of feet high, covered in a suffocating blanket of trees. At night he could feel them out there, great brooding pillars cutting off escape. It was like being in a tomb.

Penpraze watched as the young waitress behind the counter doled out coffee and rubbery scrambled eggs. He felt the stirring of an erection. She was sixteen or seventeen, a local. Too much makeup. The tight-fitting light-green terylene uniform she wore caught in the cleft of her buttocks as she moved, and he could tell she knew exactly what the men in the room were thinking. Just like the whores in Saigon. His erection faded. Looking. It was better that way. Just looking. Those times when he'd actually done it the experience had been cold, lifeless. A function, like taking a leak. He'd rather jerk off. You didn't waste time that way.

Penpraze finished his coffee and shifted on the vinyl stool. Screw it. He had more important things to think about. Like the job. He smiled and wondered what the girl would do if she knew he was an agent. Undercover. He turned his head casually and looked at the people around him. What would any of them do? Probably fall off their goddamn stools. They were like a bunch of sheep. Heads full of nothing but their boring work and a quick piece while they sat around drinking their coffee and stuffing their faces. Little did they know who sat right beside them at the counter. He looked at his watch. Eight forty-five. Time to go.

His orders had been simple and explicit. On arrival in Revelstoke he was to register at the McGregor. There would be a reservation already made. Then he was to rent a truck, preferably a four-wheel-drive type, using his own driver's license. He was then to drive the truck to his spot in the motel parking lot, leaving it there, a postcard of the Los Angeles city hall on the dashboard shelf. Under no circumstances was he to drive the truck. Between eight-thirty and eight forty-five each morning he was to check for further orders. They would be placed in a small envelope under the seat. While waiting for the orders he was to learn as much as he could about the Revelstoke area, paying particular attention to the Mica and High Revelstoke dams.

He had followed the instructions to the letter. He had spent his three days asking questions of everyone who would stop to listen. On two occasions he had visited the B.C. Hydro field office in the town in an attempt to get information on the dam.

Penpraze finished his coffee and paid the check, winking heavily at the waitress when she gave him his change. She ignored him. He shrugged, went out through the side door of the coffee shop, and crossed the parking lot to the truck. Even this early the sun was bright, the sky cloudless.

He reached the truck, hauled himself up into the cab, and sat there for a moment, staring at the yellow brick wall of the motel.

He reached into his jacket and took out a pair of aviator sunglasses. He put them on and checked himself in the rear-view
mirror. Perfect. He shrugged slightly, feeling the weight of the
battered secondhand .38 in its makeshift shoulder holster. Moving only his eyes, he checked the rear-view mirror again, then
the side. Nobody around. He felt down between his legs and his
heart began to pound furiously as he felt the slim package
wedged between the springs. He slid it out, taking care to keep
the envelope below the level of the window. He slit the edge of
the envelope with his thumb and drew out the single sheet of
paper. As he read it, he let a slow smile form on his lips. This
was it.

He read the instructions through twice and then pushed in the
dashboard cigarette lighter. When it popped out again, he put
the glowing element to the rim of the sheet and watched as it
flared briefly, peppering the floor of the truck with a fine gray
ash. He started the truck, slammed it into reverse, and backed
out of the parking space.

Five minutes later he reached the abandoned graveyard at the
northern edge of the town and turned right, up the old Big Bend
Highway. He glanced at the large green sign beside the road:

MICA DAMSITE
TOURIST SERVICES
85 MILES

He floated at the bottom of the pit, no arms, no legs, no eyes.
Voices came faintly, echoing down shadowed corridors, the ringing of dull clappers on muted bells.

Later, he might have known time was passing, in the brief seconds when he imagined himself seeing faces hovering, heavy and
bloated, lips moving. But each time the pain would come, and he
would let himself fade back to the safe blackness of the pit.

"Umm," said Kane. His lips parted stickily. There was a sour
burnt taste in his mouth. His tongue seemed to be filling his
mouth. He began to drop away again.

"Mr. Kane." The voice was firm. A man.

"Umm," said Kane. The pit shrank away and disappeared. He
opened his eyes.

"My name is Dr. Shillington," said the fuzzy pink orb above him. "You are in a private room in Doctors Hospital. The date is July the first."

"So what?" mumbled Kane thickly. There was a split in the pink circle. For some reason Kane could smell starch. Fresh sheets. Ludicrous.

"Mr. Kane," said the voice insistently.

Shillington? He didn't know anyone named Shillington. With the thought came a wave of nausea. It felt as though he was going backward on a locomotive, the bed lurching wildly. He clutched at the sheets.

"Some vertigo is to be expected, Mr. Kane," said Shillington.

The sensation faded after a few seconds, but the doctor's face was still a pink blob.

"My contacts," Kane whispered hoarsely. "Get me my contacts." Without his contacts he was helpless as a baby. For some reason, he found he wanted to cry.

"In due course, Mr. Kane. You've had quite a time," said Shillington soothingly. "How do you feel?"

Kane thought about it. His left side felt as though it had been steamrollered and the right side of his head sent pain lancing behind his eyes each time he moved. He reached up a hand and felt thick layers of gauze.

"I feel terrible," he said.

"Good," said Shillington, smiling again. "You're lucky to be feeling anything at all. I'll have the nurse bring you your contact lenses and we'll get you some pain killer. Do you feel up to a little social life?"

"Who wants to see me?" asked Kane.

The pair of dark caterpillars at the top of Shillington's head arched. "A very attractive young woman, as a matter of fact."

"Send her in," said Kane, and then closed his eyes.

Two efficient nurses fussed around Kane for the next few minutes, and then Charlene Daly peeked around the door and came to stand at the end of the bed.

"Hi," she said, and swallowed.

Kane tried to smile. "Hi," he said weakly. "How do I look?"

Chuck wrinkled her nose. "Awful," she said. "But it could

have been worse." Her voice was strained, and she swallowed again.

"That's what the doctor told me," he said. "Did it rate a story in the *Intelligencer?*" He put on a Walter Cronkite voice. "Mr. Jon Kane, noted engineer and geologist, was beaten and robbed when he interrupted burglars in his home." He stopped. Chuck was frowning, and there were tears welling up in her eyes.

"They weren't burglars," she said.

Kane looked at her, confused. He tried to smile again, and bits of broken glass dug into his temple.

"They sure as hell weren't trying to get me to contribute to the Cancer Drive," he said, puzzled. "It was just bad timing, that's all. I mean, I should have—"

"Goddamn it! I said they weren't burglars! Burglars don't burn down people's houses with blowtorches!" Chuck was crying now, her knuckles white as she gripped the rail at the end of the bed.

"I did that myself," said Kane, the pain throbbing in his head as he remembered. "It fell out of my hand and set fire to the curtains."

"Oh, for Christ's sake! What was a blowtorch doing in your living room in the first place? That's what the fire marshal wants to know. No, sorry. I didn't mean it like that." She wiped tears away with the back of her hand, and sniffed. "Sorry, but they got your office as well. Your office manager went in on Tuesday morning and the whole place had been demolished. They'd even broken into the office safe. They ransacked a few other offices on the same floor, to make it look good, but it was you they were after."

"Was it you that found me at the house?" asked Kane, straining to remember. Nothing. Blank.

Chuck nodded and smiled, avoiding his eye. "Yeah. They should make me Girl Scout of the Year. I gave you mouth-to-mouth and everything. One of the firemen said that if I'd arrived five minutes later you would have been so much charcoal." The smile began to quiver at the corners of her mouth. "Jesus, Jon! What's going on? What are we into?" She walked to the head of the bed and collapsed into a chair.

"I'm not sure," said Kane, fuzzy. "I'd like to know what they were doing in my house, and my office."

"They wanted information. And they wanted to kill you," said Chuck. "The way I figure it they were waiting for you to come home that night. They were going to kill you and then set fire to the house."

"But how did they know?" asked Kane warily, fighting to stay rational. "How did they know when I was coming home? I didn't tell anyone how long I was going to be in Vancouver for. The only person who knew I was coming home—" He stopped suddenly and rolled his head on the pillow to look at her.

"Me," said Chuck. "I was the only one who knew." It was her turn to stop. She stared at him, eyes widening in horror. "Oh, Christ! You don't . . . you can't think that I set . . ."

Kane shook his head and waved a hand. "No, no. But you *were* the only one who knew. They must have tapped your phone. They listened in on our conversation, figured I'd gone too far, and decided to finish me off. But that doesn't make any sense either. If they were listening in, they must have known you were coming over at midnight."

"You mean they were going to get me too?" whispered Chuck, startled.

Kane nodded. "That's the only thing that fits. First me, then you when you came at midnight. Then burn the house down. But I saw them coming and they had to take a raincheck on you."

Chuck had been standing at the end of the bed. Now she came around and sat down beside Kane. She took his hand and squeezed it gently.

"You weren't first," she said finally. "Halleran was."

Kane closed his eyes for a moment, and then opened them again. "Explain," he said.

"He's dead," whispered Chuck. She squeezed his hand more tightly. "It came over the wire on Tuesday. According to the report he was refueling his plane around ten o'clock Monday night. The gas tank blew up. An accident."

Kane lay back against the pillows and closed his eyes again. It was too much. He wanted to banish it all, to begin again, to wipe off the days since he had begun his investigation. It was all madness. He was an engineer, a government bureaucrat. A tiny cog in a huge machine. Things like this happened in the movies. To spies in Berlin. Not to people like him. His mind gave up and he lay quiet, not believing. Then the anger began—a cold, furious anger that was almost overwhelming. It was true, though. They—whoever *they* were—had killed Halleran, and they had tried to kill both Chuck and him. And having tried once, they'd try again.

He opened his eyes.

"We've got to get out of here. Now," he said firmly. He sat up in bed and the pain in his skull became almost unbearable.

"Don't be stupid," said Chuck. "The doctor says you've got a concussion. He wants you in bed for at least a week. You were out cold for almost three days."

She tried to push him back down onto the pillows. He pushed her away and for the first time he realized that his left hand was swathed in bandages. He remembered touching the nozzle of the blowtorch. Everything else seemed to be working, though.

"Get me my clothes and find out if there's a back way out of here," he ordered, sitting on the edge of the bed. The room spun around him.

"Where are we going?" asked Chuck.

Kane looked up at her groggily. "Olympia," he muttered. "To throw some shit into a fan."

"What?" Chuck obviously thought he was rambling. But he looked better now.

"A promise I made Halleran." He lurched to his feet. "Now, don't just stand there. Go and get me some clothes."

The tour guide, a bored, rosy-cheeked young man with hair so blond it looked bleached, led the small group through the tunnel leading from the Richland Reservation administration center to the fast breeder, the drone of his standard speech echoing dully from the walls of the narrow, brightly lit passageway.

"The cables you see to your right carry much of the information to and from the breeder center. The cables are used for transmission of electronic data-processing material, video signals, and alarm circuitry. The large cable on our left is the auxiliary power line which carries current in the event of a power failure at the fast breeder."

The guide marched to the end of the tunnel and halted his flock before the blank doors of an elevator. He pressed the single button, and almost instantly the doors hissed open. He herded the group into the elevator. The doors closed, and a few seconds later opened again, onto the main lobby of the breeder. The guide continued his patter as they clattered across the broad expanse of floor and stopped in front of a scale model of the reactor, cut away to show the interior. He fiddled with a control panel to light small bulbs within the model, highlighting areas of interest.

"In the main lobby we have the security room," he intoned, pointing to a door on the south wall of the lobby. "Here, a continuously rotating shift of guards can watch virtually all activities within the reactor facility by way of closed-circuit television." He showed his teeth in a practiced smile. "They might even be watching us now," he said, and pointed up at the ceiling. Heads swiveled obediently upward, toward the cluster of cameras arranged to cover every square inch of the lobby, including the main doors leading outside.

"On the far side of the lobby, directly in front of us," went on the guide, "we have the doors that lead into the actual breeder." He pointed to the pair of massive steel doors, simultaneously pushing the button that lit the appropriate bulb on the model. "These doors are made of titanium steel and each one weighs some six and a half tons," said the guide, registering pride. There were oohs and aahs from the tour group. "Beyond the main doors are the laboratories and the control center." He switched on two more lights in the model, one on either side of a hallway. "The laboratories are used to perform many useful and valuable experiments with the various isotopes produced in the breeder. The control room, which is to the right on the model, is the nerve center of the whole complex. There, a few highly trained men monitor all the activities within the breeder, with the aid of one of the largest computer facilities in the United States. In the very, very unlikely event of an accident, such as a reactor blowout or meltdown, the reactor could be safely shut down from behind the control room's five-foot-thick walls." Again, the practiced we-think-of-everything smile.

"The room is hermetically sealed and has its own air-supply system. It is also equipped with a secondary power system. All the controls here are duplicated both in the main fuel loading center and within the administration building. These are all measures designed to ensure that the reactor system remains safe at all times. All the controls are tested every two weeks to make sure that everything is working properly." The guide pressed another button, and a light went on in a larger room on the model. "What you see here is the main fuel assembly and loading area. The room is more than seventy feet across and has a ceiling fifty-two feet high. The room is separated from the control center and the laboratories by an air lock"—another button, another light—"which prevents radioactive contamination by people within the fuel-loading chamber. It is in the fuel-loading chamber that the bundles of fuel rods are loaded into the 'honeycomb,' the large circular area you see in the main wall of the reactor at the far end of the room. Above the honeycomb on the ceiling you can see a number of catwalks. These are used to check the liquid coolant pipes. These white tubes. In reality, those pipes are more than ten inches in diameter. The liquid sodium they contain is used to carry heat away from the reactor to the heat exchanger building, next door. The liquid sodium is heated to approximately five hundred degrees Celsius during the process."

"What's that in Fahrenheit?" asked someone in the group.

"Nine hundred and thirty-two degrees," responded the guide instantly. There was always someone. He turned away from the model and led the tour toward the doors leading into the main reactor area.

Max Rudnick, standing behind the video switcher in the security room, watched over the man's shoulder as the cameras in the lobby ceiling looked down on the tour group.

"Bring it in a little on the east camera," he said softly. The switcher thumbed a control and the tour group grew larger on the monitor screen as lens zoomed in. The back of Vince Snyder's head filled the screen.

"Long-haired fucking freaks," muttered Rudnick.

"It's going to be a lot easier than I thought," said Vince Snyder. They had left the fast breeder an hour and a half ago. Now he, Paula St. George, and Ronald Bateman were having a late breakfast in the dining room of the Richland Motor Hotel.

"Why's that?" asked Paula around a mouthful of egg. Bateman chewed sullenly at a piece of rye toast. For the past week Paula had been flirting openly with Snyder. Bateman knew matters were reaching the point where he was going to have to say something, but he didn't know what. To tell the truth, he was more than a little scared.

"I didn't think they'd be so slack," said Snyder. "For one thing, the only burglar alarm I could see on the administration building was a foil strip arrangement on the windows. Ten years out of date. I can get us in there in five minutes."

"What's the point of getting into the administration building?" asked Bateman, annoyed. "The whole point of this exercise is to show people how easy it would be for terrorists to get into an actual reactor installation."

Snyder nodded, sipping his coffee. "Right." He smiled, patronizingly. "You may remember, Ronald, that there's a tunnel from the administration building to the breeder. Once we get into the administration building we just follow the tunnel to the elevator and ride up to the lobby. Just the way we did on the tour."

"At which point the guards see us on their television cameras and come out of their security room, guns blazing," sneered Bateman. "Very constructive."

"Why don't you let Vince finish?" snapped Paula, turning on him. "Go on, Vince."

Snyder shook his head and smiled. "Uh-uh," he said. "I want to do some more checking first, but I think I've got it figured."

"I hope so," said Bateman, scowling. "If you don't, we're dead. Literally."

Exactly twenty-six and seven-tenths miles from the sign at the Big Bend Highway, Dennis Penpraze turned the truck up a narrow logging road. The road stitched up the side of a sloping, tree-covered mountain, and soon the highway was far below him. According to his instructions he drove up the road for eleven and two-tenths miles. Exactly as his orders had said, he came to a small clearing beside the road. In the center of the clearing stood a small, windowless plywood shack, raised off the wet ground on short metal stilts.

Penpraze drove off the road into the clearing and parked the truck beside the shack. Then he cut the engine, rolled down the window, and waited, listening. After five minutes he climbed down from the truck, took the tire iron from the back and went to the door of the shack. The door was secured by a simple hasp and padlock. Penpraze fitted the tire iron under the hasp and wrenched. The screws came out of the plywood and the door swung open.

The dark interior of the shack was piled high with nearly four tons of explosives. The cases of detonators, bags of nitramite, and boxes of caps and dynamite sticks all bore the markings of the B.C. Department of Highways. Penpraze smiled, at home with the familiar shapes of the containers.

He selected the explosives with care, ignoring the kegs of black powder and the nitramite blasting agent in favor of the dynamite, the high detonation pressure primers, and the caps. He also took two reels of quarry line detonating fuse, a small case of blasting caps, and a pair of crimping pliers. He piled all the explosives into the back of the truck, covering the boxes with the tarpaulin he had purchased the day before. He reserved fifty sticks of the dynamite, piling it into the seat and covering it with his windbreaker.

When he had finished loading, he climbed into the driver's seat and headed back to Revelstoke. He made one stop at the shopping center just outside the town on the TransCanada Highway, where he went into a sporting goods store and purchased a backpack frame and a knapsack, a flare pistol and a box of flares, and a Cooey single-action shotgun and five boxes of shells. He put all the purchases into the knapsack with the exception of the shotgun, which he carried out in its box. Next he went into a hardware store and bought half a dozen six-hour clockwork cooking timers, a hacksaw, and five rolls of hockey tape. These he also put in the knapsack. He returned to the truck, drove back to the McGregor, parked, and went up to his room. By the time he had unpacked everything it was twelve-thirty. Ignoring the hunger pangs he felt, he settled down to work, whistling and thinking about the waitress in the coffee shop.

They drove down the Tacoma-Olympia Interstate, Chuck behind the wheel of her 1968 Mercedes 230-S. Kane sat in the tan leather bucket seat beside her and stared out the window as they traveled down the modern four-lane thruway that cut through the mixed forest and farmland of Pierce County. In the distance, to the east, the snow-capped cone of Mount Rainier was constantly with them, backed by the hazy outlines of the Cascade Range running along the horizon.

They had been driving steadily south for almost two hours. Kane was still in pain, most of it from the three cracked ribs he'd sustained in the fight. Even though he was tightly strapped with surgical bandage, every time he shifted in his seat it felt as though his entire lower chest was on fire. The pain in his hand was duller now, but still there. He knew that Chuck, beside him in the driver's seat of the ancient Mercedes, was maneuvering the big car as smoothly as she could in deference to his injuries. Since leaving the hospital they had hardly spoken, both of them cocooned in their own thoughts.

It was Chuck who finally broke the silence. "Jon, what would happen if the dam did come down?" she asked quietly.

Kane stared out the windshield thoughtfully. A sleek black Chrysler pulled back into the slow lane ahead of them.

"I'm not absolutely sure," he said, turning to her and wincing at the pain in his ribs. "I've been trying to figure it out myself. At best it would destroy any towns along the Canadian section of the river and cause some bad flooding in upstate Washington. Spokane might be hit pretty hard, too, if the water backed up the Spokane River." He watched as Chuck's eyes flicked to the rear-view mirror. He turned around in his seat, wincing again. A light-blue Lincoln had pulled up to within a hundred feet of their tail. He frowned. There was hardly any traffic on the highway. Why would a car like that be tailgating them? But Chuck was talking again.

"You said 'at best,'" said Chuck. "If that's the best you could expect, what's the worst?"

Kane turned around in his seat and leaned back gently against the comfortable headrest. "It's called the House of Cards," he said, and closed his eyes. "It's a theory that's been around for quite a while. The theory states that, on a major system if one dam comes down and the slope is steep enough, the flow of water will take out all the other dams. Like a card house falling down. There was a bit of discussion about it at the Teton hearings in seventy-six, but there's never been anything like that. No one has ever really given it much serious thought."

"Could it happen on the Columbia?" asked Chuck.

Kane sat up in his seat and reached for the package of cigarettes on the dashboard.

"I think it could," he said, lighting up. "The slope is steep enough, especially between the Mica and the border. According to the little bits and pieces of information I could pick up, the river drops two feet a mile."

"That's not much," said Chuck.

"Are you kidding? That's one hell of a lot. The Colorado River doesn't drop half that per mile, and look at how fast it flows."

"If you put it that way," said Chuck. "But it's still hard to imagine."

Kane nodded. "I know. That's the problem we're going to have in Olympia. It's going to be tough convincing a lot of bureaucrats that a dam the size of the Mica could actually collapse." He caught a flash of color out of the corner of his eye. The Lincoln was pulling out to pass. Behind it was another Chrysler, identical to the one in front of them.

"Have you figured out who you're going to talk to yet?" asked Chuck.

Kane nodded. The Lincoln seemed to be pulling out very slowly.

"Someone in the governor's office, I think," he began.

The Lincoln had pulled up directly beside them. The Chrysler behind them had moved up to within twenty feet of their rear bumper. Kane spun around in his seat. Ahead of them the first Chrysler was slowing down, its brake lights flaring.

"Chuck!" he yelled, realizing what was happening. At that instant the Lincoln veered to the right, taking a broadside swipe at them. The car bucked and slued half onto the shoulder. The Chrysler behind roared forward, slamming into their rear end, the impact sending Kane into the dashboard. He bit back a scream as his ribs hit.

Chuck dragged the wheel to the left, bringing the heavy car into the Lincoln. The solid steel bumper of the Mercedes caught in the wheel well of the Lincoln, peeling back the fender and slicing the right front tire to ribbons. The Lincoln went into a screeching drift away from the Mercedes, struck the median divider, and flipped over it, rolling end over end. On the third roll it burst into flame and disintegrated. Chuck ignored it. She rammed her foot down on the gas, whipping the Mercedes into the slot vacated by the demolished car. The Mercedes rocketed into overdrive, the two four-barreled Bosch carburetors slingshotting them forward into the passing lane ahead of the lead Chrysler.

Directly ahead the median narrowed and disappeared as they neared the single-span bridge over the Nisqually River. Chuck glanced quickly into the rear-view mirror and then over at Kane, who was doubled over in agony. She looked into the mirror again. The two Chryslers were no more than a hundred feet behind them. She looked ahead. The bridge was free of traffic.

"Split shot," she muttered to herself. She reached down with her right hand and palmed the shift lever out of automatic and into a lower gear. The engine shrieked and the car slowed abruptly. She put her right hand back on the wheel and reached down with her left, dragging the emergency brake handle forward. Then she jammed the brake pedal to the floor.

The Mercedes went into a smoking four-wheel slide and skidded to a rocking stop on the bridge, straddling both lanes. The drivers of the two Chryslers reacted instinctively and swerved to avoid a collision, the first going left, the second right. The cars burst through the guard rails almost simultaneously, arching out into space and plunging down into the placid waters of the Nisqually, sixty feet below.

Kane sat up, groaning. It felt as though someone had hit him with a sledge hammer. His head was pounding furiously and he felt a wave of nausea sweep over him. He controlled it and turned to Chuck. She was sitting rigid, eyes glazed, knuckles white as they clutched the leather-covered steering wheel of the stalled car.

"Fine," she said. "Those years of pool playing finally paid off." Her voice went thin and cracked and she fell forward over the wheel, sobbing. She was still shaking an hour later when Kane drove her past the city limits of Olympia, the State Capitol Dome at the city's center like a beacon in the late afternoon sun.

Getting anyone to do anything in any capital city is difficult at the best of times. Kane discovered that on the eve of a holiday weekend it was next to impossible. By four-thirty the city was virtually deserted, and the few officials left were less than enthusiastic about getting involved with a wild-eyed man in a soiled seersucker suit and a bandage-swathed hand. If it hadn't been for his federal I.D., he wouldn't have got past the security guard at the front door of the Legislative Office. As it was, the various people he talked to looked at him as if he were mad and shifted him along quickly, insisting that the next man along the line was the one he really wanted to talk to.

Finally, after almost an hour of the traditional civil service runaround, Kane lost his temper. In a surprisingly short time he found himself in the governor's office.

Gloria Cullen, the governor, was already out of the city, having fled to her summer home in Puget Sound earlier in the day, but her executive assistant, a hard-faced woman in her mid-thirties named Eleanor Sweet, was still at her desk.

Kane decided to throw caution to the winds and explained the whole thing to her, from his initial suspicions to the demolition derby on the coast highway. The story took the better part of an hour and more than once Kane thought Eleanor Sweet was about to call for the men in white coats, but he plunged on, Chuck beside him filling in the blanks here and there.

"Preposterous," said Sweet coldly when he finished.

"But true."

"If it wasn't for the fact that you appear to have bona fide identification, I wouldn't hesitate to throw you out of this office," said Sweet. "Given your credentials, however, I must admit I'm not quite sure what to do. Frankly, your story sounds completely insane. What *proof* have you, Mr. Kane?" She brushed a speck of nonexistent dust off her crisply tailored tweed jacket.

"All you have to do is check with the hospital in Seattle, and with the state police. I'm sure they've found the wrecked cars by now," said Chuck, desperate.

"And what would that tell me?" asked Sweet. "Except for the fact that your friend Mr. Kane was recently in the hospital suffering from a variety of ailments that he could have incurred in a dozen different ways, and that the two of you were witnesses to a multiple automobile accident."

"For Christ's sake, don't be so stupid," snapped Kane. Eleanor Sweet's face stiffened, and he saw he had made a tactical error. "Look," he pleaded more gently, "why would we tell you a story like that if it wasn't true? What in God's name could we get out of it? If you accept the fact that I am who I say I am, then the least you can do is check out my story. The governor has to be informed immediately. If something isn't done and pretty damn quick, we may all be in a lot of trouble."

Sweet still appeared unconvinced.

"Well?" asked Kane. "Do you contact the governor or do we go elsewhere?"

"Elsewhere?" said Sweet, smiling frostily. "And where, pray, is that?"

"The *Post Intelligencer*," said Chuck. "Or maybe right onto the wire services."

"I see," said the executive assistant, pursing her lips.

Kane leaned forward, spreading his hands imploringly. "Believe me, Miss Sweet, that's the last thing I want to do," he said. "A story like that could start a hell of a panic. People might get hurt. But if it's the only way, then we'll do it. One man has already died. They've tried to kill Miss Daly and me on two different occasions. This whole thing has to be aired, now, before it's too late."

Kane sat back on the couch, his hand gingerly holding his bandaged ribs. Sweet looked at them, considering the situation. After a long pause she nodded.

"All right. Let's see if we can come to an agreement. For the sake of argument, let us assume your story is true. In that case your lives are in danger. Therefore you must be protected. On the other hand, you may be a pair of raving lunatics, going through this farce for heaven knows what purpose. I must have time to check out your story before I contact the governor. Agreed?"

"Agreed," said Kane. Chuck nodded.

"Good," said Sweet, reaching for the phone on her desk. "I'm going to arrange for you to be taken to a motel and kept under guard. If your story checks out, I will contact the governor as soon as I can. If you are lying, I'll have you thrown in jail for public mischief. Understood?"

Chuck and Kane nodded silently, and Sweet began to dial.

For some reason Kane was worried. He knew the story had to check out. But what if it didn't? He was silent as he and Chuck were driven through the town by an impassive chauffeur and escorted to separate but adjoining rooms in the Olympic Motel, not too far from the water. It was a small motel, and except for them, almost completely empty. They had been given rooms at the end of the motel farthest from the office, and the rooms on either side were vacant. An unmarked police car sat across the street. The building backed up against a large automotive supply shop, so there were no windows in the rear of the rooms. It looked as if they would be quite safe, especially since Chuck's rather conspicuous car had been taken to the police garage and wouldn't be sitting outside, like a beacon.

"It's hard," began Kane hesitantly, as they lay naked together on the bed in his darkened room.

"What is? Apart from the obvious?" asked Chuck, nuzzling his neck.

Kane laughed. "Your name," he answered.

"What's wrong with it?"

"Well, how am I supposed to say, 'I love you, Chuck'? I mean, it doesn't sound right."

"It sounds fine to me," she said, turning his head and kissing him lightly. "Better than Charlene, anyway. Why don't you try it again?"

"I love you, Chuck."

"I love you, Johnny." They lay still for a moment, touching softly.

"I wonder if it would hurt my ribs too much?" whispered Kane, turning on his side and sliding his good hand around Chuck's smooth, narrow back.

"I don't think so," she whispered, pulling him in close to her. She slid up against him, her legs parting, and guided him into her, her thighs clamped tightly at his waist. She began to move slowly, rocking him gently, pressing him farther and farther within her. He felt the touch of her lips at his ear and then heard her voice, singing softly, almost without a tune, the sound and the movement carrying him away from all the worries that surrounded them. He closed his eyes and wished desperately that they could hold the moment forever.

PART TWO:
HOUSE OF CARDS

Chapter Six

JULY 4

Colonel William D. Canterra, "Wild Bill" to his friends and "that crazy son-of-a-bitch Canterra" to his superior officers, gave the F1-11 its head, letting it climb high into the midnight sky. Almost forty thousand feet below him the lights of Spokane glimmered softly, the small patch of brightness almost lost in the surrounding blackness. Canterra didn't pay any attention to the city or to the other faint beacons of civilization on the surface of the earth. What the groundhogs were up to was no concern of his.

Although his mother had denied it emphatically, Canterra was positive he had been conceived in an airplane. There was no other way to account for his intense love of anything that flew. By the age of three he was helping his father build kites in a basement workshop, and by eight he had graduated to powered scale models. When he was ten, his parents finally gave in to his constant pleas and took him on a sightseeing flight wheeling over his hometown. The day he turned thirteen he joined Air Cadets, and on his eighteenth birthday he enlisted in the Air Force.

After a month at the flying school his instructors realized they
had a prodigy on their hands. Some people were born to com-
pose great symphonies or design magnificent buildings. Canterra
had the knack with airplanes. Anything that flew, Canterra
wanted to fly, and fly it he did. Bombers, transports, prop planes,
helicopters, gliders. Anything.

In Vietnam he flew his favorite, the F1-11. A lot of his flying
buddies thought the huge swing-wing fighter-bomber was a
death trap, but for Canterra it was love at first sight. He piled up
more successful sorties than any other pilot in the war. After that
he flew in Rhodesia and later in a NATO squadron based in Ger-
many. He wound up in the United States, a full colonel, an in-
structor in the same school he'd started in.

The administrative work was tedious, and within a few
months the challenge of trying to make aces out of green pilots
was gone. Canterra began lobbying with a few strategically
placed friends in the Pentagon, and after almost a year of nagging he got results. He was offered the job of setting up a preci-
sion flying team to be based on the West Coast and using F1-11s.
The Air Force was still taking a lot of flack about technical problems with the jet, and a stunt team seemed like the ideal of
showing off just what the aircraft could do. The only stateside
base capable of dealing with maintenance and repairs was Merton AFB, just north of Spokane, a Strategic Air Command unit
under the command of General Vaughn Hartington. When it
was pointed out to Canterra that he'd have virtually unlimited
flying time he jumped at the job.

To avoid upsetting the regular schedule of the base, Canterra
had confined his own flying activities to night flights, preferring
the solitude of the night sky to the crowded daylight hours. He
logged the trips as checkouts, but Hartington knew better. The
aircraft had been test-flown for hundreds of hours before deliv-
ery and there was no need for further vetting. He let the situation ride, though, correctly assuming that a contented Canterra
in the air was better than a frustrated Canterra on the ground.
Since his arrival at Merton, the twenty-seven-year-old flyer's
dark good looks had already got him into trouble with more than
one of the officers' wives. Hartington, despite some misgivings,

had decided that it would be politic to ignore the midnight aerial rambles.

Canterra was at play, sending the massive swept-wing fighter-bomber cavorting like a supersonic corkscrew. When he reached his maximum altitude he turned the jet northward to the saw-toothed granite jaws of the Canadian Rockies. The bleak and almost totally unpopulated area was the only place he could practice his high-speed dives without terrifying the people below. The night shift radarmen at the Canadian Forces Base in Chilliwack had become accustomed to the twisting antics of the lone aircraft on their screens, and were happy to accommodate his practice runs as long as he continued to announce himself each time he entered Canadian airspace. Canterra, for his part, enjoyed the fact that the operators could see his work reflected in their scopes, and he played to them as an entertainer plays to his audience. He looked at the array of instruments in front of him. When he had run through his checklist he yanked back on the right-hand throttle arm and hurried north to begin his performance, traveling at almost fifteen hundred miles per hour.

Eight miles below Canterra, a small rubber raft powered by a quiet but powerful electric outboard was approaching the upstream face of the Mica Dam. The four heavily equipped, black-garbed men in the raft had been airlifted to a point eight miles from the dam, at the confluence area of the Canoe River. The plane that had brought them waited there, ready for their return.

The leader of the squad looked at the luminous dial of his watch. It had been almost an hour, and now they were in sight of the dark shadow that marked the crest. If everything went according to schedule they could be back at the plane well before dawn. From there the four men would be taken to a rendezvous point in Nevada, flying low to avoid radar detection, change planes, and make for Mexico, their final destination. In Mexico City they would receive the second half of their payment. Then they would disappear. Unknown to the four, and to the pilot of the waiting aircraft, a device had been installed in the engine compartment, geared to detonate forty-five minutes after the next ignition of the engine. The men would disappear, but not the way they intended.

There was a muffled crunch as the raft bumped the gravel slope of the upstream face. The four scrambled silently out of the raft and began the short twelve-foot climb from the water to the crest of the dam.

Vince Snyder lay fully clothed on the bed in his room at the hotel. He was tense, listening. Something had awakened him from his light sleep. He lifted his arm and looked at his watch. It was only one o'clock. Three hours before they were to make their start.

He heard the sound again. A soft tapping at his door. He slid soundlessly off the bed and padded across the room. The knock came again, more insistent this time.

"Who is it?" he whispered.

"Paula. Let me in," she answered, her voice muffled behind the door. He unlocked it and peered out into the brightness of the hallway, squinting with the sudden loss of his night vision.

Paula St. George was dressed in a short electric-blue kimono jacket. Her long legs were naked. She hopped nervously from one foot to the other.

"For Christ's sake, would you open up!" she hissed, looking up and down the hall. Snyder opened the door fully, and she hurried in, closing the door behind her and leaning up against it. Snyder glanced down as the fold of her kimono slipped open, revealing a patch of thigh. Paula made no move to cover herself.

"Couldn't sleep?" asked Snyder, smiling in the darkness. Paula said nothing. She stepped forward and wrapped her arms around his neck, pressing her lower body against his groin. The kiss was full and left no doubt about her intentions. His lips parted under the repeated attacks of her probing tongue. He let the kiss go on for a moment and then pushed her away, holding onto her shoulders.

"Ronnie-boy get opening-night jitters?" he asked.

She ignored him and reached for his belt buckle, undoing it and letting her hand slide down over his flesh.

"Shut up," she whispered icily.

He reached for the cord binding her kimono and untied it, letting his hand play over the long curve of her hip and then travel upward to the curve of her breast, his thumb pressing the hard, dark knot of her nipple.

"Is he sleeping?" asked Snyder. She nodded. Together they moved toward the waiting bed.

In the next room Ronald Bateman lay staring at the ceiling, listening to the faint rustlings that came to him through the adjoining wall. He reached out a hand and let it touch the bare sheet where Paula had been.

He listened as the sounds from the next room grew louder, the rustlings giving way to deeper sighs and finally to a steady, rhythmic hammering of the headboard, counterpointed by the easily recognizable moans of her pleasure. He clenched his teeth, his eyes squeezed shut, and he prayed for the sounds to end. But the sounds kept on minute after minute.

Ronald Bateman wanted to die. He lay there, stiff with hatred. Then he realized. He didn't want to die. Quite the reverse. For the first time in his life Ronald Bateman wanted to lash out, to fight. Ronald Bateman wanted to kill.

Muscles aching and eyelids dropping with fatigue, Dennis Penpraze reached Vancouver an hour before dawn. He followed the twisting ribbon of the TransCanada as it meandered through the Coast Range and came down along the edge of Deep Cove, the most inland reach of Burrard Inlet. He followed the water west, past the refineries at IOCO, and eventually reached Hastings Street. The truck was the only vehicle on the empty, brightly lit avenue of strip joints, used car lots, and massage parlors.

He reached the center of the city, turned up Burrard, cutting across the business district, and then rolled over the Burrard Bridge. The only signs of life were a cruising taxi and an empty bus mindlessly covering its deserted route.

He continued along the water of the inlet, past Kitsilano and the blank-faced split-levels of Point Gray at Spanish Banks, finally coming to the rising bluffs of the university campus. He climbed the steeply canted road, and slowed at the summit, watching the water side of the road. When he spotted the parking bay his instructions had mentioned, he pulled into it, cut the engine, and doused the lights. The lot was deserted, the dark line of the trees that surrounded it quiet. There was no wind. He picked up the heavy bulk of the packframe and, hoisting it onto his shoulders, headed across the grass verge and down the steep path that led to Wreck Beach, at the base of the high clay cliffs.

When he reached the bottom he paused to catch his breath. Directly in front of him was the rolling surf of the inlet, lit every few seconds by the sweep of the Point Atkinson light four miles away on the far shore. Above the lighthouse the dark shadows of the last mountains of the Coast Range frowned for the last time before they ran down to the sea at Horseshoe Bay. He adjusted the pack, turned left, and began to trudge along the sand. The tower would be about a mile down the beach, at the mouth of the inlet.

The gun towers on either point of the inlet had been Vancouver's response to the Second World War. During the war years they had been equipped with heavy naval guns, but now they stood empty, forty-foot concrete pillboxes, a convenient spot for lovers' trysts and a handy surface for the graffiti of bathers on the beach.

As he reached the tower, the first flush of dawn came up behind him, rising over the mountains and spreading a gray haze over the sleeping city. In the dim light he read the large letters slopped on the pitted concrete in white paint. GO HOME they said.

He smiled. That was exactly his intention. He pulled open the creaking metal door at the base of the tower and went in, bolting it behind him. He climbed the stairs to the enclosed platform with its wide slit facing the beach and the sea beyond and settled down to wait. His instructions had said that the truck would be picked up within a few minutes of his arrival and the boat would come for him at midnight the following day. He would have preferred to while away the extra day in a motel room, but his orders had been clear. He was to be in the tower no later than the dawn of the fourth, and he was to stay there, no matter what. He dropped the pack gently to the floor, pillowed his head on it, and slept.

The man from Langley worked his way methodically through the apartment, removing some things, replacing others. A copy of *The Blaster's Handbook*, a DuPont publication, was inserted into the small shelf of books in the kitchen, as well as a copy of the *Mica Dam Construction Review* and a Rand McNally *Road Atlas of Canada*. *The Dambusters* by Paul Brickhill was placed on the toilet tank. A copy of the collected works of Thoreau was removed and a Mexican left-wing press edition of *Das Kapital* put in its place in a stack of books beside the bed. A worn copy of the *Environmental Handbook* was laid open on the rumpled sheets. A poster of Andreas Baader was taped to the back of the kitchen door. A manila envelope stuffed with newspaper clippings describing a variety of terrorist activities during the past four years was placed in the bottom drawer of the bureau. A post office box number scribbled on the wall beside the telephone in the hall was carefully sponged off, and the tiny listening device removed from the telephone itself. A crumpled envelope bearing the logo of the British Columbia Hydroelectric Authority was dropped on the floor.

By 6:00 A.M. the stage was set. The man from Langley let himself out of Dennis Penpraze's apartment, closing the door softly behind him and stripping off the thin surgical gloves he had worn throughout the operation.

Chapter Seven

JULY 4

6:30 A.M. PACIFIC DAYLIGHT TIME
9:30 A.M. EASTERN DAYLIGHT TIME

The naked young man was bending over him, the huge blade of the sword swinging in a flashing arc. The razor-sharp tongue of metal came closer and closer, and Rudnick cowered as it approached, struggling against the ropes that bound him, his mouth opened in a scream that couldn't be heard above the roaring cheers of the thousands of people in the stadium around them. The young man paused, made an elegant bow to the audience. Then he stepped forward, moving in between Rudnick's spread-eagled legs, raising the weapon high above his head. The baying of the crowd surged louder as the broadsword slashed down. In the last second before it struck, Rudnick realized with horror that he had wet himself in fear. As the edge of the sword cut into his flesh, thousands of bells burst into a mad carillon, marking the moment of his death.

Rudnick's eyes snapped open. The jangling of the telephone six inches from his head tore at the alcohol-swollen membranes of his skull. He rolled over on the couch and slapped at the phone on the small end table, sending it spinning to the floor. He lay there for a moment, breathing heavily, trying to will away the awful pounding in his head. Finally he reached down and picked up the phone, holding the receiver up to his ear. He could hear a voice calling his name. It was Haberman, his assistant.

"Uh, Jes . . ." began Rudnick, the words dissolving into a deep racking cough that wrenched at his gut. He groaned as the pain surged up. The spasm passed. "S'time?" he managed finally.

Haberman's voice was grotesquely wide awake. Rudnick could almost see the young man's pink chipmunk face and the big, almost hyperthyroid eyes.

"Almost six-thirty, Mr. Rudnick. Sorry to bother you, sir. I know you're not on duty but I thought it was important, we've got a problem here, sir, I think."

"Jesus, Haberman, slow down!" Rudnick tried to sit up, but the pain in his head knocked him down again. Even the faint dawn sunlight coming weakly through his living-room window was enough to make him squint. He tried again. This time he got as far as his elbows.

"Yes, sir. Sorry, sir," Haberman was saying.

"And lower your voice. You're screaming in my ear."

"Yes, sir." Haberman was sure that he'd hardly been speaking above a whisper, but he knew better than to argue with Rudnick. He dropped his voice even more. "As I said, sir, we have a problem." He paused, unsure.

"Yeah?" said Rudnick. His voice was thick, and he cleared his throat. "You going to keep it a secret or what?"

"No, sir," said Haberman. "We've lost contact with the breeder, sir."

"What the hell are you talking about, Haberman?" snarled Rudnick. "What do you mean, lost contact with the breeder? What's happened, the thing get picked up by a goddamn UFO or something?"

"No, sir," said Haberman nervously. "Not that, sir. I was in main security with Danby and Bellows, they're on the night shift this week—"

"I know who's on night shift, Haberman, I make up the fucking roster. For Christ's sake, get on with it!"

"Yes, sir," Haberman swallowed. "Like I said, I was in main

security and all of a sudden the monitoring line to the breeder went out. We tried to cut in the auxiliary but we couldn't get a thing, sir."

"So you lost the video feed. So I am not the maintenance man, Haberman. Is that all, now."

"No, sir. I did call maintenance, Mr. Rudnick. They checked it out and they found the cable in the access tunnel was burned through."

"Burned through?" said Rudnick. "What the hell are you talking about?"

"Right through. With acid, it looks like."

"Son of a bitch!" hissed Rudnick, his head throbbing as he swung his feet onto the floor and began looking for his shoes.

"Yes, sir," said Haberman.

"Have you tried getting breeder security on the phone?"

"Yes, sir. Couldn't get anything. The phone lines are in the same cable as the video feed, and they don't answer on the radiophone."

"Goddamn!"

"Yes, sir. I thought I'd better call you before I went and had a look, sir."

"I'll be there in twenty-five minutes. Don't move a muscle. Stay right where you are, Haberman. Don't go anywhere near the breeder. You got that?" Rudnick could feel his headache disappearing as the adrenaline pumped through his system.

"Yes, sir. Is there anything else, Mr. Rudnick?" asked Haberman.

"Yeah," said Rudnick, standing up beside the couch. "Wake up the Kraut and tell him what's happening."

"You want me to call Mr. Kellerman?" whispered Haberman, horrified at the prospect of waking the chief administrator.

"You got it. If I have to get up at six-thirty for this, so does he. Tell him it looks like someone's bust into his precious reactor."

"You think that's what's happened, Mr. Rudnick?" asked Haberman.

Rudnick grinned. "It sure as hell isn't pixies, Haberman," he said, and slammed down the receiver.

Five minutes later Rudnick, dressed in the clothes he had fallen asleep in, was tearing through the sleeping streets of Richland, the bubble flasher on the roof of the station wagon blinking wildly, the siren under the hood wailing in the cool dawn air.

At 4:50 A.M. it had still been pitch dark. Snyder, Paula St. George, and Bateman, all three of them dressed in black from head to foot, had completed the inflation and assembly of the black rubber dinghy. By 5:15 A.M. they had landed on the western banks of the Columbia at the river edge of the Richland Reservation's Storage A site. Then they ran across the wet, clinging soil, heading southwest toward the reactor compound perimeter wire. At 5:25 A.M. they crossed over the radiation leak area. In the darkness, they did not see the CAUTION–RADIATION HAZARD signs posted by Rudnick's men.

They had reached the perimeter wire at 5:31 A.M. They followed the wire, running out of range of the floodlights, until they found themselves at the northwestern corner of the compound. They crawled underneath the fence at the point where the spur rail line entered the compound. Then they crossed the deeply shadowed area of the old reactor facilities, keeping close to the walls of the abandoned buildings. By 5:40 A.M. they had reached the administration building.

Bateman, his jealousy forgotten for the moment, watched in fascination as Snyder deftly sliced through one of the basement windows with a glass cutter and bridged the foil circuit with a prefabricated line he had made from material purchased in a Richland hardware store. The bridge completed, Snyder simply kicked in the window. Snyder let himself down into the building, followed by Paula St. George. Bateman went in last, first handing down the pack containing the mock bombs as well as a sawed-off shotgun, purchased in the same hardware store as the material for the bridging circuit, the glass cutter, and the other equipment.

They found themselves in the boiler room of the building, surrounded by pipes, furnace vents, and air-conditioning paraphernalia. Snyder, walking in the lead, clicked on a pencil flashlight. They followed the narrow beam through the maze of humming machinery and ductwork until they found themselves in the wide basement hallway they had come down on their tour. They went down the hallway quickly, ears alert for the

sound of guards or a watchman. Except for the normal sounds of
the building there was nothing. Kellerman, the chief administra-
trator, had long ago decided to opt for electronic security. The
only guards in the building were cozily ensconced in a monitoring room on the main floor. Of the fifteen cameras in the administration building, fourteen were on the first, second, and third
floors. The fifteenth was in the basement, overlooking the tunnel
entrance. Unfortunately its obsolete photon gun had burnt out a
week before and hadn't been replaced. The tunnel entrance was
blind.

The tunnel itself was night-lit: only one overhead fluorescent
in four was on. The three paused as they reached the entrance.
Bateman pointed silently to the overhead camera on its swivel
mount. The dead-eyed lens was pointing down the tunnel.
Bateman bent over and Snyder climbed up on his shoulders, bal-
ancing precariously, one hand holding a pair of wire cutters, the
other grasping Bateman's shoulder. Bateman felt slightly nause-
ated by the touch of the other man's groin on his neck. He closed
his eyes briefly and tried to concentrate on the operation at
hand. Snyder reached up and snipped the wires to the camera,
then touched Bateman lightly on the top of the head. Bateman
leaned down again, and Snyder hopped off the heavier man's
shoulders. He looked at his watch and nodded.

Snyder knew enough about security installations from his in-
surgency training to realize that in a television setup there were
never as many monitors as there were cameras. In a good setup
each camera would be patched into the main security facility on
a regular schedule. Snyder was assuming that there was at least
a fifty-fifty chance that they would have time to get to the
breeder before the tunnel camera was turned on. It was a calcu-
lated risk. It had worried Bateman, but Snyder had assured him
that any facility still using foiled windows would probably still
be somewhere in the Iron Age when it came to security.

The three raced noiselessly down the tunnel. At 5:56 A.M. they
reached the elevator doors. Paula held out the pack to Snyder.
Still breathing hard, he reached inside and drew out two small
glass vials, their ends plugged with wax. He took the vials over
to the thick bundle of cables clamped to the wall, then motioned
to Bateman, who pressed the heat-activated elevator call button.

The compartment was already on the lower level and the doors swished open immediately. Paula stepped into the elevator carrying the pack and the shotgun. Bateman stood in the elevator opening, wedging the door open with his foot, watching as Snyder went to work on the cables.

On the tour Snyder had correctly deduced that the thick bundle of cable high on the wall carried the main current, while the thinner, lower bundle of color-coded wires carried the alarm-system line, the television monitor co-axials, and the telephones. Snyder tapped the ends of the two vials sharply against one of the bracket clamps holding the lower bundles and poured the fuming nitric acid over the wires. Almost immediately Bateman's nostrils were filled with a foul odor. As he watched, the wires began to smoke. The rubber insulation dripped away, then the bright metal cores turned green and dissolved. Coughing, Snyder hopped into the waiting elevator as Bateman moved his foot away from the door, simultaneously punching the up button on the control panel. Bateman frowned as he saw Paula hand Snyder the shotgun.

"Only birdshot," Snyder had assured him when he'd shown him the weapon in the motel.

"It's the complete opposite of what we want to achieve!" Bateman had yelled, furious. "It's not just the fact that Greentree is nonviolent, or that I'm against guns of any kind. It's simply that it's dangerous. We're coming down to their level!"

"What the fuck are we supposed to do, say 'Pretty please, we want to take over your reactor'? Be realistic!" Snyder had retorted. In the end he had won out. Now, as Bateman watched Snyder expertly snapping the pump action and removing the safety, he felt the cold realization that he had made a fatal mistake. If Snyder had ever had any intention of trying to achieve any kind of humanitarian goals by occupying the reactor, something Bateman doubted anyway, they had dissolved the minute Vince's fingers had closed around the trigger of the snub-barreled Remington. With the shotgun in his hands Snyder was in his element, and his element was violence.

The ride up in the elevator seemed endless, although according to Snyder, who had timed it on the tour, it took only six seconds. Snyder knew that the time lapse was critical. As soon as the guards in the security room realized that their alarms were out of action, they'd come out of the room with their asses on fire. He was counting on there being enough confusion while they tried to figure out what was wrong to give him the time he needed.

The doors swished back and Snyder leapt out of the elevator in a running crouch, the other two close behind him. He fired upward from the hip, the thunder of the shotgun filling the lobby as he took out the overhead cameras, shattered electronic components scattering wildly into the air, coming down like a metallic hailstorm. Snyder pumped the shotgun as he ran and fell into a crouch ten feet in front of the door to the security room.

The three guards had reacted quickly, heading for the door within a split second of seeing Snyder on their monitors. They weren't quite fast enough. As they poured out the door, they found themselves staring into the black muzzle of the Remington.

"Trick or treat?" grinned Snyder. The men, all of whom had been reaching for their holster flaps, raised their hands. Silently, Paula and Bateman disarmed the three and then tied them up with lengths of thin clothesline from the pack. They dragged the men back into the security room. Snyder checked the knobs, then took a bunch of keys from one of the men. He went to the television control board and, after a quick check of the switches, began flicking through the camera locations until he found the one for the reactor control center. He sucked his teeth, staring at the flickering image. It was as he had predicted. There were only two men in the room, monitoring the computers and the reactor operations. The facility was operating on a skeleton staff over the long weekend. It was also apparent that the tour guide had been right when he'd referred to the control center as being hermetically sealed. The two men seemed completely unaware that anything had happened.

"Let's move it," said Snyder crisply, motioning to Bateman. The two went out of the security room, leaving Paula standing over the three bound guards with one of their own pistols in her hand.

Snyder and Bateman opened the large doors leading to the

laboratories and the control center. They walked quickly down the brightly lit, metal-floored hall and stopped in front of the control center's emergency exit. The tour guide had been quite specific. Normal access to the control center was through the air lock at the end of the hall. In the event of an accident within the reactor, however, the men in the control room could make their escape rapidly by breaking the thin lead seals on the emergency exit. "Although the reactor control center houses many millions of dollars worth of equipment," the guide had said proudly, "the safety of the men and women who work here always comes first."

Bateman and Snyder stood back against the far wall and ran at the door. They hit it solidly with their shoulders and it burst inward, one of its hinges snapping. Snyder leveled the shotgun at the two white-faced technicians. A few moments later they had joined the guards in the security room.

Snyder locked the door to the room and the three began placing the "bombs." Ten minutes later the job was complete and the fast breeder was theirs.

It was 6:36 A.M.

Charlene Daly kept her eyes squeezed tightly shut, refusing to admit to the weak fingers of light that were beginning to creep insidiously around the edges of the drawn curtains on the other side of the room. The scuttling rodent sounds that had filled her dreams continued. Mice. There were definitely mice in the room. She flung out an arm to warn Jon, but her hand felt nothing but the slippery nylon fabric of the empty pillow. Chuck had an instant of panic. Then she opened her eyes and rolled over. Kane, already dressed, was seated at the writing table by the connecting door scribbling with a pencil on a sheet of paper. That explains the mice, she thought, and heaved a sigh of relief.

Kane turned at the sound, his face drawn and worried. "Go back to sleep," he said tersely, and turned back to his writing.

"What the hell are you doing?" asked Chuck groggily, peering at the clock on the bedside table. "God! It's only twenty-five to seven!" she groaned.

"Just go back to sleep," said Kane again, without turning. He continued to write furiously. Chuck sat up in bed and reached for her cigarettes.

"You were giving me nightmares," she said, lighting one. "You sounded like a battalion of field mice."

"Sleep!" said Kane, glaring at her over his shoulder.

"I'll go back to sleep when you tell me what you're working so hard at," replied Chuck, dragging on her cigarette.

Kane threw down the pencil and stretched. "I've been trying to figure it all out," he said, walking across the room and sitting down on the edge of the bed. He tapped out one of his own cigarettes and lit up.

"Reach any conclusions?" asked Chuck.

Kane scowled. "Yes. I've decided that I'm clearly not as bright as I thought I was. The whole thing is crazy. None of it hangs together."

"Try it out on me," suggested Chuck. "I'm a journalist. Journalists are good at coming up with wild hypotheses."

"All right," said Kane. "Riddle me this: I come up with what I first thought was a pretty harebrained idea about the possibility of multiple collapses on the Canadian Columbia. I try to do some sniffing around and I get nowhere. Then I dig a little deeper and suddenly people start getting upset. Then someone tries to kill me. They do kill Halleran. Which would suggest that my idea wasn't so crazy after all. Right?"

"So far so good."

"We try to get in touch with someone who can do something about the situation, and they try to knock us off a second time. When we finally get to someone in authority, we get shunted off to a motel in the boondocks with Bert the Guard out there to make sure we don't get into trouble." Kane jerked a thumb over his shoulder toward the window.

"So?" shrugged Chuck. "What's to figure out?"

Kane leaned over and stabbed his cigarette viciously into the ashtray. "Why?" he shouted.

Chuck frowned. "Why what?"

Kane stood up and began pacing back and forth across the room. "Why are they doing all this?" he asked, exasperated. "Because I've fallen over something they wanted to keep secret? Bull shit! How do you keep a monster slide like that a secret?

Stopping me from blowing the whistle on them won't keep the slide from coming down!"

"I see what you mean," mused Chuck. "It would only make sense if they wanted to solve the problem somehow, without attracting any attention."

"Which is impossible," said Kane. "I thought of that. But there's no way they could shore up the slide without just about emptying the reservoir, and that would open up the whole can of worms. There'd be a full-scale inquiry."

"Which they would not enjoy." Chuck leaned back against the pillow, shutting her eyes. Kane went to the window and peeled the curtains back slightly, looking out over the vacant parking lot and the quiet street. The unmarked car was still there. A beefy, red-faced plainclothesman was reading a paperback and drinking coffee from a thermos cup.

"Time," said Chuck, her eyes still closed. "Time," she said again. "They seem to be in an awful hurry." She puffed on her cigarette and squinted through the cloud of smoke at the ceiling, thinking. "Try this for size," she said after a moment. "Whoever these people are, they want us out of the way, and fast. They know the slide is going to come down, and they know we know. They're going to sit back and let it happen, and when it does they'll call it an act of God, and we won't be around to tell anyone different. If your theory about a multiple collapse is right they'll be in bad trouble, but maybe they're hoping it won't happen, and that the only damage will be in Canada. How does that sound?"

"As far as it goes it's okay," said Kane. "But it doesn't work. For one thing, if they simply let the slide come down they'll be faulted for not knowing the slide was there in the first place, and if they did know it was there, if their initial geological reports showed a fault or a potential slide site, then they could be hit really hard. I think that's what's happened. I think they've known that there was a fault there right from the beginning, but the Canadians went ahead and built anyway, to keep to their obligations under the treaty. The Canadian dams, or their basic locations at least, were chosen by the U. S. The Canadians had their own plan but we wouldn't go for it. We eventually convinced them to build the dams where we wanted them for the optimum water-storage capacity. Now the chickens are coming home to roost. If my guess is right, the Corps of Engineers, or Reclamation, ran a study on the possibility of multiple collapses after the Teton Dam collapsed in 1976, and they found out that the Columbia system would go if the Mica came down. I remember reading some of the material from the Teton Dam hearings held by Congress after the disaster, and they skirted the whole issue of multiple collapses. I don't think they'd ever even considered the possibility of a multiple collapse until the Teton came down, and by then it was too late, at least as far as the Columbia system was concerned, so they kept their mouths shut."

"But the slide is going to let the cat out of the bag," said Chuck.

"Exactly," said Kane. "They must know there will be a slide. The silt I saw proves that. And somehow we're getting in the way of whatever it is they're trying to do to stop it."

"But what?" asked Chuck. "If they had some way of stopping this slide from coming down, they'd have done it long ago."

"They have two choices," said Kane. "One: they bring down the slide slowly, so that it doesn't raise a flood wave capable of topping the dam and eroding into the core. Two: they open up the spillway and the discharge tunnels and let the water out as fast as they can. That would lower the level in the reservoir and maybe prevent the slide from creeping any farther. But I think it's too late for that."

"So?" shrugged Chuck, sitting forward on the bed and butting her cigarette into the ashtray. "Maybe they thought up something you haven't considered."

"There isn't anything else!" exploded Kane. "Opening the spillway is the only way of lowering the water level, and even that might not be fast enough. They had the floodgates wide open at Vaiont for almost a week before *that* slide came down, and it didn't do any good at all." Kane frowned and rubbed the palm of one hand along his stubbled jaw. "No. The maximum spillway capacity for the Mica, according to the material Halleran gave me, is 246,000 cubic feet per second. To do any good they'd need about five times that volume of water passing out of the reservoir to lower the water level, and there's no way in the

world they could do that. I mean, unless they were absolutely insane and—"

Kane's eyes widened and the blood drained from his face. The
vision that had appeared in his mind's eye was too horrifying to
believe. But he had to believe it. It was the only thing that made
any sense, the only thing that the people who were after them
could do to prevent a massive flood wave like the one at Vaiont,
and the multiple collapse of all the containment structures on the
Columbia. It was a hideous compromise. A small disaster to
avert a larger one.

"What is it?" asked Chuck, urgently, staring at him. "What's
the matter?"

"Mother of God!" whispered Kane, "I think they're going to
blow up the Mica Dam!"

Chapter Eight

JULY 4

8:55 A.M. PACIFIC DAYLIGHT TIME
11:55 A.M. EASTERN DAYLIGHT TIME

It never failed to excite him. Each time Norm Taylor, chief maintenance engineer, walked the crest, as he did every morning before settling down to the charts and schedules that were the nitty-gritty of his job, the vastness of his charge sent a thrill through him. The Mica was the biggest in the world, and it was his job to keep her fit. Most of his time was spent making sure that the drainage tunnels and the outlet works and the hundred and one other small details of the dam were in order, but he walked the crest each morning to let the simple size of the dam get to him.

As he strolled down the narrow asphalt strip that ran from one side of the dam to the other, he was a flyspeck on a mountain. To his right, beyond the outlet works tower, the reservoir stretched away, deep and placid, the tourmaline waters reflecting the mountains crowding its banks. On his left was the gorge, an eight-hundred-foot drop down the steep gravel and shot-rock slope. As he neared the center of the dam he walked to the edge and looked down.

At the bottom he could see the dark line of the access road running along the toe of the dam to the newly built power-houses, once again the largest in the world, buried deep in the rock of the western abutment. Taylor looked back the way he had come and stared at the arcing ribbon of the spillway, and the upturned throat of the flip bucket at its base. He was relieved that today was the day for the opening of the flood-gates. The reservoir was higher than it should have been, and the snowpack melt and the heavy rains had narrowed the safety margin severely.

Well, it didn't matter now. In another hour the waters of the massive lake behind the dam would begin flowing through the powerhouse gates as well as down the spillway, easing the pres-sure and at the same time generating the hydroelectricity that was the reason for the dam's existence in the first place.

He looked down the southern face of the dam again, at the in-sectlike forms of the big Caterpillar tractors lined up on the ac-cess road, each one, seen from his vantage point, no larger than his fingernail. He wondered what he looked like from down there, then laughed. He'd looked up from below before. You saw nothing but a rearing cliff of rubble the height of a seventy-story building, filling your vision. The figure of a single man on the crest was a mere irrelevance. He continued his walk.

Just beyond the center of the dam he tripped on a small pro-trusion in the road. He stopped and looked back, frowning, won-dering if the winter frost had buckled the road. But surely he would have noticed something like that before. He looked closely, but couldn't see anything amiss. Then he saw it; a little ridge in the pavement, not quite the same color or texture. He bent down for a closer look.

The lump was smooth, not pebbled like the asphalt around it, and the protrusion was almost perfectly circular. He touched it with the tip of his index finger, and the finger came away smudged. What the hell was it?

He reached into the pocket of his work shirt and drew out a small penknife, flipping open the blade. He dug it into the lump. It went in easily, as though through unhardened putty. He worked away at the lump, chipping out flecks of the black sticky substance. He looked around as he worked and noticed that the lump was not unique. There were at least two dozen of them that he could see, neatly spaced about four feet apart, in a double row from one shoulder of the road to the other. The blade of the knife struck something and he stopped. He dug in with his fingers, pulling away the last of the material, and his heart jumped to his throat. He leapt to his feet. It was a blasting cap. He'd seen them, used them, a thousand times before. He turned and started to run.

The explosion came when he was still no more than ten feet away. Norman Taylor died instantly, his body and brain vaporized before he realized that there had been an explosion.

The thunder of the detonation never had a chance to fade. Hard on its heels came a hideous bellow as water roared through the newly opened gap and formed a plume of foam that arced out over the downstream face of the dam. At the moment of the explosion the trench had been twenty-four-feet wide and seventeen-and-a-half-feet deep. Within ten seconds the eroding force of the water had widened it to almost forty-five feet and cut into the compacted till as far as the core area twenty-five feet down.

The heart of the dam was being torn out in chunks and spat into space, each passing second widening and deepening the keyhole, the water hacking into the dam like a hammered wedge in softwood.

As men began streaming out of the spillway control house to the crest, the roadway began to sag around the lip of the rupture, large slabs of the black asphalt breaking off and falling into the torrent, only to be sent flying out into the gorge by the incredible pressure of the flow. Several of the men recognized the frightening possibility of what they were seeing and reacted, turning back to the control house. The only way to stem the almost inevitable catastrophe would be to open every available outlet, easing the pressure along the crest. But the worst was yet to come.

The slide zone had been much closer to collapse than anyone had imagined. The detonation of the more than two hundred pounds of explosive not only ripped into the Mica Dam, it also sent a strong shock wave through the water of the reservoir. Within a few moments the tremor reached the base of Mount Dainard, eight miles upstream, shaking, even though only slightly, the already-fragile balance at the underwater toe of the slide area. It was enough. The mountain moved.

The slide area included a section of the south face of Mount Dainard two and one-quarter miles long, a mile and three-quarters high, and almost eight hundred feet thick. This entire land mass, 900 million tons of earth and rock, sheared away from the side of the mountain and plummeted into the waters of McNaughton Lake.

The displaced water rose into a towering wall, 745 feet high, which sped across the lake. As it moved, the wave scoured the western face of Mount Cummins, on the east bank of the reservoir, flensing the soil down to bedrock. As this water crashed into the lake again, it created another wave, which followed the giant wave already headed toward the dam at more than 150 miles per hour.

This swell thrown up by the slide rose almost five hundred feet higher than the crest of the dam, reaching the upstream face four minutes after the initial explosion. The dozen or more men standing on the crest were obliterated, their bodies crushed as the swell broke against the dam.

The concrete grouting that welded the earthfill structure to the mountain walls on each side was subjected to pressures in excess of twenty tons per square foot. Within seconds it failed, allowing the entire dam to slide forward on its downstream toe. The remains of the upstream heel rose as the great mass of water wedged the base upward.

As the wave broke above the crest, the half-mile spillway was torn away from the east bank like rotted cardboard. The dam began to sag. At that instant the second wave, created by the rebound off Mount Cummins, burst on the upstream face and opened up a gaping wound in the center of the dam. A few seconds later the structure dissolved in a seething welter of boulders, silt, and mud. With the obstacle removed, the monstrous wave, a surging wall of water, 620 feet high, traveling at 96 miles per hour, and fueled by a lake 135 miles long, began its headlong journey down the Columbia to its final destination—the Pacific Ocean, a thousand miles away.

It was 9:05 A.M., Pacific Daylight Time.

Chapter Nine

JULY 4

9:15 A.M. PACIFIC DAYLIGHT TIME
12:15 P.M. EASTERN DAYLIGHT TIME

In the broadloomed and antique-crammed office of Dr. Hans Kellerman, the chief administrator of the Richland Nuclear Reservation, Max Rudnick looked and felt like a bull in a china shop. He sat precariously on one of the slender-legged Queen Anne chairs and waited for Kellerman to speak. The short, white-haired chief administrator stood at his window, staring down at the hive of activity in front of the administration building. A dozen police cars from both the Richland sheriff's office and the state police littered the road in front of the building. Haberman and three or four others from the Richland Security Force were directing the uniformed men to the breeder. Kellerman turned away from the window and sat down behind the ornately trimmed seventeenth-century table he used as a desk. He looked at Rudnick.

"You have yet to repair the cable in the access tunnel?" he asked. The German accent was stronger than usual.

Rudnick nodded. "I checked them myself. Eaten right through. Smells like nitric or sulphuric."

"And you have not gone into the reactor yet?"

Rudnick nodded again. "No. I thought it best to wait for the state boys. The guards and the technicians in the breeder security room said there were only three of them, two men and a woman, but one of them had a shotgun. I figured to hold off until I talked to you."

"Thank you," said Kellerman. "You have checked the location of these people on the monitors?"

"They're in the reactor control center. One man, the one with the shotgun, looks about thirty or so, maybe a bit younger. The other guy's got a bit of a pot, curly dark hair, maybe thirty-five.

"Girl's tall, dark haired. Mid-twenties. The guy with the shotgun's the only one that looks dangerous."

Kellerman eyed him coldly. "They are all dangerous, Mr. Rudnick. You have called the FBI?" It was more a statement than a question.

"No, sir," replied Rudnick curtly. "I think we can handle this without their help."

Kellerman shook his head. "It is not a matter of what you think, Mr. Rudnick. This is a federal reservation. The FBI must be brought in. By law. Is that clear?"

"Yes," said Rudnick, leaning back in the flimsy chair. "But that means publicity, you know."

Kellerman reddened. Over the years, the Hanford-Richland Works had come under fire a number of times, mainly because of the large number of accidents that had occurred there. Publicity was a sore point with him, and Rudnick knew it.

"Publicity or no publicity, call them in. Now. Have you discovered how these . . . individuals entered the reactor compound?" he asked, changing the subject.

Rudnick shook his head, smiling tightly. "Not yet. Haberman's sending out a crew when he gets finished with the state boys. I've got a pretty good idea, though. I laid it all out in the last report I sent you, the one just before the leak." Rudnick controlled a feeling of grim satisfaction. As soon as he had arrived at Richland, he had made it abundantly clear that he thought the security arrangements were in dire need of upgrading. Over the past year he had been giving most of his attention to the problem of a terrorist action against the reservation, his interest spurred by a recent Oak Ridge ERDA bulletin on the possibility of plutonium hijacking. But Kellerman had ignored the reports. As far as he was concerned the possibility of anyone breaking into Richland was too remote to worry about. He had put down Rudnick's requests for increased budgets as a crude attempt at empire building. Well, thought Rudnick, he would regret it now. His reports were still on file and would make damning evidence at the investigation that would certainly result from today's events.

"I believe you suggested that the most likely infiltration point would be at the river," replied Kellerman, trying his best to summon up the contents of the report in his mind.

Rudnick nodded, leaning forward in his chair. "Yeah. They probably followed the perimeter fence up from the water. Odds are we'll find a boat of some kind down there. It's always been the weakest spot, but I just don't have the personnel for an effective patrol system."

Kellerman ignored the unsubtle jab. "Does that mean they will have gone across the new leak area?" he asked.

Rudnick scowled. "I hadn't thought of that," he muttered, annoyed with himself. "I'll get a rad squad out."

"I suggest you do so immediately," said Kellerman, pleased that he had scored. "If these people are contaminated it puts an entirely different light on things."

"Yeah," said Rudnick to himself. It was bad enough having those creeps in there, but if they were hot it would make getting them out ten times harder. On top of that, the longer they waited to figure out a way of springing them, the more they were going to contaminate the reactor control center.

"I would also appreciate it if you would inform me when the cable has been repaired in the access tunnel. We will have to take over the reactor from the auxiliary control here. We have been on automatic program for the long weekend. The reactor is still cycling. It will have to be shut down."

Rudnick raised his eyebrows. Shutting down the reactor was not only time consuming, it was also incredibly expensive. It would take weeks to get it back up to optimum working capacity.

Kellerman stood up and gave a brief nod of dismissal. The

meeting was over. After Rudnick had closed the door behind
him, the chief administrator turned and went back to the window and gazed out beyond the wide patch of brown earth that
lay between the road and the southern perimeter fence. The
early morning sun was beginning to warm the barren terrain on
the far side of the fence. The sky was a cloudless, watery blue.
Kellerman knew the day was going to be hot. He was suddenly
aware of the burden of his sixty-three years. He felt a nervous
tug at his cheek and stiffened, controlling it. He looked into the
sky again. There had been another day like this, almost forty
years ago. A day that had changed his life.

He had returned from a three-day pass and found Peenemünde in ruins, von Braun and the others wandering dazedly
through the twisted, smoking wreckage of one of the greatest
research installations the world had ever seen. Somehow Kellerman had managed to survive that day and the horrors that followed, but he had been young then, barely into his twenties.
This was different. This time there would be no new career.
Even if, by some stroke of luck, the terrorists were removed
without difficulty, the publicity would ruin him. He would be
forced to resign, or at best accept an early retirement. It was
ironic that in the end it would probably be Rudnick's reports
that would brand him an incompetent. Rudnick, of all people!
There had been a time in his life when people like that fat Polish
fool would have been less than nothing to him, useful for only
the most menial of tasks.

Kellerman turned away from the window. He walked stiffly
back to his desk and sat down. He looked around his office for a
moment at the beautiful things he had collected over the years.
Then he reached for the telephone.

"They look very realistic," said Bateman, staring at the bomb
taped to the main console in the reactor control center. The device was in two parts: a six-inch ball of a plastic substance
whose flattened base had two protruding nipples and, connected
to each nipple by a wire, a black box the size of a package of
cigarettes.

Paula, sitting beside him in front of the console, looked at him
sharply. "What's that supposed to mean?" she asked.

Bateman, eyes burning with anger, looked across at Snyder, who was standing by the burst emergency exit doorway, looking out into the hall, his shotgun cradled under his arm.

"Why don't you tell her, Vince?" he snapped.

Snyder turned slowly, the shotgun coming out from under his arm, his fingers wrapping around the trigger. He smiled coldly.

"So you figured it out," he said.

Bateman nodded. "It came to me in a flash of divine inspiration while I was sitting here," he sneered.

"What the fuck are you two talking about?" said Paula, turning around in her seat.

Bateman laughed hollowly.

"Lover boy, over there. He's been taking us for a nice long ride. I always wondered what he was doing it for." He sighed. "At first I thought he was leading you along just because he wanted to get into your pants. I figured his motives were out of place, but after a while I got swept along myself by the whole thing. I should have seen it a lot earlier. He's fucked you in more ways than one, Paula. He's fucked both of us."

"Vince?" said Paula, turning toward him. Snyder shrugged. She looked back at Bateman, questioningly.

He held her eye, his round face earnest. "You wanted excitement, maybe you wanted a new bedmate. I wanted—oh, Christ, I don't know, I guess I wanted to be what you wanted me to be. What is it for you, Vince? Money?"

Snyder nodded, his smile turning into a broad grin.

Bateman felt his stomach contract with rage. "How much?" he asked. "A million, two million? How much does that sick little mind of yours want?"

"I'm a man of simple tastes, Bateman," answered Snyder from across the room. "Five hundred grand."

"And what about us?" asked Bateman.

Snyder made a seesawing motion with his free hand. "That depends," he said. "Get in my way and I'll blow you away. Be nice and maybe I'll cut you in. Your girlfriend isn't half bad in the sack. I could get used to her."

Paula lurched out of her chair, a screech hissing through her clenched teeth. She threw herself toward Snyder, fingers curved into claws. As she approached, Snyder snapped the shotgun around. The heavy sawed-off butt struck her full in the mouth and she collapsed onto the floor, groaning.

Twenty feet away Ronald Bateman sat very still. When he spoke his voice was quiet. "I'm going to kill you, Vince," he said slowly, staring into the other man's eyes.

Snyder grunted. "No, you're not," he said, his voice mocking. "You don't have it in you." But as he looked into Bateman's eyes he saw suddenly that he just might be wrong.

At 9:09 A.M., four minutes after the first wave reared over the Mica Dam and began moving down the high-walled canyon, the water reached the Mica townsite. The wave filled the canyon and squeezed upward more than seven hundred feet, a roaring, foam-shattered wall that obliterated the trailers, the tourist motel, and the A-frame church within seconds. High-tension cables and telephone wires flailed in the air for a moment then disappeared into the raging flood. Communication with the city of Revelstoke was severed as the entire town disappeared in a fleeting instant. There were no survivors.

The flood wave, 670 feet high and traveling at 93 miles per hour, began creating its own weather system as it plunged southward. Warm air at the base of the wave was forced upward, cooling rapidly and forming a giant shroud of mist that feathered back over the sloping body of water behind the face.

The wave chewed at the rock and soil on either bank, undermining the canyon walls and creating earthslips that sent thousands of tons of debris sliding down into the fuming water. Entire hillsides began to move as the earth shuddered with the wave's passage. Boulders the size of houses were flung into the wave, trees were uprooted and pounded into matchwood as the flood accomplished in minutes what the normal erosion of the river would have taken a million years to do.

Carl Turcott, his wife and his five children, driving in a late-model station wagon, had been on their way to the Mica Dam. They were on holiday—Carl from his insurance brokerage and his wife Margaret from Carl's mother, who lived with them but had chosen to remain in Vancouver rather rather than endure the horrors of traveling with the five children. Neither Carl nor anyone else in the car knew anything about the laws of hydrol-

ogy, but at 9:19 A.M. on that morning they were witnesses to one
of that science's fundamental principles.

A given volume of water, no matter how fast it is flowing, can-
not increase its rate of flow down a given channel beyond a certain point. If the channel suddenly constricts, the water rises
rather than increases its speed.

Sixteen miles below the townsite the Columbia Canyon con-
tracts. As Carl maneuvered through a hairpin turn at that point,
he and his family came face to face with the wave as it rose a
further 230 feet into the air. The wave leaped up and began
tearing away entire forests and vast acreages of topsoil above the
canyon rim. Carl Turcott's station wagon joined the wave's burden of death.

Thirty-seven minutes after the abrupt termination of the Tur-
cotts' holiday the flood wave reached the newly completed High
Revelstoke Dam. The five-hundred-foot wall of earth and concrete held the rushing water for a few moments, forcing it to rise
even higher than before. The impact was so extreme that some
of the workmen on the dam and within its honeycomb of drainage tunnels were actually shaken to death, their bones shattered
by the vibration before the water swept what was left of them
away. Much of the grouting that fixed the sides of the dam to the
canyon walls was still unfinished. Fourteen seconds after the initial impact, the dam dissolved into its component rocks and mud,
adding still more to the huge burden of debris that the wave
contained within its length.

Dwayne Cutler, the owner of the Esso service station on the
TransCanada Highway just beyond the bridge crossing the Columbia, was the first resident of Revelstoke to see the wave. His
station lay on the western outskirts of the town and from the
pumps you could see upriver to the CPR bridge and beyond to
the point where the river disappeared around a bend. Cutler had
just filled the tank of a tourist's car and was wiping his hands,
idly looking northward, when he realized that something was
wrong. The ground beneath his feet was vibrating slightly. At
first he thought it was caused by the passing of one of the large
lumber trucks that were constantly rolling by the station, but
there was no truck. Then he realized that the vibration was more
widespread. The big sign on the Gulf station a hundred yards

down the highway was swaying gently back and forth, and he could hear his tools rattling on the shelves inside the station.

As he stood there the vibration grew stronger, accompanied now by a distant thundering sound that seemed to be coming from up the river. He peered northward and blinked in surprise. A giant cloud of fog was descending on the town, and for a moment he thought they were about to be hit by some kind of freak summer storm. The thundering increased, and as he watched, the cloud began to spread, fitting itself to the contours of the small bowl-shaped valley. It was only when he saw the CPR bridge disintegrate that he recognized the wave for what it was. He barely had time to turn and begin running toward the office station before the wave struck. As the pumps were torn out of their footings, a spark ignited the giant storage tanks beneath the station. The explosion was snuffed out instantly by the furious passage of the water.

The water hammered into the city, swallowing people, automobiles, and buildings as it went, grinding brick and stone to mud and rubble. It demolished the pulp mill, the freight yards, three waiting freight trains, the roundhouse, and the passenger station.

But still the flood could find no peace. The widening valley slowed its progress only momentarily. For a brief instant the height of the wave dropped as the water filled the valley. Then, as it reached the southern limits of the town, the banks closed in again, funneling the water into the narrow, high-sided canyon lifting the wave back to almost its original height.

Within six minutes of leaving Revelstoke the wave struck the still waters of the Upper Arrow Lake. As it hit the upper reaches of the lake its nature changed. It approached at an extreme angle, digging deeply into the lake's deep waters, and created a swell that began running the length of the lake. The wave was no longer a high, turbulent wall. Now it was a huge humped-backed beast that swept down the lake, gathering the shoreline into its hungry maw: farms, trees, summer cottages, small boats, people, animals, and among others the entire towns of Mount Cartier, Shelter Bay, Galena, and Nakusp. Once again, there was no warning.

The swell, more than 350 feet high, rose even higher as the

water shallowed toward the end of the lake. Then it burst into Lower Arrow Lake, thrusting downward, witnessed only by the dark tree-carpeted mountains on either side, repeating its destructive course. The towns of Makison, New Burton, New Faquier, and Needles all disappeared beneath the water, towns that had been moved when the Hugh Keenleyside Dam was built and the depth of the Arrow Lakes artificially increased. Again there was no warning, and again, almost no flood protection procedures had been used.

At the southern end of the lake an obstacle stood in the path of the swell. The Keenleyside Dam was the heaviest of the Canadian dams on the Columbia. It was a dual structure, two-thirds of it earthfill like the Mica, the last third concrete.

Compared to the Mica it was a small dam, rising less than 250 feet above the floor of the lake. The swell struck its face and rolled over it, topping the structure by more than a hundred feet, dissolving the earthfill portion and bludgeoning the smaller concrete portion into nothingness, releasing the waters of the Upper and Lower Arrow, and adding their volume to the volume of water released by the collapse of the Mica and the High Revelstoke.

Beyond the Keenleyside, the river narrowed once more and the swell became a wave again, thundering down the ancient riverbed toward the United States border.

The wave reached the town of Castlegar, inundated it, and rolled on. Ten minutes later it reached the town of Trail. Trail, like Revelstoke, had been built in a small valley, but in Trail's case there were a few lucky survivors. The airport, used by bush pilots and by the small local flights of Pacific Western Airlines, was built on a high plateau. As the wave steamrollered over the town one of the controllers in the Trail Airport tower managed to send a distress call before the power went out. The call was picked up by an Air Canada jet on its way west, and the pilot relayed the message to Vancouver International Airport.

As the wave, now 640 feet high, tore into the small village of Columbia and crossed the border into the United States, the first vague and confused warnings of the approaching catastrophe began to circulate.

Chapter Ten

JULY 4

10:30 A.M. PACIFIC DAYLIGHT TIME
1:30 P.M. EASTERN DAYLIGHT TIME

At 6:25 A.M., twenty minutes after Dennis Penpraze entered the gun tower on Wreck Beach, a panel truck emblazoned with the University of British Columbia's rising sun crest and the words "Physical Plant" had pulled into the parking alcove beside Penpraze's rented pickup. A tall, curly-haired man wearing overalls got out of the UBC vehicle and walked over to the pickup. He removed the explosives and loaded them into his own vehicle, leaving behind one of the boxes marked "B.C. Department of Highways." Then he opened the door and climbed into the cab of his own truck, peeling off the thin surgical gloves he had been wearing. He nodded silently to his partner behind the wheel and they drove off through the weak dawn light, heading toward the university grounds, half a mile farther up Marine Drive. The entire procedure had taken less than ten minutes.

At 6:45 A.M. the duty officer at the Royal Canadian Mounted Police Detachment on West Seventy-third Avenue in Vancouver had received a telephone call, which was automatically recorded: "Good morning. My name is Dennis Penpraze. At pre-

cisely 9:00 A.M. this morning there will be an explosion at the
Mica Dam. The dam will be completely destroyed. I am fully
aware of the extreme seriousness of this act, but man has raped
the land for too long, and the injustices done by man to the
world he lives in must be redressed. The fall of the Mica is part
of my plan. Do not waste your time. There is nothing that you
can do to stop what I have begun. If you require proof of my ac-
tions, you can check the parking lot above Wreck Beach. I will
be waiting below in the gun tower by the sea, which is the beginning and which is the end. This is my only communiqué.
Soon I will be dead, but the land shall live, and even by my
death I shall succeed, my flesh and my blood returning to the
soil from whence they came."

Understandably the duty officer assumed that the call was
from a crank, but when he replayed the tape of the conversation,
something about the wooden, almost mechanical voice worried
him. He dispatched a patrol car to the Wreck Beach parking lot.
He then placed a call to the Revelstoke RCMP Detachment. His
opposite number there told him that there were no patrol cars
available to check out the story, but that one would be sent out
as soon as possible. The Vancouver officer asked if the Revelstoke detachment had a helicopter available. The Revelstoke
duty officer explained that they did have a helicopter but it had
been loaned to the National Parks, which was conducting a
search for a bear that had been terrorizing the campers at Gla-
cier National Park. The two men agreed that it was probably a
hoax anyway, but the duty officer dispatched a patrol car.

At 7:15 A.M. the officer in the patrol car radioed back to the
detachment and made his report. According to him the bed of
the pickup truck contained a crate that looked as if it might once
have contained explosives. The duty officer sent out a three-man
identification unit, and the RCMP bomb squad was put on
stand-by.

At 7:30 A.M. the Vancouver duty officer phoned Revelstoke
and advised them of the change in the situation. The Revelstoke
duty officer managed to contact one of his patrol cars and sent it
up the Big Bend Highway to the dam. Even at high speed the
trip would take almost two hours. The Revelstoke duty officer
then tried to reach the B.C. Hydro Office at the Mica townsite,

but a recording informed him that the office would not be open until 9:00 A.M. and then listed the times of that day's tours.

At 8:10 A.M. the pickup truck was identified as a rental out of Revelstoke. The identification unit returned to the detachment, bringing the papers with them. The patrol car officer remained with the truck.

After discussing the situation, the duty officer decided to assign four investigators on a surveillance detail. Two men would watch the truck from a safe distance and the other two would take up positions on the beach itself, disguised as sunbathers. The bomb squad would remain on alert.

While the surveillance detail swung into operation the duty officer went to the communications office. The name and address on the rental form were telexed to the FBI district office in Los Angeles, California.

As Dennis Penpraze's name began to rattle out of the Teletype machine in L.A., a small Chris Craft cast off from the docks at False Creek. The boat puttered slowly out past the Crystal Beach Coast Guard station and the forest of West End high rises across from it, moving out into Burrard Inlet. Completely unaware of the activity his presence was generating, Dennis Penpraze slept.

"Shit!" roared Kane, slamming down the telephone. "How many is that?"

Chuck, sitting cross-legged on the bed with the Olympia telephone book in her lap, did a quick count. "Nine. One left," she said, looking up at Kane, who was sitting at the desk on the far side of the room.

"No answers and wrong numbers," he scowled. "Where the hell is she?" He picked up the receiver. "Give me the number."

"C. M. Sweet. 357-3362," answered Chuck, peering down at the book. Kane began to dial once again.

It was their last hope. So far they had tried the capitol, the governor's office, and the main government information number with no response. The city was empty for the holiday weekend. Kane had gone so far as to call in the plainclothes policeman in the car across the street to ask him if he had an emergency number for Sweet. He didn't. All he knew was that he was to watch them until the governor's office told him differently.

Kane put down the receiver.

"Well, that's it," he said gloomily.

"No luck?" asked Chuck.

Kane shook his head and began drumming the fingers of his good hand on the desk top.

"We could run through the ones that didn't answer before. Maybe someone's home now," suggested Chuck.

"Why bother?" said Kane, grimacing. He stood and went to the window.

"Well, we can't just give up," said Chuck. "She's got to be somewhere."

She tossed the directory onto the bed and lit a cigarette. "You said yourself these people are going to make a move soon. Maybe it's going to be today! We've got to keep trying, Jon, if we—"

Kane, peering out through the curtains, motioned for silence. "Hang on," he said quietly. "I think we have visitors." A black Cadillac limousine had pulled up beside the unmarked police car, and their guard was talking to someone in the passenger seat. As Kane watched, the guard stood up, nodded, and got back into his car. The limousine began to move, swinging into the motel parking lot.

"They're coming here," Kane said quickly.

"Who is?" asked Chuck, getting up off the bed and padding across the room to join him by the window. The Cadillac pulled into the parking space in front of their room. A moment later the governor's executive assistant stepped out.

"Sweet!" said Kane, amazed.

Chuck looked down at herself. "My God!" she wailed. "I don't have any clothes on!" She leapt across the room and disappeared through the communicating door into her room.

Kane was at the door as Eleanor Sweet knocked. He opened it, and Sweet, dressed in a severe linen suit and carrying an attaché case, came into the room.

"Christ!" said Kane. "We've been trying to get you for the past two hours. We figured out exactly what—"

Sweet held up her hand. "We can talk later, Mr. Kane. Please gather your belongings and come with me." Chuck, dressed now in her jeans and a work shirt, came into the room, struggling into her suede jacket. Sweet gave her a quick look and turned back to Kane. "Miss Daly will remain here," she said crisply.

Chuck stopped in her tracks, the jacket dangling from one shoulder. "What the hell are you talking about?" she snapped. "I've been with Jon right from the beginning of this."

"I'm sorry," said Sweet. "Mr. Kane is required for a special briefing with the governor. You are not. Frankly, you would be in the way. You will remain here. Under guard."

"It's happened, hasn't it?" said Chuck. "The dam's come down and you're trying to cut me out of it. The biggest goddamn story of my career and you're cutting me out!" She turned to Kane. "Tell her, Jon," she pleaded. "Tell her I'm going along."

"It's not for Mr. Kane to decide," said Sweet, her hand reaching nervously for the tight bun of dark hair that lay against her neck. "It is a matter of security. National security. You will remain here."

"Do as she says, Chuck," said Kane softly. "You'll be safer here anyway." He came forward and put his hand on her shoulder. She shook it off and turned on him, eyes blazing.

"Chauvinistic crap!" she snarled. "I go the limit with you. I pull your damn hide out of the fire, literally. I almost get killed because of you. And now you tell me this is where I get off?"

"Chuck," began Kane.

"Screw you!" she yelled. She turned on her heel and ran back into the other room, slamming the door behind her. Kane stood helplessly, staring after her.

"Mr. Kane," prompted Sweet. She was at the door, her hand on the knob. Her voice was surprisingly gentle. "Mr. Kane, we don't have any more time."

Kane nodded. He put his hands in his pockets and followed her to the limousine. A few moments later they were on their way to the governor's mansion.

"Have you found them yet?" said the man from Langley into the telephone.

"Yes," said the voice three thousand miles away. "A motel on the outskirts of town. There's a problem, though. The prime's just been taken off in a limo."

"The girl?"

"Still there. So's the guard."

"Pick up the girl. She might be useful. We'll deal with the other later."

"The guard?" asked the voice on the other end of the line.

The man from Langley gingerly prodded at a razor nick on his chin. "Terminate," he said. Then he hung up the phone and began looking for his styptic pencil.

The ceiling speaker in the reactor control center crackled. Snyder looked up. "About fucking time," he muttered. He glanced across the room. Bateman and Paula St. George were sitting against one of the big computers. Paula's hand was pressed to her mouth, a trickle of blood seeping between the fingers, her head resting on Bateman's shoulder, eyes closed.

The speaker crackled again, followed by a nervous metallic voice.

"This is Dr. Hans Kellerman, chief administrator of the Richland Nuclear Reservation. If you wish to talk, please go to the central console and open the switch directly below the microphone."

Snyder looked up at the camera perched on its mount high on a corner wall and grinned. He went to the control console and flipped the switch, angling the gooseneck microphone so that he could talk and look into the camera simultaneously.

"Morning, Dr. Kellerman. My name is Snyder. How you feeling?" There was no response from Kellerman. Snyder shrugged and went on. "Okay, no small talk. Right down to business."

Snyder removed the bomb from the console and held it up to the camera. "This is what you call an explosive device," he said, as if giving a lecture. "Half a pound of the best black-market gelignite. Also a couple of ordinary blasting caps and a single-crystal citizen's band receiver. That's the little black box." Snyder put the bomb back on the console and took a gray box about four inches square out of his jacket pocket. "This is a transmitter. Fifteen crystals, fifteen bombs. I can set them off one at a time or all at once. Boom! Kiss your little installation here good-by. You got that."

There was a long pause; then Kellerman's voice came through the speaker. "Yes. I presume you have some demands."

Snyder smiled up at the camera. "You bet, Dr. Kellerman. I want quite a few things actually. First off, I want $500,000 worth of gem-cut diamonds, all of them between two and seven on the AGS scale and all of them between .8 and 1.4 carats. I used to run them when I was in Rhodesia with the Berets, so don't try to fuck around. I brought along a loupe just to keep you honest." He brought a small jeweler's eyepiece out of his other jacket pocket and held it toward the camera. "You should be able to get the stones from Consolidated Diamond Distributors in Seattle." He took a deep breath and let it out with a hiss. "While you're doing that," he went on, "you can work on getting me one of the state police helicopters. One of the big ones, a Jetranger maybe. And a pilot. Don't plan on any shit there, either. The transmitter in my pocket is good for up to fifty miles. The pilot or anyone else tries anything and I blow the whole fifteen." Snyder looked up at the camera, his face hard. "You understand me?"

After a brief silence Kellerman responded. "Yes. I understand. We'll do as you have requested."

"Good," said Snyder. He grinned wolfishly and let the shotgun swing around until it was pointed at Bateman and Paula St. George. "You don't come up with the diamonds and the helicopter sometime in the next four hours and I waste my two hostages here. After which, I start broadcasting."

"We were under the impression that the two other people were partners in your . . . escapade," Kellerman's metallic voice said.

"Yeah, so were they," Snyder grinned. "But they're not. So get on it, Kellerman. Four hours." He flicked off the microphone.

In the reactor securing room a few hundred feet away, Kellerman slumped in his chair, staring bleakly up at the silent monitor. Rudnick, seated beside him, relit his cigar and puffed thoughtfully. He watched the screen as Snyder took up his post at the emergency exit door again. Behind Rudnick, the two Richland sheriff's deputies were quiet. The other man in the room, a bomb-disposal expert from the Washington state police, leaned over Rudnick's shoulder for a better look at the device on the control console in the reactor control room.

"Is what he said about the bombs possible?" asked Kellerman. The tall, middle-aged explosives expert stood back and looked at the screen. Then he nodded.

"I'd say it's more than possible. I'd say it's a hundred per cent. I've heard of those things. They say it was invented by a radio freak in Vietnam who wanted to frag one of his superiors by remote control. Crude, but it'd probably work all right."

Kellerman turned to Rudnick. "Do you have any suggestions?"

"I thought I was out of this," said the security chief, edging his cigar into the corner of his mouth. "You said you wanted to bring in the FBI."

"That is correct," Kellerman said stiffly. "However, I was unable to contact the Spokane FBI office. There appears to be something wrong with the phones."

"What about Portland?" offered Rudnick.

Kellerman nodded. "Yes. I did contact them. But there is the time element. Their people will not be here for at least two or three hours at best."

"Ummn," said Rudnick, looking back at the screen. "I get you. You think that whatshisname—Snyder?—you think he might go off the deep end and blow the bombs, right?"

"It had occurred to me," replied Kellerman.

"Me too," said Rudnick. "I think he's crazier than shit. Anybody with a brain in his head would know he couldn't get away with it. As soon as he gets out of range with that transmitter of his, the pilot of the helicopter could bring him down in the backyard of Walla Walla Pen."

"So what do you propose?" asked Kellerman. Rudnick opened his mouth to answer, but before he could begin the door to the security room burst open and a wild-eyed Haberman appeared, breathing hard.

"Mr. Rudnick! The rad squad just reported in!"

"And?" said Rudnick, knowing what the answer was going to be from the expression on his assistant's face.

"Right through the leak, sir! Those people are all hotter than hell!"

The flood wave's entrance into FDR Lake differed from its earlier pattern through the Arrow Lakes. Instead of plowing directly into the basin, the wave skittered across its northern end, much like a car skidding on an icy patch of road. When the burden of the floodwater became too heavy, the face of the wave sank, propelling a huge swell forward as it collapsed into the placid blue water.

The swell, fueled by the size and speed of the original wave and further augmented by the waters of the Arrow lakes, thundered down toward Grand Coulee. Its face was approximately two hundred feet above the normal surface of the water, angling back in a blackish curve of heaving water. Its back, humped like a primeval creature, fanned out behind, forming swirls and eddies that reached back for miles. Anything within a quarter mile of either bank was swallowed by the wave and eventually thrown back in a thick gray-green layer of silt and ooze. The riverbed was bulldozed by the circulating currents within the main body of the swell, further adding to the mass carried by the wave.

As it turned the dogleg at the Spokane River and began to head westward, debris and silt, gouged up from the bottom, was thrust into the mouth of the Spokane, blocking it solidly. Soon the tributaries of the Spokane began to back up, flooding back to the city of Spokane itself.

Beyond the Spokane River the banks of FDR Lake became steeper, the width of the river narrowing as it headed into the deep-cut gorges that threaded through the arid basaltic plateau. The swell maintained its westward thrust, surging down the man-made lake, its sides gouging into the banks, chewing a thousand summer homes and small boat marinas into pulp, the mangled and dismembered bodies of first hundreds, then thousands, of holiday makers whirling grotesquely among the wreckage.

A renovated paddlewheeler, the *Oregon Lady*, her decks crowded with more than four hundred schoolchildren, somehow managed to ride out the giant swell and top the immense crest, its twin paddles gnawing at empty air. But as the vessel slid down the sloping back of the swell, her blunt bow was sucked downward by the massive undertow, digging so deeply she actually struck the silted bottom of the lake. A few seconds later the screams of the terrified children were silenced forever as the secondary swell behind the main body rolled over them.

By the time the swell had traveled halfway down the lake, it was 312 feet high and traveling at 82 miles per hour; a black-faced horror, sweeping toward the immense dam that blocked its path.

It was 11:18 A.M.

Chapter Eleven

JULY 4

11:30 A.M. PACIFIC DAYLIGHT TIME
2:30 P.M. EASTERN DAYLIGHT TIME

The President of the United States paced anxiously back and forth across the spacious office in the executive block that had once been Richard Nixon's favorite workplace. He walked with an easy loping step, his sneakers hissing on the highly polished cherrywood floor. Every few moments he stopped and examined the tearsheet in his hand. He had always respected Gloria Cullen, for her native intelligence as well as her political shrewdness, but when she had phoned to advise him of the situation in Washington State he had momentarily doubted her sanity. He stared at the flimsy. It was a confirmation from NOAA—the National Oceanographic and Atmospheric Administration. Gloria Cullen hadn't been crazy after all.

SATELLITE CONFIRMS WIDESPREAD FLOOD ACTIVITY CEN-
TRAL BRITISH COLUMBIA. EVIDENCE OF EXTREME DISTURB-
ANCE IN AREA F.D.R. LAKE/GRAND COULEE ADVANCING
SOUTH AND WEST/PRESIDENTIAL PRIORITY THIS INFORMA-

TION NOT TO BE DISSEMINATED WITHOUT EXECUTIVE
AUTHORITY./NOAA HOUSTON.

The President's mouth twisted into a sour smile as he scanned
the last line. He knew perfectly well that the media hounds
would be hammering on the White House door within the hour,
howling for some kind of statement. He glanced at his watch. Almost two thirty-five. He frowned, his smile disappearing as
quickly as it had come. Walter was late, and so were the others.

He turned to the large bulletproof picture window that overlooked the West Lawn, his frown deepening as he recalled
Gloria Cullen's fears about Richland. Until their conversation he
had been unaware of the terrorist take-over, but now, with the
news of the flood, the Richland crisis had risen tenfold.

The President was well aware of the dangers of the Richland
waste dump, and also the possibility of a catastrophe at the fast
breeder if efforts weren't made immediately to shut it down in
the face of the approaching water.

He stared out over the manicured lawns and prayed that
Grand Coulee would hold. If it didn't, they were all going to be
in a lot of trouble.

Charlene Daly parted the curtains and looked out onto the motel
parking lot and beyond it to the street. She tapped her foot im-
patiently. The guard was still there, on the far side of the street,
sitting in the unmarked car. He had finished his paperback. Now
he was munching an apple and reading a magazine.

"Damn," she said, letting the curtains fall back and slumping
onto the couch. As she lit her twentieth cigarette of the day she
wondered if Bert ever went to the can. She was fuming with rage.
She had to get out. There was a story going down, her story, and
she was missing it, while every hack in the world was getting the
goods.

"Damn, damn, damn!" she repeated. There had to be a way
out of the motel. She stubbed out the cigarette, and reached for
another one. The pack was empty.

"Son of a bitch!" she yelled. She stood up, stomped through
the doorway between the two rooms, and pulled her purse off the

chest of drawers. She rummaged through it, looking for a cigarette. Then she stopped, her eyes growing wide.

It was so bloody obvious. She stared at the doorway she'd just come through, then spun around, to the far wall. There it was. Another connecting door. The rooms were probably all hooked together, from one end of the motel to the other. She walked quickly across and tried the handle. Locked, of course. She stood back, took a deep breath and ran at the door. At the last moment she leapt into the air, her legs high.

There was a splintering crash as she connected. The momentum of her leap carried her into the middle of the next room where she landed with a bone-crunching thud on the floor. The room was empty, thank God.

"Idiot!" she growled to herself. She tried to remember how many units there were between her room and the corner of the motel. One more? She went to the window and peeked out. The guard was working his way through a doughnut. He was already at least fifty pounds overweight. Chuck made a clucking sound with her tongue. Probably drop dead in the middle of a Sara Lee one night on patrol duty. She checked the parking spot for the room next door. Empty. She wondered what she would have done if the room she'd crashed into had been occupied. "Hi! I'm just escaping from protective custody, pay no attention." The whole thing was crazy. She gathered herself together and made another jump. Once again the connecting door gave way easily, and this time she landed on her feet. She looked toward the end wall of the room and smiled. A window, combination glass and screen. Perfect!

She ran back through the shattered doorways to her own room and gathered up her coat and purse. Then she went back to the end room, dug through her purse, and found her nail file. Within five minutes she had sliced a hole through the screen big enough to crawl through. Moments later she was outside on the narrow grass strip at the end of the building, well out of the guard's line of sight. She pelted across the strip of asphalt that ran beside the motel, jumped the low wooden fence on its far side, and ran quickly up the narrow alley beyond. She came out of the alley and onto the sidewalk in front of the automotive supply shop that backed onto the motel. A moment later she hailed a taxi and was gone.

Rudnick inched forward through the narrow sheath of the galvanized-steel ventilation duct, his breath fogging the clear plastic visor of his radiation suit. The pain in his stomach was still there even after a double dose of the pain killers in his office. The pain didn't matter, though. What was important was the fact that he was back in action. The Kraut hadn't taken much convincing, even though going in through the vents was a grandstand play if ever there was one. Maybe he just wanted to wrap the whole thing up with as little publicity as possible, or maybe he believed that this Snyder punk really was going to blow the reactor up. Rudnick didn't care one way or the other. The point was, he was actually doing something again. He was living!

His crawling pace was agonizingly slow. He had entered the ventilation system from the maintenance room that led off the tunnel. According to the plan he had four long sections of vent and three elbows to get through before he reached the main stackpipe that led up to the floor of the fuel loading chamber. The third elbow was just ahead. He hoped the guy from maintenance was right about the cleated ladder in the main stack. It'd kill him if he had to shimmy up, especially when he was wearing this goddamn suit. The thick lead-lined fabric was making him sweat like a pig. Twice he'd almost passed out.

He reached the last elbow and squeezed around it cautiously, taking care on the knife-sharp edges of metal where the pipe was coupled together. If he tore the suit and then went into the contaminated control center, he was as good as dead.

Five minutes later, his muscles aching and his breath coming in ragged gasps, Rudnick reached the end of the pipe and the bottom of the main stack. He paused for a moment and rested. Sweat was soaking him under the suit, running into his eyes and making it hard to see. His head felt as though someone were hitting him repeatedly with a two-by-four, and both his hand and his stomach were on fire. Christ! He was falling apart. He took a deep breath and reached up with his good hand, feeling for a rung. He sighed with relief as his gauntleted hand closed over one of the U-bolts that ran up the pipe. He pulled himself into

the stack and began to climb, the riot gun tethered to his leg
with a length of cord banging hollowly with each slow upward
step.

Kane sat at the far end of the boardroom table in the administrative suite of the governor's mansion. Somehow Sweet had
managed to find him a suit that fit reasonably well, and he'd
changed in the office washroom. At least he didn't have to suffer
the embarrassment of appearing in the crumpled and blood-
stained clothes he had been wearing when he left the hospital.
He still felt self-conscious in the presence of the solemn group of
VIPs at the table. And on top of his self-consciousness, there was
the nagging certainty that the attempts on his life had their origins in high places. As he was introduced to the other members
of the briefing session he was disturbingly aware that one of
them, perhaps more, was at least peripherally involved in the
tangled conspiracy that depended for its success on the deaths of
Kane, Daly, and Halleran.

He immediately discounted Crawford, the paunchy Air Force
colonel on his left. According to Governor Cullen, Crawford had
been brought in from Merton AFB to handle reconnaissance liaison. He had also ruled out Dr. Sloane Wilson, the gray-haired director of the Pacific Emergency Planning Council. Kane knew
that Wilson had taken the job as EPC director because he had
reached retirement age at the University of Washington, where
he'd been professor emeritus of environmental science. An aca-
demic down to his horn rims and wrinkled gray flannels.

Kane looked up the table. Manfreddi. What about him? It was
possible, certainly. The weasel-faced deputy chairman of the
Bonneville Power Authority had certainly been with the BPA
long enough to have been privy to any secrets surrounding the
Canadian dams. Or Hammond, alone on the far side of the table
from Wilson and Manfreddi. General Curtis D. Hammond,
thickset and jowly, was the regional commander of the Army
Corps of Engineers. The Corps, in conjunction with the Bureau
of Reclamation, was directly responsible for the preliminary
work on almost every major dam in the United States and had
been involved with all the dams on the Columbia. If anyone had
been close to the Columbia treaty and the building of the Ca-

nadian dams, it was Hammond. But that was crazy. If Hammond was involved in the cover-up, then the Bureau was too, as well as God knows how many other people in D.C. And that was ludicrous. He might as well say that Gloria Cullen was involved to boot.

She certainly had the background for it. From mayor of Spokane, to state senator, to governor, all in the space of less than ten years. There was even a rumor going around that the fifty-four-year-old spinster was making plans for the presidential nomination next time around. You didn't go that far that fast without a few dark corners in your past, and a few compromises and favors owed as well. This was getting ridiculous, he thought. There were more important things to think about. The possibility of having a couple of states wiped off the map, for instance.

He looked down the table at Cullen. She was finishing a whispered conversation with Eleanor Sweet, who was sitting in a chair behind her, looking as if she might have been her sister. Each member of the group at the table had put forward his thoughts on the problem, and they were now waiting for the governor's recommendations.

Cullen nodded to Sweet and turned her attention back to the table. Her normally pleasant face was deeply lined with worry. When she spoke her voice was tense and brittle.

"Gentlemen," she began, clasping her hands in front of her. "Miss Sweet has just informed me that the flood wave is now within fifty miles of Grand Coulee. We have little time to prepare, and no time to investigate the origins of this disaster. Mr. Manfreddi has assured us that Grand Coulee will hold and that at worst we can expect nothing beyond widespread flooding in the northern part of the state. Mr. Kane, however, disagrees, and frankly, his arguments are forceful. Without reflecting adversely on Mr. Manfreddi's expert opinion, I am afraid we must move on the assumption that Mr. Kane is correct and that the Grand Coulee Dam will fall."

Cullen looked down the table at Sloane Wilson. "Doctor, I suggest you implement the contingency plans for small-town evacuation as soon as possible. According to the time frame put forward by Mr. Kane I don't think we have to worry about Portland for the moment, but evacuation procedures will be discussed when I meet with Governor Blake. On the telephone Governor Blake suggested that we establish our headquarters in the EPC offices in Portland. Unless there are any objections, that is what I propose." There were assenting nods from around the table. The Portland EPC had a fully equipped emergency communications system and an auxiliary power generator as well as a number of other emergency facilities including a direct telecommunications satellite link.

Cullen poured herself a glass of water from the jug in front of her and drank. Then she went on. "I think we are all in agreement that our most urgent priority in the event of the Grand Coulee Dam collapsing is the safety of the Richland Nuclear Reservation. You are also aware of the difficult situation the reservation is already facing. My assistant will be informing the administrator of Richland about the possibility of a flood. As an engineer, and as a person familiar with the setup at Richland, I would ask that Mr. Kane oversee operations there. I understand Colonel Crawford can provide transportation."

Crawford nodded. "I came in on one of our F1-11s," he said. "With our best pilot. If that helicopter is still on your back lawn I can have Mr. Kane in the air within fifteen minutes. As long as you clear a section of highway for him at Richland, there shouldn't be any problem landing. He'll need about a mile of blacktop."

"Excellent," said Gloria Cullen, standing. "If there is nothing else, gentlemen, I suggest we get on with it." She nodded and pushed back her seat. She and Sweet left the office together and the briefing session broke up.

As Kane headed for the door, following Crawford, he brushed past General Hammond who was talking to Manfreddi. As he passed, Kane's eyes met Hammond's for a brief instant. Kane felt a chill run up his spine. As a young boy he'd once seen a photo essay about the shrike in a magazine for naturalists. The Butcher Bird. One of the photos had shown the bird's larder—its warm-blooded prey impaled on the needlelike spikes of thorn bushes. The shrike's eyes had been cold and lifeless. The eyes of a killer. Like Hammond's.

The general stepped aside and Kane went by, his heart pumping with the panic rising in him. As he hurried after Crawford and away from Hammond's frigid glance, Kane wished desperately that he hadn't left Chuck behind at the motel.

Charlene Daly had been gone from the motel for less than ten minutes when two shabbily dressed men appeared at the end of the street. They separated at the corner and began walking toward the motel on opposite sidewalks. The man walking on the side farthest away from the unmarked police car moved with a decided limp. As the man approached the motel, the guard looked up from his magazine and watched his progress. Distracted, he didn't notice the other man until it was too late. The second man reached the door on the passenger's side of the police car and swung it open, reaching into his half-open shirt with the other hand and bringing out a silenced Centennial Airweight pistol. The guard turned at the sound of the door opening and the man shot him four times. The bullets struck with a wet, slapping noise in the chest, neck, and head. The man on the other side of the street, his limp gone, walked over to the car, opened the door on the driver's side and got in, pushing the dead man into the center of the seat. The other man put the pistol back into his shirt and got into the car, sitting beside the corpse, propping the body upright. They drove off.

Thirty seconds after the car had turned the corner, a second vehicle appeared, heading in the opposite direction. The car slowed as it reached the motel and turned into the parking lot, coming to rest in front of the room recently vacated by Chuck. Three men, dressed in almost identical dark suits, got out of the car and went to the door. One of them knocked and then waited. After a few moments he tried the door. It opened and the three men went into the room. They reappeared almost immediately, returned to their car and drove away.

The state police helicopter bringing Kane and Crawford from the governor's mansion clattered over the perimeter fence of Olympia Airport and set down within twenty feet of Wild Bill Canterra's midnight-black F1-11. The jet was the synthesis of all Kane's fears of flying. It was obscene, squatting on the tarmac like a winged serpent from a nightmare. It was seventy-six feet long from the stiletto point of its nose cover to the razorback edge of its tailfin. Its wings were fully extended for takeoff, but once aloft they would swing back tightly against the thick fuselage, the trailing edges almost meeting the broad, flat triangles of the ailerons jutting from either side of the gigantic Pratt and Whitney engines in the tail.

As Kane stepped stiffly down from the helicopter a dark-haired man in a molded black pressure suit climbed out from under the open cowl of the cockpit and came down the short ladder hooked to the side of the aircraft. Kane ducked as the rotors of the helicopter began to whirl and the machine lifted off taking Crawford back to the mansion. The man in the pressure suit came forward, helmet under his arm, and extended a black gauntleted hand. Kane had almost expected that the man's face would be black as well. It wasn't. In face it was almost ghostly pale, the eyes large and gray.

"Mr. Kane?" said the man in a soft southern drawl. Kane nodded and took the proffered hand. The grip was firm beneath the leather glove.

"That's right," said Kane.

The pilot smiled. "My name's Bill Canterra. Wild Bill to my friends."

"Is that right?" said Kane weakly, wondering if the nickname was a reflection of the man's private life or his flying skills.

"Got a pressure suit for you in the bird," said Canterra, smiling.

"Oh, good," said Kane. He swallowed hard, and followed Canterra across the runway to the jet.

Chapter Twelve

JULY 4

A bead of sweat trickled down Dr. Hans Kellerman's temple to his cheek. He brushed it away, keeping his eyes fixed on the monitor screens in the security room. Beside him, Haberman fiddled with the zoom control, bringing the image of the vent grating closer. So far there was no sign of Rudnick.

"How long has it been?" asked Kellerman tersely.

Haberman looked at the clock above the monitor screens. "He's been in the vent system for twenty-five minutes. It should be any time now, sir." Kellerman's eyes went to the screen showing the interior of the control center. Snyder was still at the emergency exit door, the other two against the bank of computers. Kellerman checked the other screen again. Still nothing. Where was Rudnick?

The call from the governor's office had shaken the administrator deeply. He'd had enough to cope with, but the take-over of the fast breeder paled against the prospect of a flood such as the one the governor's assistant had described. Rudnick had to succeed. The acid had fused the cables in the tunnel beyond repair, making a reactor shutdown from the auxiliary control center impossible. In his mind's eye Kellerman again saw the smoking wreckage of Peenemünde. He knew that it would be a million times worse here. If the reactor wasn't shut down and the fuel rods were not removed, the sodium coolant would have to keep flowing to prevent the reactor from overheating. The thought of even one of those massive conduits bursting in the face of a flood was simply too terrifying to consider. Sodium, especially in a superheated liquid state, is violently explosive when combined with water. And there are several hundred tons of it flowing in and around the reactor core at any given moment. The blast would literally blow the roof off the core, rupturing the zirconium-clad containment vessel. When the zirconium combined with the sodium and water, the chemical reaction would cause a second, even more powerful, detonation as a tremendous volume of free hydrogen was created instantaneously. It wouldn't be a nuclear explosion, but the result would be the same: a deadly mushroom cloud of lethally radioactive debris.

The governor's assistant had explained that if Grand Coulee collapsed they would have two or three hours at best before the flood wave reached the Richland Reservation. Even if Rudnick succeeded in recapturing the reactor control center there would barely be enough time.

"There!" exclaimed Haberman, pointing at the screen, his hyperthyroid eyes bulging. Kellerman looked and picked up a movement on the monitor showing the vent grille. Sitting forward anxiously, Kellerman watched as the grille moved up and back and Rudnick struggled out of the main stack.

"Schnell, schnell!" whispered Kellerman. On the screen he saw Rudnick untying the cord and picking up the riot gun.

There was a sense of unreality to it all. If he tried, Kellerman found he could almost believe that the scene he was watching was taking a place in a fictional suspense drama. But it was real, happening only a few hundred feet away.

Haberman pulled back on the zoom control as Rudnick shuffled clumsily toward the air-lock/decontamination chamber door in his radiation suit. Kellerman frowned. The security man's movements were slow and clumsy, and even masked by the bulky suit, he looked exhausted. He watched as Rudnick fumbled with the heavy lock wheel on the door. Finally, it opened and Rudnick stepped into the chamber, disappearing from the screen.

Kellerman turned to the other monitor. Snyder hadn't moved; he still stood at the emergency exit door, his back to the air-lock entrance. The sawed-off shotgun was still cradled in his arms. Kellerman stole a quick glance at the clock.

"He's been in the chamber for almost two minutes now," said Haberman in a whisper.

"What's taking him so long?" said Kellerman, more to himself than to Haberman. "It shouldn't have taken him more than a few seconds to open the door to the control center."

On a regular television program the scene would have been done in slow motion. In reality it was over in a split second. Snyder began to turn, his lips moving as he talked to the two others in the room. At the same moment the air-lock door burst open. Kellerman had a fleeting glimpse of Rudnick's burly, white-clad form as the man exploded into the room, riot gun held high. Snyder, already half turned, spun around, raising his own weapon. The two men fired simultaneously, Snyder dropping to the floor and Rudnick lurching back against the dials and flashing lights on the control console. Rudnick fired a second time as he went back. The monitor screen in the security room flashed white, then went blank.

Haberman frantically flipped switches on the control panel, but it was no use. The second slug from Rudnick's gun had neatly demolished the camera.

There was a pause, during which neither Haberman nor Kellerman breathed. Then from the speaker on the wall in the security room hissed static. Kellerman closed his eyes and prayed that it would be Rudnick's voice. It wasn't.

"That was really stupid," said Snyder, his words edged with venom. "I mean really, really stupid. Your man in the funny suit took a load of buckshot in the shoulder, in case you're interested. He's not dead, but he will be if you don't stop screwing around. Remember, Kellerman, I've got three hostages now, and one of them belongs to you. No more talk, no more bullshit." There was a deafening roar as Snyder shot the speaker in the control center off the wall, then silence.

"Dear God," whispered Kellerman, turning to Haberman, his face ashen. "What do I do now?"

Big Bob Taggart looked out the picture window in the Green Valley Coffee Shop, shaking his head with disbelief. In his more than forty years at the Grand Coulee he'd never seen anything like it. The whole goddamn town was empty, including the coffee shop.

"Bunch of chickens," he snorted, his loud, beer-furred voice echoing in the vacant restaurant. He slurped at the lukewarm coffee he'd appropriated from the machine behind the counter and stared out at the gigantic structure that had been his place of employment for almost his entire working life. From where he sat he could see the whole dam.

It was 4,000 feet across and 550 feet high. At its base, deep beneath the still-placid water of the Columbia, it was more than 500 feet thick, narrowing to thirty feet at the crest. The structure was made of steel-reinforced concrete and was grouted deeply into the brittle volcanic cliffs and the riverbed. There wasn't anything in the world going to move Grand Coulee, he thought. No way.

"Nobody asked *me* if she was going to collapse," said Taggart, peeved. He'd come to Coulee Dam in the beginning, back in 1933, along with a thousand other hungry men eager to work on Franklin Delano Roosevelt's monumental WPA make-work project. He was seventeen when he started, working as a water boy for the men at the concrete plant. By the time the dam was finished in 1942 he'd been over every square inch of her, and he'd also been promoted all the way up to maintenance man. He took a few years off to fight in the Pacific, and then he was back. He'd been there ever since, and in that time he'd slowly climbed the ladder to his present position as plant foreman. He knew the guts of Grand Coulee as well as he knew the strawberry veins in his lined and weathered face. Grand Coulee collapse? It was just plain stupid. No flood somewhere in Canada was going to so much as scratch the old girl. If the other people in the town wanted to believe what some white-collar pansy in Olympia told them, that was their business. He was staying, come hell or high water. He chuckled at the joke.

"Hell or high water," he said aloud, savoring it. He slurped coffee and sat back in his chair to wait.

Two miles upstream from the dam, the swell charged onward, rising in the narrow basaltic canyon until it stood 310 feet above the normal water level, racing toward Grand Coulee at seventy-two miles per hour.

Taggart felt the approaching swell long before he saw it. The mass of water had set the entire floor of the canyon into shuddering motion. Behind the counter in the coffee shop the dishes and cutlery began to rattle louder and louder as the vibration increased. Then the counter itself started shaking, the napkin dispensers toppling over as it moved. Taggart frowned, confused, as the floor beneath his feet began to move. They'd said a flood, not an earthquake. He stood up, unsure of what he should do. He looked out toward the dam again and then he saw it.

The full size of the swell wasn't visible as the hideous mound of water turned the final corner and surged toward the dam. The swell's effect reached as far down as it did up, a line of compression racing ahead of the main body reaching invisibly for the dam. It was this unseen force that struck first. The spillway, all 1,600 feet of it, crumbled under the onslaught of the pressure line, instantly releasing a huge spurt of water that sprayed down across the base of the dam, taking the shattered remains of the flood gates with it, battering down on the generating stations below.

Taggart stood, his mouth a silent O of amazement, a stain spreading darkly over the crotch of his work pants as his mind took in the full extent of what he was seeing.

Then the main face of the swell struck, and the dam, acting as a giant breakwater, forced the wall of water higher and higher until it reared 680 feet above the crest, entirely filling Taggart's vision, blotting out the sky. To Taggart, staring up at the wave, eyes wild, it seemed as though the wave paused for a moment at its highest point, suspended above him like an unspeakable theater curtain. Then the curtain fell.

Ten million tons of water crashed down on the town of Grand Coulee in a roaring avalanche of boiling spray that completely drowned out Taggart's single muted squeal of terror. The roof of the motel and coffee shop was slammed into the ground as though swatted by the open palm of an angered giant. Taggart died, his body bursting like a piece of overripe fruit under the weight of the roof and the sledge-hammer blow of water that followed it.

The grouting on either side of the dam began to pull out of the cliffs. Thirty seconds after the initial strike, the left and right sides of the dam separated from the volcanic bonds that had held the structure in place for more than forty years. In a slow, ghastly pirouette the two sections, each a thousand feet long, twisted and collapsed, dropping ponderously into the whirling maelstrom of the flood. The greatest obstacle in the way of the water's race to the Pacific had been obliterated. The Grand Coulee Dam was gone.

The only consolation, thought Kane, is that from this high it all looks unreal, like a roadmap. He looked down through the curving plexiglass cowling of the F1-11 at the ground, sixty thousand feet below, the fields and desert plains of southeastern Washington melting into a green and yellow blur, shot here and there with brilliant swatches of blue. The only identifiable landmarks were the wrinkled gray skin of the Cascade Mountains and the narrow thread of the Columbia. Straight ahead he could see the earth curving away in front of them. Kane was amazed at how good he felt. Hardly scared at all. He pressed the throat switch on his ill-fitting pressure suit and turned toward the helmeted figure of Canterra at the controls beside him.

"This isn't half as bad as I thought," bubbled Kane.

Canterra turned toward him, his eyes smiling above the oxygen mask that covered the bottom half of his face. He flipped on his own microphone and his voice came rattling into the head phone in Kane's helmet.

"Best way to live there is," he said happily. "It also might have something to do with the fact that you're suckin' in almost pure oxygen," he added. "Makes you kind of giddy if you aren't used to it."

"Oh," said Kane, mildly disappointed. He was sure that he was finally getting over his fear of flying.

"Touch 'fraid of heights?" asked Canterra. "Can't understand that. I get vertigo when I'm on the ground. Hell's bells, I'd go even higher if I could. Even thought of being an astronaut once. But they only give you automatics. Takes all the fun out of it. I like to wiggle a bit, y'know." He tugged the yoke slightly and the jet yawed, traveling at almost a thousand miles per hour. Kane shut his eyes. "Sorry about that," said Canterra.

After a while, Kane opened his eyes. Ahead he could see the bulk of what had to be the Canadian Rockies. He wondered how far they were from the Grand Coulee. He looked down again, but he couldn't make out any details.

"How much longer?" he asked.

Canterra checked the bristling instrument panel in front of him. "Well," he drawled. "We should be over Idaho in a minute or so."

"Idaho?" asked Kane, frowning behind his oxygen mask.

"Well sure," said Canterra, sounding surprised. "This thing doesn't have what you might call a narrow turning circle. Not this high anyway, and with the wings back. I thought we'd kind of sneak into potato country and then swing back low over the dam. I come over it this high, you won't see a thing." After a few seconds Canterra checked the instruments again and nodded. "Okay. This is about right. I'll take it slow, just in case you want to keep your breakfast. Down we go."

Kane gripped the sides of his contour seat as Canterra began pushing the yoke forward, turning it gently at the same time, sending them into a shallow dive. With the other hand he eased back on the twin set of throttles between the seats, slowing them down as they fell. As they dropped toward the ground he cut in the swing-wing actuator.

They made a long banking turn high above the ice-blue dog-leg of Coeur D'Alene Lake in Idaho, sweeping down, the wings now fully forward, passing over the city of Spokane at seventeen thousand feet, traveling at more than six hundred miles per hour.

"That oughta rattle a few windows," said Canterra as they went over the city, heading west. Kane was too frightened to look, sitting petrified in his seat. At sixty thousand feet it was easy to imagine that you were in a dream. At ten thousand things were only too real.

They dived even lower as they moved west above the Spokane River. Kane gritted his teeth, concentrating on the spinning needle of the altimeter on the instrument panel in front of him. Out of the corner of his eye he saw Canterra's hands, deft and sure on the controls as he brought them still lower.

"Five hundred feet!" yelled Canterra, and jerked a thumb downward. "The Columbia!" There was a pause and then Canterra's voice crackled into the headphone again.

"Sweet Mother of Christ!"

Kane summoned up the last remaining shreds of his courage and looked out beyond the black wedge of the wing. What he saw was a vision from the inner reaches of hell.

The churning water, brown and yellow with its load of silt and soil, was covered by a swirling scum of debris that danced in the glittering sunlight. Bodies, hundreds of bodies, broken and maimed, demolished shards of homes, docks, marinas, boats of all sizes, all being carried in a frenzied race down the wildly flowing river.

Canterra had slowed the huge fighter-bomber to just above stall speed, the shattering roar of its twin tailjets echoing back from the rising heights of the basalt cliffs that surged up on either side. The pilot nudged the yoke gently as they negotiated the final turn toward the dam that people called the eighth wonder of the world.

But they came too late. The wave had been there before them.

By the time Kane and Canterra made their overflight there was nothing left to show that the river had ever been held back in the ancient volcanic canyon. The water roared on, unhindered, the torrent 110 feet higher than normal.

"You want to make another pass?" asked Canterra, as they pulled up and away from the damsite. Kane shook his head mutely, his brain still trying to cope with the concept of a force that could destroy a dam like Grand Coulee. Finally he spoke, his voice barely audible through Canterra's headphone.

"No," he said. "There wouldn't be any point. Just get me to Richland as fast as you can."

The tall, conservatively dressed black man with the salt-and-pepper hair stood on the observation deck of Portland International Airport and watched as the Western Airlines shuttle flight from Olympia came in low over the waters of the Columbia and landed on one of the runways that crisscrossed the mud flat on which the airport lay.

A few moments later he spotted the woman answering the description put out by the Olympia team as she climbed down from the airplane and crossed the narrow strip of the apron. He double-checked the description. It was her. Short, red haired, wearing a tan leather jacket, and carrying a shoulder bag. Satisfied that he had her marked, he left the observation deck and went to one of the plastic phone kiosks on the main concourse.

The phone was answered on the first ring. "Yes?" said the voice on the other end.

"Bonner," said the black man. "She's in Portland. Jacket, bag. Nice ass. Now what?"

"Follow her," said the voice. "If you get a chance, pick her up. Hobbs with you?"

"Yeah," said Bonner. "Him and Lachlan. Lachlan's in the parking lot. Hobbs'll shadow her from the arrival gate."

"You shouldn't have too much trouble, but just remember this is the broad that took out Flexhaug, Havers, and Reid. She's got balls."

"Yeah," said Bonner. "If we pick her up, what then?"

"Take her to the place in Parkrose. Hold her there. I'll call you. We'll move her to Seattle later."

"Yeah," said Bonner. "Anything else?"

"No," said the voice.

Bonner hung up and went out to the concourse, spotting Charlene Daly almost immediately. His partner, Hobbs, was thirty feet behind her.

As the taxi pulled away from the terminal and headed down Fremont toward the city center, Chuck smiled to herself. Things were getting pretty hectic, and that was just the way she wanted it. The hurt of being left behind by Jon still rankled, and being back on the job made it easier not to think about him. She turned the events of the past couple of hours over in her mind, wondering if she hadn't acted too hastily. Once away from the motel she'd taken a taxi directly to the airport. She'd thought of phoning her boss at the *Post Intelligencer*, but her flight had been called and there hadn't been time. She supposed she could have called when she arrived in Portland. To hell with it, she thought. It was her story and hers alone. Nobody at the paper would have believed her anyway.

The taxi weaved through the early afternoon traffic of Union Avenue, carrying Chuck south through the high-rise business district. Chuck knew that if the House of Cards scenario actually came about, Portland would be the center of most of the disaster activities, being the largest city on the Columbia. She figured that a logical place to begin would be the local office of the Emergency Planning Council. She'd come into contact with the EPC during the droughts of 1976 and 1977 and knew the council had regional offices all over the country, set up to handle all kinds of emergencies. She'd looked up the address of the Portland office while she was in the airport.

The cab finally came to a stop in front of the small five-story building on Division Street that held the EPC office. Chuck got out and gave the driver his fare, barely noticing the dark blue Pontiac that had pulled up at the curb. She was climbing up the steps to the main door of the building when she heard someone calling her name.

"Miss Daly?"

She turned and found herself looking up into the smiling face of a middle-aged black man, his temples shot with silver.

"Yes?" she said, smiling. Then the smile vanished. There was no way anyone should have known where she was. She turned to run, but the man's hand snaked out and grasped her by the elbow. She saw a second man coming toward her up the steps and struggled, trying to worm her way out of the black man's grip. Then she felt the pin prick of the needle in her side and the world collapsed around her.

Bonner and Hobbs took her down the steps quickly and pushed her into the back of the waiting Pontiac. Lachlan, the driver, made an unhurried U-turn on Division Street and headed toward the freeway.

It was 12:55 P.M.

Chapter Thirteen

JULY 4

Max Rudnick sat on the floor with his legs straight out in front of him and his back against the computer banks. His hands were tied painfully behind him. His radiation suit lay in a crumpled heap on the far side of the room. Bateman and Paula St. George sat on the floor a few feet away. Snyder was back at his post by the emergency door, Rudnick's riot gun on the floor beside him; the sawed-off shotgun in his hand.

Rudnick had regained consciousness only a few minutes before, and had been immediately engulfed in pain. His shoulder stung where the buckshot had come through the lead-lined suit; his ruined hand was in agony from the tightly wrapped coils of his own belt. He was aware of a pain in his side. He had a vague memory of Snyder kicking him. When he coughed, he tasted the copper tang of blood in his mouth and his stomach was on fire.

He had realized that he was as good as dead. The abandoned radiation suit was proof of that. He would certainly have received a lethal dose from the three people in the room. The floor where they had been walking was probably burning with hard radiation.

The truth of it was, he didn't give a shit.

He thought about it, sitting there, feeling the bits and pieces of his tired body, the pain in each. Maybe he had been feeling this way for a long time, even as far back as leaving the police force. Maybe his life had ended that night in the alley, and all of this was just a living dream, a nightmare before death.

He thought about the radiation. Most of the waste in the leaking underground tank was cesium 137—a common nuclear waste, not terribly toxic and with a half-life of only thirty years. But there was another waste product in the tank—radioiodine 131, a lethal isotope with a half-life measured in millennia rather than decades. The radioiodine had been accidentally produced in excessive quantity during an experiment in one of the fast breeder labs. ERDA regulations stipulated that materials such as radioiodine could not be buried in large quantities in any one site, but Kellerman hadn't had any alternative, so it went into Storage A.

Now it was in Rudnick. Eating him alive from the inside out, the hard radiation slicing through tissue and organs, killing him and the others in the room cell by cell. The other three would feel the effects first: they'd come in direct contact with the waste. Rudnick might live a day, a week, maybe two weeks, but he would die.

He looked across at Snyder. There was already a sheen of perspiration on his thin face. It could be just the tension, thought Rudnick, but maybe he was already beginning to fry.

Rudnick grinned. "Hey!" he boomed, summoning up his strength.

Snyder's head jerked round at the harsh sound of his voice and he whipped up the shotgun.

"Starting to feel a little bit queasy?" asked Rudnick, taunting him.

"What the fuck is that supposed to mean?" snarled Snyder, frowning.

Rudnick laughed. The sound changed to a hacking cough and bright red blood splashed across the front of his shirt.

"You didn't wonder why I was wearing that?" asked Rudnick when he recovered, nodding toward the limp radiation suit.

"What about it?" asked Snyder, his voice skeptical. Out of the corner of his eye Rudnick could see the young woman and her baby-faced friend watching him intently.

"It's a radiation suit," explained Rudnick calmly. "We wear them to keep from getting contaminated."

"So?" asked Snyder belligerently.

Rudnick laughed again, careful to keep it controlled. "So why do you think I was wearing it, punk?"

"Maybe you think it's Halloween. How should I know?" snapped the blond man. "Why don't you get to the point."

"The point is that you're all little walking reactors. You've been contaminated. They had a bad leak and you walked right through it on your way in here. I ran an instrument check. You're carrying a dose of at least 1,500 to 2,000 rads. I can see it from here. That's not a sunburn you've got on your face."

"You're full of shit!" said Snyder.

Rudnick shrugged, trying to ignore the pain that plucked at his hand. "I don't care what you believe, Snyder. It happens to be true. If I was you I'd be praying, not waiting for Kellerman to show up with any diamonds." He paused, gritting his teeth against the fire in his stomach. Jesus, how hard had Snyder kicked him? The pain faded for a moment and he went on. "The only way you're going out of here is in a lead-lined coffin."

Snyder raised the shotgun and worked the pump action back and forth.

"Shut up!" he yelled.

Rudnick smiled. "Worried?" he asked solicitously.

Snyder's eyes narrowed and he stepped forward quickly, advancing on Rudnick with the butt of the weapon held like a club. "Shut your fucking mouth!" he yelled. "Just shut up and sit there before I beat your brains in!"

"Okay, okay!" said Rudnick quickly. He wasn't ready yet. He wanted to push the punk, but not too far. Not yet.

"Much better," said Snyder, stopping. He reversed his hold on the shotgun and moved back to the emergency exit door. Rudnick waited for a few moments and then got to work on the belt that bound his hands. He was prepared to die of radiation poisoning, but not before he'd had the satisfaction of dealing with Snyder.

Charlene Daly opened her eyes and found herself staring up at a yellow ceiling with sequins in it. A crack ran across her line of vision, edged on either side with a damp stain.

Slowly, as the drug loosened its grip, she began to remember things. The flight to Portland, the taxi journey, going up the steps to the main door of the building, and then that black smiling face. With the memories came fear. These were the same kind of men who had tried to kill her on the coast highway, and there was no reason to think they were any less violent than their colleagues. Except for the fact that they hadn't killed her right away. That was frightening in itself. What were they waiting for?

She sat up gingerly, swinging her legs over the side of the bed. The room was almost empty of furniture; other than the iron bed she was sitting on there was only a small unpainted chest of drawers and a single blue-painted kitchen chair. The walls were the same faded yellow as the ceiling and the floor was covered with worn green linoleum. The small window across from the bed had been boarded over with an irregular rectangle of plywood. The only light came from a ruffle-shaded lamp on the chest of drawers. The scarred panel door facing her across the room was closed.

The drug had left her with a crashing headache, and as she rose to her feet she groaned. She got to her feet but a wave of dizziness broke over her and she sat down again abruptly.

She looked down at her wrist. Her watch was gone. She didn't have the slightest idea how long she had been under.

She stood up again, trying to ignore the pounding of her head. This time she made it to the door. She tried the knob. Locked.

She put her ear to the door and listened. A radio was playing Burt Bacharach music somewhere below and there were two, no, three, voices. She went back to the bed and sat down.

All right, she thought, let's go over it. So I've been kidnapped, not killed. Why? You kidnap someone because you want something. What did they want? Silence, of course. They wanted to make sure that Jon kept his mouth shut. Jon's safe with the gov-

ernor's people, so they'd have a hard time killing him now, or
even later. It would be too obvious. They're holding me hostage
and demonstrating their power. Spill the beans and we slit the
lady's throat.

She remembered the eyes of the black man. Dead. Cold. He
wasn't in it for his jollies. He was a businessman. He'd kill her
the way someone opens a letter. Suddenly she was very, very
frightened.

She pulled herself together, dragging herself back from the
edge of panic, and took a deep breath. She'd just have to escape
again. Twice in one day. She laughed, then stopped herself. Too
close to hysterics.

She got down on her hands and knees and put her ear to the
floor. The radio was even clearer. The music shifted to the special effects sound of a clattering Teletype. A news report.

"Good afternoon, it's one-thirty and this is Kevin Bell with a
K-VAN news update." Well, at least she was still in Portland.
"Rumors of a dam collapse in the Canadian Rockies early this
morning have now been confirmed by our Vancouver corre-
spondent. At approximately nine o'clock this morning the Mica
Dam, a headwater dam on the Canadian Columbia, was the
scene of what appears to have been a massive landslide.

"Waters released by the dam collapse have caused widespread
flooding in the Canadian cities of Revelstoke and Trail, British
Columbia, and there have also been some reports of flood damage on FDR Lake in Washington.

"Attempts to confirm reports of damage on the American side
of the border have so far been unsuccessful, and there may be
some connection between the Canadian flooding and the sudden loss of hydroelectric power observed in some parts of Washington and Idaho. K-VAN reporters in Salem have been unable
to reach Governor Blake for comment, and the Emergency Planning Council here in Portland has so far declined to make any
statement on the extent of the disaster, which according to some
sources will rival that of the Teton Dam collapse in 1976. This is
Kevin Bell, K-VAN news."

Chuck levered herself up, wincing as the floorboards creaked
under the linoleum. She sat down on the bed. The panic began

to rise again but she forced it down. The cat was out of the bag. She had to escape—fast.

At one thirty-five, the F1-11 came to a screeching halt on a stretch of highway seven miles from Richland Reservation. Fifteen minutes later Jonathan Kane was in Dr. Hans Kellerman's office. Kellerman had located his waste storage manager, Vernon Hilts, and after brief introductions the three men got down to business. Hilts, a short, leathery man in his mid-fifties, had been born and raised in the Richland-Pasco area, working mostly in heavy-equipment construction jobs. Kane was more interested in Hilts's estimation of the situation than in Kellerman's.

"According to the ERDA regulations you don't have to bury your waste any deeper than four feet," said Kane. "Do you keep to that or do you take it deeper?"

Hilts scowled and looked out of the corner of his eye at Kellerman, seated behind his desk. "We stick pretty close to the four foot. Too much to dispose of to go much deeper. Matter of logistics," he explained.

Kellerman coughed. "We deal with a large amount of waste here at Richland, Mr. Kane. We have a schedule to maintain."

"I see," said Kane, trying to control his anger. He'd never met Kellerman, but the Richland reports he'd been receiving at the OESI office suggested that he was a by-the-book type. "How far out do you have waste buried?"

Hilts shrugged. "About three-quarters of a mile, a mile from the reactor compound. A few thousand acres. We're always expanding."

"What kind of waste do you have farthest out?" asked Kane. "Hard or soft?"

"Soft, mostly," said Hilts. "Contaminated clothing, bits and pieces of equipment that have been in hot areas too long. That kind of thing. All of it's in fifty-gallon drums."

"And the hard material is closer to the compound?"

Hilts nodded. "The big tanks are in A, B, C, and D mostly. The solid waste, too. There are some pools for cooling fuel rods inside the fence but they're pretty well empty now."

"So we concentrate on the tank areas close to the fence," said Kane. "I'm going to need as much heavy equipment as you can rustle up, Mr. Hilts. Dozers, front-end loaders, backhoes, whatever you can give me. And men to drive them. How fast can you get it together?"

Hilts grinned. "One step ahead of you, Mr. Kane. I've already called in my crews. Machinery's being fired up now."

"Excuse me," interrupted Kellerman, "but as chief administrator I must insist that your priority be the breeder reactor. We are in the midst of a difficult situation there, as you know. If there's a flood, the breeder will be the most vulnerable, especially if we can't shut it down before the water comes."

Kane frowned. "Look, Dr. Kellerman," he began. "I know you're the chief administrator here and that Richland is your responsibility. But I'm the one who sets priorities in this case. We're going to have to raise coffers as high as we can around the main storage site. The breeder isn't the most vulnerable as far as I'm concerned. The core is contained in a steel and concrete casing that is supposed to be able to withstand an impact equivalent to a thousand tons of TNT. The waste is buried in four feet of sandy loam. We worry about the waste first, the breeder second." Kane stood up.

"Mr. Kane!" Kellerman's voice was high, the German accent more pronounced. "The Richland fast breeder is a United States federal installation that has cost in excess of one and a half billion dollars. I insist that you give it priority!"

Kane stepped forward and leaned over the desk, his palms flat on the gold-tooled leather surface. "Dr. Kellerman," he said, his voice quiet, "your last report, which I might add was almost useless because of your so-called 'security regulations,' included a statistical chart. The chart said you had almost four million gallons of waste on hand at Richland. I also happen to know that there are also a few hundred tons of Cyclon B, Sarin, Tabun, and other assorted nerve gases dumped here by the Chemical Corps a few years ago. Right now, Dr. Kellerman, I don't give two hoots in hell about your one-and-a-half-billion-dollar reactor. I care a lot more about what's going to happen if all that poisonous shit out there gets into water that could eventually percolate through the water tables of the entire Pacific Northwest and land up in the Pacific Ocean. This flood has already killed a great many people, Kellerman. I want to keep it from killing too many more." Kane straightened up. "I've been beaten, burned, and attacked by automobiles at seventy miles an hour, Kellerman. And it's because of people just like you. People more interested in covering their asses than the country they're supposed to be serving. So screw your reactor. The waste comes first, and that's final!"

Kellerman rose from his chair, his entire body quivering with rage. "Mr. Kane, you are an insolent fool! This is my installation, not yours, and you will do as I say. I know nothing about what you have been saying. I know only that I have a responsibility to keep the Richland Reservation, and especially the fast breeder, intact. In case you are unaware of the fact, the breeder has been operational for almost eighteen months. It has a fuel load of approximately sixty-seven thousand kilograms, ten per cent of which is enriched plutonium 239. Ten per cent, Mr. Kane! That is more than eight tons of plutonium! Do you have the slightest idea what that could do if it was released into the air or water! *Lieber Gott*, Mr. Kane!" Kellerman sat down again, almost in tears.

Kane was shaken. The operational reports he had received each month had told him that the breeder was on-line, but they had contained no mention of the vast quantities of plutonium on hand. Plutonium—Pu-239—was by far the most deadly element known to man, emitting a constant stream of alpha radiation and with a half-life of almost twenty-four thousand years. An ounce would be enough to wipe out New York City. Eight tons dispersed into the atmosphere would be enough to annihilate the entire United States.

Faced with the decision, Kane hesitated. The Grand Coulee had gone. The flood was coming. If the waste was buried only four feet down, the water would undoubtedly scour it to the surface. On the other hand, if he didn't do something to protect the breeder there was a chance that the containment vessel would rupture, spewing plutonium to the four winds. The devil and the deep blue sea. He groaned soundlessly. He couldn't take the chance.

"All right, Kellerman. The breeder first." He turned to Hilts. "Come on, we've got work to do." He walked quickly out of the office, followed by the waste storage manager, leaving Kellerman alone behind his desk.

The flood bore down through the flattening gorges below the Grand Coulee. The dams between Grand Coulee and Richland were all relatively small structures and hardly broke its stride. In most cases the dams were simply grouted into the rock or soil on either bank, and the water cut around one side or the other dealing with the rest as if it were an afterthought. First the Chief, Joseph, then the Wells and the Rocky Reach dams crumbled under the onslaught of the thundering current.

Dr. Wilson and his staff at the Emergency Planning Council had worked as quickly as they could to establish a communications network, but in most cases that network depended on the telephone. Thousands of lines and dozens of exchanges had been obliterated by the wave, and the system was in chaos. The EPC was forced to rely on a jerry-built web of radio relays. It was not very successful. Citizens' Band users, who might have been invaluable in spreading word of the flood, merely compounded the communications problems. As they picked up the police calls, the airwaves became jammed with hundreds, then thousands, of contradictory messages and frantic appeals for help or information. Only the largest centers, like the county seat at Wenatchee, benefited from any warning. In that town an evacuation program was hastily put together, and at least some of the inhabitants were moved to higher ground before the wave, by now slightly more than eighty-five feet high and traveling at sixty-seven miles per hour, lashed into the small city and scraped it clear off the map.

By 1:45 P.M. the flood had reached and mounted the Rock Island Dam and was less than seventy miles from Richland.

Chapter Fourteen

JULY 4

Charlene Daly had succeeded in removing two of the three-inch nails from the square of plywood, but she had broken six of her own nails in the process. Her fingers were raw and bleeding after more than an hour of what was clearly futile work. It would take her a year to get the plywood off the window. Still there wasn't a hell of a lot else to do.

She had just begun work on the third nail when she heard footsteps climbing the stairs. She tiptoed away from the window and sat down on the bed, legs tucked up and arms wrapped around herself, hiding the condition of her hands as the door opened.

It was the black man. He stood in the doorway, knowing there was something wrong. The stubby barrel of the revolver grew out of his hand like a lethal extra finger. He looked around the room sharply. When he saw the chipped corner of the plywood he looked back at Chuck, smiling. On anyone else's face it would have been a pleasant grin. On this man it was a threatening gesture.

"Been working hard, have we?" he said.

"Screw you," said Chuck hotly. She took her hands out from under her arms and began sucking on her fingers to ease the pain.

The man laughed. "You've got a dirty mouth, sweetheart."

Chuck took her fingers out of her mouth and sneered. "Double screw," she said. "In spades."

The smile vanished. "Careful," he said.

"Of what?" threw back Chuck. "My language? You going to spank me or something?"

"We could maybe do better than that," he said, pointedly looking over her body.

Chuck barged on undeterred, sensing that she had got under his skin. "*We*, as in whatever agency you work for, or *we*, as in black?" she asked. "Incidentally, is it true what they say about nigras?"

The man's lips pressed into a thin line, his finger tightening on the trigger of the pistol.

"I thought all you agency types had to be Harvard grads," she went on. "Or Yale at the very least. How'd you get on the team? A bit of the ol' tokenism maybe?"

"Who said anything about any agency?" He was back under control now, businesslike and almost urbane.

"Oh, come on!" she scoffed. "What do you take me for, a complete idiot? CIA, NSA, DIA—what the hell's the difference? You certainly aren't from the Peace Corps. You kidnapped me because you want Jon Kane to keep his mouth shut, right? Somehow you and the rest of your spook friends got involved in this Mica thing, and now you're trying to use me to get yourselves out. Well it won't work, buddy. The whole thing is going to backfire, and it's mouse shit to a million that it's going to backfire all over you."

"I don't know what you're talking about," said the man. "So why don't you shut up and save it, okay? And get ready to go. We'll be moving out of here soon." He backed out of the doorway closing the door firmly behind him.

Chuck looked scornfully around the bare room. "Sure buddy, I'll pack a bag!" she called after him. Then she began to cry.

Jonathan Kane and the waste storage manager stood together on a mound of earth and surveyed the progress of the coffering operation. Under Hilts's expert and often profane direction, the work had gone smoothly. A rampart of dirt had been built up to a height of ten feet around the breeder, completely encircling it. A second, even higher wall had been pushed up in a concentric circle around the first, leaving a dry moat some fifty feet wide between the two. Kane hoped that the water would strike the outer circle and expend most of its force there. If it did get past the outer wall, the inner wall would prevent it from entering the breeder building. Kane tried not to think about the fact that by walling in the breeder he was burying the terrorist and his three hostages alive. According to what Hilts had told him, the four people in there were already as good as dead.

On the far side of the old reactor compound, dozens of bulldozers and backhoes worked steadily to coffer the storage areas. The machine operators had all been issued antiradiation suits, and it had been a wise precaution. Already more than a dozen rusty steel drums had been disinterred, their seams bursting and the contents spilling onto the ground. No one had the slightest idea what the drums had once contained, and how radioactive they were. Kane prayed that they weren't part of the U. S. Chemical Corps dumping.

"Going pretty good," said Hilts beside him. The walkie-talkie in the man's hand crackled incoherently with orders passing from the crew leaders to the teams on the bulldozers.

"Let's hope it's enough." Kane looked out over the giant reservation, searching the northern horizon for some sign of the approaching flood.

"It'll have to do," said Hilts. "If you're right, there's no time for anything else. Walls around the big tanks are twelve feet high now, and the equipment we got here isn't going to take it much higher." He squinted up into the cloudless sky. "Hot, too. We've had a couple of faintings on the 'dozers. They won't be able to keep it up for much longer."

"They won't have to," said Kane grimly. "There's less than an hour left. Tell your people to keep going for another ten minutes and then pack it up. I want everyone out of here in plenty of time."

"Right," said Hilts, a note of relief in his voice.

As Kane walked back toward the administration building a state trooper caught up with him.

"You Mr. Kane?" The trooper was young. His eyes were invisible behind his dark blue sunglasses.

Kane nodded. "That's right," he replied.

"Message for you on the radio," said the trooper. "Take it in my cruiser if you like."

Kane trudged after him to the police car parked in the swarm of other official vehicles that surrounded the installation and slid into the passenger seat, his shirt sticking uncomfortably to the vinyl upholstery. He found himself actually yearning for the cool interior of Canterra's jet. The trooper thumbed the microphone switch on his radio and spoke, his voice crisp and businesslike.

"Come in HQ, this is state police two five niner. I have your Mr. Kane in the car here. You can go ahead with the relay from Portland." The trooper released the switch and waited. A few seconds later there was a crackle of static and the interior of the car was filled with the monotone voice of the dispatcher.

"Thank you, two five niner. Relay message for Mr. Jonathan Kane from Dr. Wilson at EPC Portland. Message is as follows: Regarding NOAA request. Satellite surveillance shows disturbance moving beyond vicinity of Rock Island Dam. Computer analysis places disturbance in your area within seventy-five minutes. Disturbance is believed to have a front of approximately one thousand yards and a mean average height over a computed mile of 86.4 feet. Suggest immediate withdrawal from your area and evacuation of all personnel. Please return to Portland EPC immediately. Message ends. That's it, two five niner."

"Thank you, HQ." The trooper clipped the microphone to its holder and turned to Kane. "Anything you'd like from us?" he asked.

Kane shook his head. "No. Talk to Kellerman first, but I get the feeling you and your friends should get the hell out of here."

"Shit about to hit the fan, sir?"

"That's about the size of it, Trooper," said Kane.

The young man nodded. "I got a wife and a three-year-old boy," he said. "We live in a little place in Kennewick. They going to be all right, sir?"

Kane looked at him, wondering how many wives and babies had already died. He shook his head. "No. Sorry. Get them out. East if you can. Walla Walla maybe. Stay away from the river, a long way away."

The trooper frowned, then tried to smile. "Thanks, Mr. Kane. Appreciate the tip."

Kane shook hands with him, then climbed out of the cruiser and ran head-on into Haberman. The bug-eyed security man was sweating heavily.

"Mr. Kane?" he said, his voice thin. "We've got a problem."

"No kidding?" said Kane. He looked at Haberman, irritated. The loose mouth was hanging open, and he seemed at a loss for words. "What can I do for you?"

"It's Dr. Kellerman, Mr. Kane, uh . . ."

"Well, what?" yelled Kane, his temper finally breaking.

"He's . . . shot himself, Mr. Kane. I went to his office to ask him about evacuation procedures and I found him at his desk. His head, uh, his head was just about gone, Mr. Kane. I saw the gun. It looks like an old World War Two Luger or something. I was wondering what I should do about it, Mr. Kane. With Dr. Kellerman gone I guess you're in charge, aren't you, sir?" The bulging eyes pleaded with him.

"Oh, God!" moaned Kane. He thought for a moment. "Yes. All right. Leave Kellerman where he is. There's nothing we can do anyway. Start spreading the word that it's time to get out. I want this place empty inside of half an hour. Now, if you'll excuse me?" He turned away and went back to Hilts and the breeder, running.

They were almost out of time.

Ronald Bateman sat huddled on the floor of the control center, eyes closed. Outwardly he was quite still, but every muscle in his body was tense. Even with his eyes shut, he could sense the presence of the others in the room with him. He listened to the pounding of his own heart and to the rushing of the air in and out of his lungs. Each intake of breath was an effort of will. He wondered if it was the first symptom of the radiation sickness, or simply the terror that was mounting within him. It was as though all his nerve endings were on fire, straining, urging him to do something, anything, to ease the pressure.

He followed no train of thought as he sat. The seconds passed one by one, each entirely independent of the next. Every few moments he had a vision of his hands at Snyder's throat, or Paula's, his grip tightening. Once he had a brilliant image of the two copulating, their bodies oiled with sweat, and it was all he could to to keep from bellowing with rage.

He opened his eyes. The harsh glare of the overhead fluorescent lights made him squint. He looked around the room. Nothing had changed. Snyder was still by the emergency exit, shotgun hanging from his hand, Rudnick's short-barreled riot gun at his feet. Bateman turned his head slightly. Paula seemed almost asleep beside him, her eyes closed, head sunk low on her chest. A few feet beyond her sat the fat security man, his face mottled and gray. He, too, seemed asleep, eyes closed, his breath coming in bubbling wheezes. Bateman stared at Rudnick, willing the heavyset man to notice him. Finally it worked. The cropped head turned sluggishly, the eyes blank, the mouth tight with pain. Bateman wondered if the man was capable of making an attempt on Snyder. It was only then that he realized what he was contemplating.

The two men looked at each other for a long moment as Bateman tried to make Rudnick understand. He let his eyes shift towards Snyder and back again. Rudnick looked confused for a moment. Then one bushy eyebrow lifted and he nodded, barely inclining his head. Bateman returned the signal and then looked pointedly down at Rudnick's hands, hidden behind his back. Rudnick smiled thinly and lifted his arms. He had managed to loosen the belt considerably. The security man let his eyes travel up the far wall above the control console to the IBM clock. Bateman followed his glance. It was two twenty. Rudnick mouthed the word "five." Bateman nodded and looked over at Snyder. The blond man seemed not to have noticed their pantomime; his concentration was focused on the hallway beyond the emergency door. Bateman closed his eyes again and began a silent countdown wondering if he was marking off the last few moments of his life.

When he reached 250 he stopped counting and opened his

eyes. He looked up at the clock. The count had only been a few seconds off. Less than thirty seconds to go. He moved his left leg up slowly, ready to spring. He waited for Rudnick to make his move. Rudnick's eyes were closed, and once again Bateman wondered if he would be able to do anything. It didn't matter. He'd take on Snyder alone if he had to.

As the thin red needle of the second hand crossed the numeral five on the clock, Rudnick fell sideways with a low moan, slamming into the sleeping form of Paula St. George. She started as she felt Rudnick's weight against her and her eyes flew open. When she saw Rudnick, she began screaming, pulling away, letting the man fall to the floor, his arms still behind him. At the sound of her scream Snyder turned, raising his weapon.

"What the fuck is going on?" he grated.

Bateman looked at Rudnick and grimaced. "I think he's dead. He looks pretty bad."

"Yeah?" said Snyder, cradling the gun under his arm. "Well, we'll just have a look-see." He peered down the hallway then came across the room. He stood over Rudnick's prostrate form, drew back his right foot and brought it viciously forward. Before it could make contact Rudnick slithered around on the floor, amazingly quickly for a man of his size. He brought his own leg in behind Snyder's left leg and kicked hard, sending Snyder flying backward, shotgun shells spraying from his pockets. Bateman lunged upward and threw himself on Snyder, fighting to get at the windbreaker pocket and the detonator. Snyder brought up the shotgun and clubbed him away, but Rudnick fell on top of him, grabbing for the weapon. Behind them, Paula St. George began screaming again, hands up to her shattered mouth.

Pain lancing into his shoulder from Snyder's blow, Bateman crawled forward and tried to get his hand in between the struggling men. He dug into Snyder's jacket, his fingers scrabbling for the detonator. He couldn't pull it free.

"I can't get it!" he screamed. "I can't get it!"

Snyder pulled away and he and Rudnick rolled toward the bank of computers. As they came toward her, Paula St. George scrambled to her feet, trying to get out of their way. The two men stood up, still locked in a bear hug. Seeing another chance,

Bateman moved in and looped an arm around Snyder's neck, squeezing with all his might. Snyder loosened his grip on the shotgun and rammed his elbow into Bateman's ribs, sending him tumbling backward, gasping for breath. At almost the same instant there was a thunderous roar as the shotgun went off.

Paula St. George, less than a yard away, took the full blast in her face and chest.

The blast threw Rudnick and Snyder apart, the shotgun falling between them. Snyder fell heavily against Bateman. Before he could regain his footing, he saw Rudnick reaching down for the shotgun. Snyder turned and raced for the emergency door. He reached it, scooped up the riot gun almost without pausing, and ran for the air lock. Before Rudnick could reload the shotgun with the shells scattered on the floor, Snyder was gone.

Bateman rose to his feet and saw Paula for the first time. He rushed toward her with a small, birdlike cry.

Rudnick blocked his path.

"Not now," he gasped. "No time now. Get out to the lobby, tell them!"

Bateman ignored the order and stepped around him. He looked down at Paula. She had fallen face down, hiding the full extent of her wounds. Bateman stripped off his windbreaker and crouched down, covering her head and the oozing puddle of scarlet around it. He stood up, smiling wistfully. Then he turned and left the room, pushing aside the barrier by the emergency exit. Rudnick began reloading the shotgun.

A few moments later, Bateman's owlish figure reappeared at the emergency exit doorway. He was shaking with silent laughter.

"What is it?" asked Rudnick, gripping the shotgun tightly as another wave of pain surged up from his stomach. "Where . . . ?"

"Walled in!" giggled Bateman. "Right out of Edgar Allan Poe!"

"What the fuck are you talking about?" said Rudnick, advancing on him menacingly.

Bateman held up his hands, still laughing. "Look for yourself! We're sealed up!"

Rudnick brushed past him, walking as quickly as his shaky legs would allow. The fight with Snyder had used up most of his remaining strength. He knew he didn't have much time left before the pain finally put him under. He went out into the corridor. A few moments later he saw what Bateman had been laughing about.

The double glass doors leading to the outside of the building were bulging inward from the pressure of the earth piled up against them. There was no sign of daylight beyond.

Rudnick scowled, confused. What was Kellerman up to, for Christ's sake? He shuffled weakly across the lobby, Bateman close behind him. His shoulder had begun to bleed again during the fight with Snyder and his shirt sleeve was crimson to the elbow. He stopped a few feet from the doorway and stared.

"Jesus!" he muttered. Abruptly he turned on his heel and went back across the lobby into the security room. He sat down in front of the monitors and looked blearily down at the control panel for the exterior cameras. The cameras, six of them, were fitted with wide-angle lenses and were located high on strategic corners of the breeder. Normally they would have given Rudnick a clear view of the area immediately around the building. He keyed the cameras in rapidly, one after the other. The screens remained dark.

"What's happening?" asked Bateman from behind him. The hysteria was gone from his voice.

"Dunno," wheezed Rudnick thickly. He tried the cameras again. The monitors were still blank. "Looks like Kellerman's buried the whole fucking place. Christ only knows why."

"Maybe it's just at the front entrance. He might have had the cameras disconnected or something," suggested Bateman.

"Why would he do that?" asked Rudnick.

Bateman shrugged. "To scare Snyder, maybe?"

"I doubt it," said Rudnick. He checked the power source meter, though, just in case. There was still current reaching the cameras, and the cameras were returning a signal. He shook his head. "I can't figure it," he muttered. "It doesn't matter though. We've got to get Snyder first."

"Why?" asked Bateman. "According to you we're all dead of radiation poisoning anyway. Why chase him now?"

Rudnick gave a rasping laugh. "Because Snyder still has the detonator. He can still blow this place off the map. We may be dead but I'm goddamned if I'm going to let him spread radioac-

tive fallout over half the state." He turned to look at Bateman
again, a glint of fire in his eyes. "Not to mention the satisfaction
I'm going to get when I blow the crazy sonofabitch's brains out."

Dennis Penpraze woke, startled. A shaft of sunlight slashing
through the firing slit in the gun tower was striking him in the
face. He sat up and stretched. Then he stood and made his way
to the firing slit, stepping over the rusted track that had once
held the traversing gear of the naval gun. He looked cautiously
out of the slit, taking care to stay in the shadow.

It was a beautiful day. Burrard Inlet, its surface ruffled by a
slight onshore breeze, was swarming with sailboats and other
small craft. On the far side of the water, to the north, the hump-
backed shapes of the coastal mountains stood out sharply against
the blue of the sky.

Penpraze listened. Above the roar and hiss of the waves breaking on the sand below, he could hear voices and a dog yapping.
He tensed, panic welling up in his chest. Then he relaxed. A nice
day, a beach. Of course there would be people. He'd locked himself in securely so there was really nothing to worry about.

He turned away from the firing slit and surveyed the interior
of the gun room. It was about thirty feet in diameter, the circular stairway from the magazine below opening up beside the
remains of the gun mount. The gunner's chair was still intact,
and so was the wedge-shaped firing control box in front of it. He
went across to the center of the room and sat down in the metal
seat. Soon, for Dennis Penpraze, it was 1943 and the little yellow
men of Nippon swarmed just below the horizon. It was his duty
to keep them back, and keep them back he would with his trusty
six-inch gun.

As Penpraze sent shell after imaginary shell hurtling at the
phantom invaders, the two RCMP officers maintaining surveillance on the beach were becoming increasingly uncomfortable.
Wreck Beach happened to be the only nude beach in Vancouver,
and to avoid drawing attention to themselves, they had been
forced to strip naked. Their clothes, hand guns, and the walkie-
talkie were bundled between them on the sand. They had been
on the beach for almost seven hours now, and both of them were
burned a painful lobster red.

A mile to the east the Chris Craft bobbed lazily on the gentle swell. The tall, freckled man in the cockpit lowered his binoculars and looked at his watch. Two thirty-five. Almost time. He bent low and went through the narrow hatchway into the tiny cabin. He unpinned the June Pet of the Month from the bulkhead, opened the hinged panel she had covered, and took out a compact directional transmitter. The transmitter was tuned to the same frequency as the receiver hidden in the firing control box of the gun-tower emplacement.

Chapter Fifteen

JULY 4

2:45 P.M. PACIFIC DAYLIGHT TIME
5:45 P.M. EASTERN DAYLIGHT TIME

A continuous stream of vehicles was pouring out through the main gates of the Richland Nuclear Reservation reactor compound, acting on the evacuation order issued by Jonathan Kane. The vehicles carried the state troopers, the national guardsmen, and the last few remaining members of Kellerman's staff on hand at the complex. In addition to the personnel carriers there were a number of large trucks, all but a few appropriated from the town of Richland, which had been pressed into service to carry the radioactive isotopes and other portable sources of radiation off the reservation. They had been given instructions to make for the ERDA installation at Idaho Falls, a few hundred miles to the eastward.

By 2:45 P.M. the reactor compound was empty except for Kane and a helicopter pilot from the Washington State Police who was pacing nervously back and forth in front of his machine.

Kane stood on the outer earth wall, taking a final look around. A delicate fan of air coming out of the north plucked at their clothing and sent up small whirling funnels of dust at his feet. The sun was falling in the west now, throwing a dark pool of shadow across the buttressed reactor. Only the high dome of the containment sphere, a giant white globe of metal, was still visible, its shape flawed only by the winding helix of the maintenance catwalk. Pandora's box, thought Kane. The wind puffed dust in his face, gusting stronger. Let's just hope I've screwed the lid down tight enough. He turned away from the breeder and ran down the embankment to the waiting helicopter.

The chopper pilot had radioed ahead, and by the time they set down beside the F1-11, Canterra had wound the idling engines to a banshee wail in preparation for take-off. Kane struggled into his pressure suit, climbed up into the cockpit, and strapped himself in. A few seconds later they were howling down the makeshift runway and into the air.

When they reached cruising altitude, heading up over the mountains to Portland, Canterra locked in the autopilot and motioned Kane to turn on his intercom.

"Wanted to wait until we were in the air, Mr. Kane," said the pilot. "Uh, just before the chopper arrived I got a pretty weird message relayed from EPC Portland." Canterra paused.

"What do you mean, weird?" asked Kane.

Behind his oxygen mask Canterra frowned. "They got an anonymous call. Some guy said to pass a message along to you. He said to tell you that Miss Daly was in good hands. That mean anything to you, Mr. Kane?"

"Son of a bitch!" hissed Rudnick. He was seated in front of the monitors in the security room, his good hand running across the selector switches as he tried to locate Snyder on one of the more than twenty cameras scattered through the breeder.

"The prick has to be in here somewhere!" he muttered to himself.

Bateman, seated beside him, had come out of his shock at Paula's death to find himself consumed by an anger far stronger than any other emotion he had felt in his lifetime.

"Find him," he said. "Come on, find him."

"Ah, find him yourself," said Rudnick, coughing lightly. "He could be anywhere. We've only got one advantage."

"What's that?" said Bateman.

"He doesn't know we've been sealed off," said Rudnick still flipping through the switches, his eyes glued to the monitors. "He probably thinks there's a battalion of state cops about to come down on his head any minute. He's shitting his pants. Running scared." Rudnick coughed again, the sound harsher this time, and leaned forward, his tired eyes peering closely at one of the screens showing the inside of the fuel loading chamber.

"Got the bastard!" he yelled, his voice disintegrating into a racking cough. He recovered and wiped the blood from his lips. He pointed at one of the monitors. "Look—up there on the catwalk, in behind that pipe!" Rudnick jabbed his thick index finger at the screen, pinpointing a small square of dark fabric protruding from behind one of the giant coolant conduits that ran along beside the catwalk in the fuel loading chamber.

Bateman glanced at the screen. "So you found him," he said, looking at Rudnick's gloating expression rather than the screen. "Now what do we do?"

"We go and get him!" said Rudnick, rising from his chair.

Mike Stalling grappled with the heavy strongbox, bumping it down the stairs from the office mezzanine at the south end of the cavernous Aluminum Company of America smelting plant. He grunted as he pulled the box down the last few steps and rested for a moment. Then he dragged it toward the forklift truck he had brought from the other end of the plant. He manhandled the box onto the pallet covering the forks, his thick biceps bulging with the effort, then climbed into the driver's seat.

"Almost home!" he whispered. He started the forklift and set off down the pot lines of cooling aluminum ingot molds, heading toward the loading doors at the far end of the immense building. As he drove quickly along between the fuming rows of four-foot-square pots, he speculated on the amount of money in the box. The holiday shift usually took its overtime in cash, so there would probably be forty or fifty thousand. Enough to kiss the place good-by forever. It had been worth the danger. When the evacuation order had come in at the hands of a state trooper he acted as though he'd had the whole thing planned for weeks, hiding in one of the washrooms and waiting until the place had emptied. When he was sure that he was alone in the plant, he had come out of the washroom, gone to the office, and begun to search for the strongbox. He had finally located it in the assistant manager's cubicle.

Mike Stalling was twenty-eight, a bachelor, and had a degree in economics. His degree hadn't taken him any further than graduation. Actually, he had been lucky to get even his present job as a line worker in the Alcoa plant twenty-five miles outside of Wenatchee on the Columbia. But Mike Stalling did not feel lucky. He hated both Wenatchee and Alcoa, and for the past eighteen months his only ambition had been to get the hell out of both at the first opportunity. The flood warning was tailor-made. If it was as bad as the cop had said, the plant was probably going to be out of action for a long time. No one was going to miss the strongbox until it was too late, if they ever missed it at all.

He glanced up as he passed beneath the shadow of one of the forty-odd cast-iron "kettles" of molten aluminum suspended from the ceiling rails twenty-five feet above. The enormous vessels were filled at one of the six big smelters ranged along the sides of the plant, then maneuvered by heavy-duty donkey engines along the track to the appropriate pot line. The kettle would move slowly along the line, filling up each pot as it went, guided by the line workers.

Stalling grinned as he neared the end of the line. Even if the flood didn't do much damage, there was going to be hell to pay. The longer the kettles waited, untended, their loads cooling, the worse it would be. In another hour or so they would have cooled beyond the point at which they could be emptied. If they were allowed to cool completely, they would have to be dismantled and their loads of solid metal broken up and resmelted. Compared with what that would cost, the fifty grand in the strongbox would look like peanuts.

The flood wave, seventy-one feet high and traveling at an even fifty miles an hour, struck the Alcoa plant broadside, lifting the entire north wall off its foundations. The ninety-foot roof trusses buckled and the ceiling began to collapse, the rails holding the kettles twisting with a hideous screeching that rose above

the wild hammering of the water. One by one the kettles fell
away toward the floor.

One of the kettles hit the concrete less than twenty feet from
Stalling. It split into a dozen pieces on impact, spraying white-
hot aluminum in all directions. Several thousand gallons of the
man-made lava splashed over the forklift, the strongbox, and
Stalling. The flood roared through the shattered building, putting out a hundred fires before they had a chance to spread and
quick cooling the huge gouts of aluminum from the kettles, including the lump containing Stalling's body. The would-be thief
had been incinerated at the first touch of the metal, but the
rapid cooling left a perfect hollow mold where his body had
been, the shadow image of his screaming face preserved forever
in its monstrous tin-can tomb.

The wave moved downriver, striking the town of Vantage and
rolling over it. Seven minutes later it outflanked the concrete and
earthfill Wanapum Dam on both sides, then pushed its center
portion flat.

After a breakneck passage over the placid recreational pool of
the Priest Rapids Reservoir the flood climbed the dam of the
same name, destroying it completely.

Although the wave had spread to almost a mile in width after
its entrance onto the broad flood plain below the Priest Rapids
Dam, a number of factors conspired to keep the juggernaut on
its course.

To an observer standing on the banks of the Columbia the surrounding plain would have appeared almost perfectly level, ex-
tending for several miles to the foothills of the Cascades in the
west, and rising much more abruptly on the eastern bank. In fact
the land has, in geographical terms, quite a steep grade in cross
section looking like a flattened V with the river at its lowest
point.

Water tends to follow the path of least resistance and rather
than fight the forces of gravity the flood moved along the original course of the river. The riverbed also offered the least fric-
tional resistance; friction, in the mathematics of hydrology being
the greatest deterrent to velocity. The result was that the wave
began to assume a blunt, spearheaded shape, its face narrowed
into a rounded point that ran along the ancient riverbed, its

leading edges flaring out behind. The water now weighed more than 500 billion tons, and surface tension held the edges in a steeply curved slope on either side, looking like a vast, searching finger of volcanic lava moving at almost fifty miles per hour across the parched land.

Chapter Sixteen

JULY 4

"You were supposed to be protecting her, for Christ's sake!" yelled Kane, pounding his fist on the desk. "What the hell are you doing?" he glared down at Eleanor Sweet, seated behind the desk in the small office next to the EPC boardroom. A constant murmur of voices came from outside as people gathered for the planning meeting.

"Please sit down, Mr. Kane," said Sweet, motioning to a leather couch set against one wall. "You look exhausted."

"I don't want to sit down. I want some answers!" said Kane savagely. "I want to know why all the resources of the governor's office couldn't keep one person from getting kidnapped in broad daylight!"

"Mr. Kane. Please." Sweet gestured toward the couch. Kane remained standing, staring at her, his expression dark.

Sweet shrugged. "We have good reason to believe that Miss Daly was not kidnapped from the motel room," she began, her voice firm and controlled. "There is evidence to suggest that she left of her own volition."

"I thought you said the guard had been murdered," said Kane.

Sweet nodded. "Quite so. It would seem, however, that by the time the guard was killed Miss Daly had already gone. According to the report I received, all the connecting doors between your room and the end unit in the motel had been broken open and the window in the end unit had its screen torn out. All the doors had been broken from the inside, Mr. Kane." Sweet cleared her throat. "After further investigation it was discovered that Miss Daly subsequently used her American Express card to purchase an airline ticket. The destination was Portland."

"Here?" said Kane, bemused.

Sweet nodded again. "Apparently. The kidnappers, if they really have her, must have picked her up in Portland after she landed."

"They've got her, all right," said Kane. "It's the only assumption we can afford to make judging by past performance." He fingered the tender swelling above his temple. "So what do we do now?" he asked.

"Nothing," said Sweet. "There is nothing we can do."

He stared at her, not believing. "I'm going to pretend I didn't hear that," he said.

Sweet put her palms flat on the desk in front of her and sat up very straight. "Mr. Kane, try to understand our position," she said. "The NOAA satellite and the Seattle EPC computer predict an impact time of between 7:00 and 7:45 P.M. this evening. We have been left with a little more than four hours to evacuate the city, or to stop the flood from reaching it. The general evacuation order was given less than an hour ago, and as you are no doubt aware, Portland is already in chaos. There has not been a full-scale evacuation of an American city since the Civil War. Nobody was prepared. Our chances of finding Miss Daly in the midst of half a million evacuees are slim, to say the least, even if we could afford to divert any manpower to the search."

Kane sat down on the couch. Sweet was right. His arrival at Portland International had been like a descent into a madhouse. Thousands of people were swarming all over the terminal and the runways, desperately trying to get on the last flights out of the city.

He and Canterra had been whisked aboard a traffic helicopter

commandeered from K-VAN radio. Kane, already disoriented and
nauseous from his high-speed travel, was further sickened by
what they saw as they made the trip from the airport to the roof-
top helipad of the EPC building.

Portland was seething like a broken anthill. More than 350,000
people, almost all of them on foot, were in the streets, heading
west toward the relative safety of the hills on the far side of the
Williamette River. Hordes of frightened citizens found themselves trapped as they reached intersections jammed with abandoned cars. The mobs turned and went back the way they had
come. Anyone who couldn't turn or get out of the way fast
enough was trampled.

Everywhere, rising plumes of smoke pinpointed the hundreds
of fires that had sprung up throughout the city, the result of cigarettes hastily extinguished, stoves left on, and backyard barbe-
cues abandoned in the panic. For the most part the fires grew
unchecked; the fire department was unable to reach the blazes
through the choking crowds of people.

Somewhere in all of that was Chuck. He rubbed a palm across
his forehead. His whole body was one dull ache, with sharp
patches of pain at his head, hand, and side. But he fought it
back, forcing his brain to function logically. He looked up at
Sweet.

"Is Hammond going to be at this meeting?" he asked.

Sweet frowned. "No," she said slowly. "He stayed in Olympia,
as I recall. Something about contacting his superiors in Washington before he made any decisions."

Kane grunted, his lip curling. "It figures," he said.

Sweet looked at him quizzically, catching the anger in his
voice. "What does General Hammond have to do with Miss
Daly?" she asked finally.

"Plenty," said Kane icily. "He's up to his red neck in this
whole thing. I'm not exactly sure what his part is, or was, but
he's involved. He knew!" Kane dragged himself up off the couch.
At the door he stopped, his hand on the knob, and turned to
Sweet.

"You can be my witness. If Miss Daly doesn't make it through
this thing, if she's killed, or hurt in any way, I am personally
going to see that General Hammond is drawn and quartered."

The door slammed behind him. Miss Sweet looked at it for a second, puzzled; then she went back to work on the papers in front of her.

"Roadblock up ahead," said Lachlan, slowing the car.

Bonner, beside him, reached into his shoulder holster and took out the Smith and Wesson, hiding it on the seat with the breadth of his wide black hand. Charlene Daly leaned forward in the back seat, trying to see the roadblock. Hobbs, the third member of the kidnap team, grabbed her by the upper arm, his manicured fingers digging painfully into the muscle, and pulled her back. He had taken out his gun, too, and she felt the snub barrel pressing into the soft tissue of her side, just below the right breast.

"One peep and I'll blow your tit off," he said, smiling with his chubby wet lips.

Chuck turned to him, repulsed by his soft pink face and the faint peppermint of his breath. This one was different from Bonner. He liked hurting people.

She returned his smile. "You're the type who likes guns because you think your cock is too short. And you're probably right."

Hobbs's face reddened. "You fucking—"

"Shut up!" snapped the black man. "Take it slow," he said, turning to Lachlan. They pulled to a stop twenty feet away from the three police cars that were parked across the intersection of Northeast Halsey and 122nd in the well-to-do residential neighborhood just west of the Glendover Golf Club. Pedestrians crowded the wide sidewalks in front of the spacious houses on either side of the street.

One of the half-dozen policemen at the roadblock came toward them, gloved hand on holster, cool and efficient in his crisp uniform, his eyes protected from the midafternoon sun by a pair of sunglasses. Lachlan rolled down the window as the policeman came up to the car. He rested one hand on the roof and leaned down to look inside. Chuck felt the gun in Hobbs's hand pressing into her and kept her face blank.

"You're going east," said the officer.

"That's right," said Bonner trying for the correct blend of

polite impatience. "We have a plane at the Troutdale Airport."
Bonner wasn't lying. He had been instructed to use the small
plane to ferry Chuck to Seattle.

"No one's going east," said the policeman. "You go west, and
on foot. Out of the car, please. You can leave it right here. Lock
it and take the keys with you."

Bonner smiled. "I'm afraid that won't be possible," he said, his
hand cupping the gun on the seat. "We really have to get to
Troutdale. We'll be quite all right."

"I don't think you understand me, sir," said the policeman.
"Orders are that you go west and on foot. So out, please. Right
now!" He stepped back from the car, reaching for the door handle with one hand, the other straying toward his holster.

Bonner brought up the pistol, leaned across Lachlan and fired
three times, one bullet into each lens of the sunglasses and a
third into the open mouth.

"Go!" he snapped.

Lachlan slapped the shift into reverse and slammed down on
the accelerator. They rocketed away from the roadblock. Lachlan spun the wheel and the heavy car went into a lurching skid.
He plunged his foot down on the brake, jerked the shift up, and
they roared off the way they had come, tires screeching, weaving
through the dozens of abandoned cars on the street, sending
dozens of already terrified people scurrying to safety. As Chuck,
sobbing with terror, put her hands over her face and tried to
choke back the vomit that rose as the policeman's head was disintegrated, she dimly heard the sirens begin to wail in pursuit.

The two men walked carefully through the open air-lock doorway to the fuel loading chamber. Rudnick's eyes swept the gal-
lery high above them at the other end of the cavernous room.
The piece of fabric was still there, poking out from behind the
huge cooling pipe.

A third of the way across the room was a large rubber-
wheeled dolly used in the loading process. Rudnick and Bateman
skirted around the edge of the room, then dashed across the
polished floor to the dolly where they rested for a moment.

Rudnick carried a riot gun from the security room arms'
locker. It was identical to the one taken from him by Snyder.

He'd offered Bateman a similar weapon, but Bateman had taken Snyder's shotgun instead. If he was going to kill Snyder, he had decided, he was going to do it with the weapon that had murdered Paula. He held the gun gingerly, the weight of it unfamiliar and uncomfortable. Ronald Bateman had never fired a gun in his entire life.

As they caught their breath, Bateman felt a mild surprise that Rudnick had given him the weapon. After all, only an hour before they had been enemies. But it didn't matter now, he told himself. They were allies of the moment, their trust in each other springing from their hatred of a common foe. He shivered. The world had shrunk to the size of this one large room, and anything beyond it had ceased to exist for both of them.

Rudnick looked around the corner of the dolly. The floor of the chamber stretched out in front of them for a hundred feet, ending at the massive curving wall of the reactor core with its protruding circle of fuel bundles topped by the maze of galleries and catwalks. Rudnick had been working at the reservation long enough to know something about how reactors worked, and he could see from the number of extracted fuel elements that the core was half shut down. He looked up and saw the dangling arms of the rod grappler, suspended from its rail in the ceiling. The grappler hung well out from its normal position against the wall, almost in the center of the room.

Those hundred feet of empty floor between them and the base of the catwalk stairs were a problem. First he'd have to get across the floor, and then up those steps to the catwalk. He bent at the waist for a moment, trying to still the pain in his stomach, and grunted to himself. He might be dying, but he wasn't about to commit suicide by trying to travel across the floor in the open. He stuck his head out farther. Fifty feet away to their right, almost in the center of the room, there was another dolly. It was no closer to the other side of the room, but it might be useful. He sat back, flinching and biting back a cry of agony as his ruined hand banged into Bateman's knee. Would his body abandon him when he needed it most?

"You willing to take a chance?" he managed to whisper, his face taut with pain.

"Why not?" said Bateman. The flesh had sagged away from

the bones of his face, and when he grinned Rudnick saw the skull beneath.

"All right," said Rudnick. "There's another one of these fuel dollies about forty, fifty feet to the right. I want you to make a run for it, make as much noise as you can. See if you can attract the bastard's attention. I'm going for the catwalk. Okay?"

Bateman nodded. "Sure," he said.

"Good," said Rudnick. "Count of three."

On the last number Bateman moved, springing up and running for the other dolly in a crouching, weaving run, his rubber-soled feet slapping loudly on the floor. Rudnick lumbered toward the reactor wall, his stomach raging at him. He caught a brief glimpse of Snyder's pale face looking out from behind the conduit high above him, and then a shot boomed and echoed round the enormous room. Rudnick lowered his head and plunged on like a charging bull, expecting the tearing impact of one of Snyder's slugs with every agonizing step. There was a second blast from above, followed immediately by a third and a fourth. Then an answering volley roared from floor level. Bateman.

Rudnick reached the steps and threw himself beneath them, panting hard. He knew Bateman's shots were wasted, that the shotgun didn't have the range to hurt Snyder. Bateman had done his work well, though.

Rudnick looked up through the grillwork steps. The stairway was attached to the reactor wall by a series of L-shaped supports. If he kept close to the wall as he climbed, Snyder wouldn't be able to see him. He twisted out from under the stairs and began to climb. As he moved cautiously up the steps he felt a faint vibration coming through his feet. He frowned, wondering if the reactor had been as completely shut down as he first imagined. He'd never felt it do anything like that before. Then he brushed the thought aside and concentrated on his ascent.

When the torrent finally reached the outlying reaches of the reservation, it had dropped to a height of fifty-two feet and was traveling at fifty-seven miles per hour. What it had lost in height and speed, however, it had gained in simple mass.

As the wave slid, like mercury, over the flood plain, its base acted like the blade of a carpenter's plane, gouging out thick curls of sand and alluvial soil, slicing down to the bedrock, the pressure ripping open long-dormant fissures and faults and sending constant hammerblows of earthquake intensity into the fabric of the earth, rippling the landscape like a flag snapping in a strong wind.

The thousands of steel drums of waste buried just below the surface were scoured from their shallow graves and thrown into the thick soup of debris that had been picked up by the flood on its 800-mile journey from the Mica. Most of the drums, interred without any additional cladding, burst open. Their invisible poisons spread widely through the wave. Several hundred of the burst containers were from the U. S. Chemical Corps dumpings, so in addition to the low-grade radioactive wastes, the water now carried some twenty tons of nerve gas.

As the water reached the outskirts of the reactor compound it ran into the complex maze of holding tanks surrounded by Kane's earthworks. The diking held for perhaps ten seconds before it was swamped. Many of the tanks had been built during the austerity period of the late fifties and early sixties and were constructed with single walls of metal. Some had even been built without bottoms, the designers at the time relying on the solid bedrock beneath them for protection.

The tanks were undermined by the furious movement of the water and levered out of the soil. Walls ruptured, conduits and cooling coils fractured and burst under the strain, and half a million gallons of waste added its weight to the torrent.

Finally the water tore up the compound perimeter fence breached earlier in the day by Snyder, Bateman, and Paula St. George, and roared onward through the facility, ripping up the rail line and ramming into the abandoned buildings. The turbulent leading edge of the wave cut like a scythe through the checkerboard of tall cooling towers that had once serviced the old reactors, ripping out their foundations and sending them toppling into the mass of water behind. Finally, the wave reached the administration building, chewing it to rubble, and moved on to the breeder.

The outer shell of the Richland fast breeder had been built to withstand a force equivalent to a thousand pounds of TNT. It was a credit to its designers that the containment vessel was able to take an impact four times that strong.

The sledge hammer of water and other debris from the reactor compound bludgeoned above the outer wall and struck the face of the building with a crashing blow that shook the fuel loading chamber violently and sent a shuddering vibration deep into the core itself.

Rudnick was halfway up the stairs, when the water hit. He fell to his knees, his bad hand mashing down between the iron slats of the steps. A current of unbearable pain lashed through his arm and he screamed, his lips pulling back grotesquely over clenched teeth, his eyes rolling back until only the whites were visible. The riot gun fell from his other hand and clattered down the steps, the sound lost in the dissonant roar of the quaking breeder.

In the center of the room, high on the cathedral ceiling, the rail holding the rod grappler twisted away from its supports, the long metallic arms flailing, claws extended. The fifteen-ton servo mechanism tore away from the rail and fell in a long, curving arc, striking the dolly in front of Bateman and crushing it. One of the grappler's steel claws whipped round in a final death spasm, striking Bateman in the chest, driving his ribs into his heart and lungs.

Rudnick still lay slumped on the stairway, his mangled hand jammed between the steps. There was no sign of Snyder, but the coupling in the pipe behind which he had been hiding was now emitting a high, whistling hiss.

The wave passed on.

The man in the Chris Craft surveyed the beach, a mile distant. His high-powered binoculars brought into sharp focus every detail of the nude sunbathers, including the two RCMP officers. The man in the boat had spotted them almost immediately from the color of their skin and their obvious embarrassment. He had also seen one of them talking surreptitiously into a small two-way radio.

He put down his binoculars and looked at his watch. Three-fifty. Almost an hour past the time of the supposed rendezvous. The man lit a cigarette, then picked up the binoculars again, studying the beach. He smiled. One of the RCMP officers had risen and was walking toward the tower, studiously keeping his eyes averted from the numerous women littering his path. The policeman reached the tower and disappeared behind it. A few seconds later he reappeared and walked back to his partner. Checking the door, thought the man in the boat. Not long now.

In the tower, Dennis Penpraze was still sitting in the gunner's chair. It was still 1943, and now the Jap fleet was this side of the horizon. The only thing between the defenseless people of the city and the slant-eyed Samurai was Dennis.

"K-chow! K-chow!" whispered Penpraze, as ship after ship exploded and sank.

The command center was forty feet square. It shared the top floor of the EPC Building with the communications center next door. In the communications center the clattering of the Teletypes formed a continuous background to the voices of the thirty-odd volunteer workers manning the telephones, radios, and data links. The heavily soundproofed command center, however, was quiet; the dim lighting gave it an almost tomblike feel.

The end wall of the low room was almost entirely taken up by a giant relief map of the Pacific Northwest, including the states of Washington, Oregon, Idaho, northwestern Montana, upstate Nevada, and northern California. A variety of acetate overlays could be pulled down from the ceiling to illustrate particular features. The overlay diagraming the Columbia and its dams was now in place, the acetate scrawled with notes and figures. A dark green line indicated the path of the flood. The map was lit from above by a row of concealed baby spots.

On a low riser in front of the map was a small table with a microphone. Seated at the table, facing the room, was Dr. Sloane Wilson, the EPC regional director, flanked on the left by Governor Cullen of Washington and on the right by Governor Blake of Oregon.

Ten feet away was another table, much larger, curving gently away on either side of the map. There were no lights above the table; each place had its own high-intensity lamp. Jonathan Kane occupied the center position, directly in front of the head table and the huge map.

On his left sat Chief Robert Simm, Portland Police Department, Captain David Caldecott, Washington State Police, Captain Andrew Hancock, Oregon State Police, and Colonel Mark Lhotsky of the Oregon National Guard.

On Kane's right were Mayor Julius Delahay of Portland, Mayor Owen Melfort of Vancouver, Washington, Dr. Duncan McFadden, chief administrator of the Portland General Hospital, and Dr. Allan Brewster of the Portland Red Cross.

In the unlit area behind the large table sat Canterra, the audio technicians recording the proceedings, and the Secret Service agents assigned to protect the two governors.

For almost an hour now, they had been trying to iron out the hundreds of details requiring immediate attention. From time to time a worker from the adjoining communications center would enter silently and go to the map behind the head table. The newest information received from the NOAA satellite would be added to the map, the flood line extended and the time written in beside the new position. So far the line stretched down to a point just above Richland.

Kane was becoming increasingly agitated as he sat listening to the detailed reports and recommendations from the officials in the room. So far they had dealt with the Red Cross, McFadden's concerns about the movement of intensive-care patients and the evacuation of the Portland asylum, and the two mayors. The chairman had bypassed Kane for the moment in favor of a report from Chief Simm.

"It's getting out of hand," said Simm. "My men are reporting incidents from all over. Crazy things. It's becoming a riot."

"You have been given authority to use as much force as you deem necessary, haven't you?" asked Dr. Wilson.

Simm snorted. "Fat lot of good that does!" he scowled. "People are refusing to obey the no-car order. One of my men was shot to death by some people in a car trying to head east. East! It's insane!"

"I would agree that these are not normal times," put in Gloria Cullen from her seat beside Wilson. "However, you must be prepared for this kind of thing. This is a high-stress situation. People are bound to act irrationally. The point is that beyond these isolated incidents things are, by all reports, going exceptionally well. I'm afraid we must face up to it. You're going to lose some men, but a lot more people will be saved because of them."

"Thanks a lot," muttered Simm.

Beside Kane the pudgy mayor of Portland offered his own aside. "Yes, especially when half the city's on fire."

Wilson heard him. "Mayor Delahay, you have already been informed of the measures we have taken to deal with the fires. The Forest Service water bombers have promised that they will be here within the hour. They can load directly from the river. There's nothing more we can do until they arrive." Wilson turned away from Delahay and looked toward Kane.

"We have had input from everyone else, Mr. Kane. Now it is your turn. The best—or possibly the worst—last. I think we'd all like your over-all opinion." There were nods from the head table and the people on either side of Kane.

"You're not going to like what I have to say," began Kane uneasily.

"What we like or dislike at this time is irrelevant," said Governor Blake, pushing his wire-rimmed glasses higher on his bulbous nose. "The largest city in my state is about to be inundated by what might well be a radioactive wall of water. I think I'd like to know the worst now, rather than later. It might save a few lives."

Kane sat forward, marshaling his thoughts. He began slowly, reducing a lot of technical information to a form the others would understand, leading carefully up to what he really had to say. "Gentlemen, Governor Cullen, we're in trouble. The flood should by now have reached the Richland Reservation and there is no doubt in my mind that some, if not all, of the waste there will have found its way into the water.

"As you can see on the map, the flood plain of the Columbia widens considerably at Richland. If it was only the collapse of the Grand Coulee that concerned us we would not be in nearly as bad shape as we are now. The water behind the Coulee would cause a lot of damage, granted, but it would lose its force relatively quickly. But we have more than one dam and one reservoir to worry about. Eight have come down so far, each one adding its own mass of water to the flood. Eight dams, eight reservoirs. The water in those lakes represents the rainfall, snow-pack melt, and normal river flow collected from seven different mountain ranges in two countries and four states, draining an area bigger than France. About 250,000 square miles, in fact. And that is one hell of a lot of water.

"There are only four dams left on the system. The McNary, which is a low dam, less than two hundred feet, the John Day, much the same, The Dalles and the Bonneville, both of which are in the Cascade Range. None of those dams is going to give our flood any trouble at all."

"You're positive that they'll fail?" asked Wilson.

Kane spread his hands. "We'd be fools to think otherwise, Dr. Wilson," he answered. "Even if the failures aren't complete, the dams, all of them, are still going to be topped, which is just as bad. Look at the map. You see where the river turns west, toward the Cascades? That's the Wallula Gap. The river starts to narrow again there, and the further west you go the narrower it gets. By the time it gets into the Columbia Gorge it's less than five hundred feet across. Less, in some places. The narrower the flood plain gets, the faster that water is going to flow and the higher the wave is going to be. The dams will come down. You can bank on it. That means we're going to have radioactive water in Portland, and beyond."

"By 'beyond' I presume you mean the Pacific Ocean?" asked Gloria Cullen.

Kane nodded. "Yes. I'm not an oceanographer, but I do know that the Pacific Coast currents flow in both directions at the mouth of the Columbia—north and south. That means radiation pollution for the coast of British Columbia and Alaska, and heavy damage on the west coast of California. San Francisco, Los Angeles, San Diego, even farther. We've got enough trouble without that." Kane leaned further forward, his hands moving animatedly in the puddle of light from his desk lamp, his eyes intense. There wasn't a sound in the room.

"Look," he said, his voice fierce with emotion. "Virtually the entire Columbia Power System has been destroyed. That's a third of all the hydro power in the entire United States. Almost all of the aluminum plants in the country are, or maybe I should say were, on the Columbia. This is already the worst disaster this country has ever seen. And it's going to get worse. If we don't do something we're going to be faced with the prospect of an irradiated city that won't be habitable for the next half million years or so and a million refugees with no place to go. God knows how many corpses. Ladies and gentlemen, that flood has to be stopped. Cold. Now."

"You have something in mind?" asked Gloria Cullen dryly.

Kane looked at her grimly. "Yes. I do. And as I said before, you're not going to like it, Governor."

"Why don't you let us be the judges of that?" said Cullen softly.

Kane felt all the eyes in the room on him. He took a deep breath and let it out slowly.

"There's a place called Castle Rock, deep in the Columbia Gorge, just before you get to the Bonneville. It's a big slab of basalt separated from the mountain beside it. The rock is big, close to a thousand feet high and a little more than a quarter of a mile long. The whole area is pretty unstable geologically, a lot of shale and loose rock." Kane paused, trying to summon up the courage to tell them the rest.

"What does Castle Rock have to do with our problem, Mr. Kane?" Gloria Cullen, again, prodding.

"I want to use Castle Rock to stop the flood. In effect I want to put a new dam in its path. A dam so big that even a flood the size of this one won't be able to get past it. I can do that by bringing down Castle Rock."

"And just how do you intend doing that, Mr. Kane?" asked Governor Blake, peering at him skeptically.

"A low-yield tactical thermonuclear device of between ten and twenty kilotons, dropped between the rock and the mountain beside it. An atomic bomb."

PART THREE:
THE GORGE

Chapter Seventeen

JULY 4

4:00 P.M. PACIFIC DAYLIGHT TIME
7:00 P.M. EASTERN DAYLIGHT TIME

The gentle but insistent sound of dripping water filtered through the shrouds of unconsciousness wrapping Rudnick. His eyes fluttered, and he became aware of the sound of his own bubbly breathing, thick and fluid in his ears. He opened his eyes and found himself staring down at the metal grillwork of the step his cheek rested upon. He let his eyes focus on the floor beneath the stairs. It was now covered in water. He frowned. That was impossible. Shaking off the last vestiges of his blackout, he sat up, his back on the reactor wall.

He gingerly pulled his hand out from between the metal slats of the step below him. The tissues around the striated scars of his old wound were raw and bleeding. He should have been in horrible pain, but the hand felt numb, almost completely without feeling. He realized after a few seconds that the pain in his stomach had all but disappeared. He lifted his good hand to his forehead. It was cold, almost clammy.

Shock. I'm in shock, he thought. There was a distinct buzzing sound in his ears now, like the high-tension hum of a cicada on a hot summer day. He shook his head, but the sound remained. When he looked out across the vast room, his eyes swam and he was overcome by a nauseating wave of vertigo. He closed his eyes, and then tried again. It was better the second time, although his vision was still blurred, doubling if he moved his eyes too quickly.

He hadn't dreamed it. The floor really was covered with water. He could see rivulets of it pouring out from the open airlock door. The water was three or four inches deep. He turned his head. Bateman, lying face down amidst the remains of the dolly and the fallen grappler, was half covered, one arm floating free, waving back and forth in the unseen currents. Beckoning.

He's the lucky one, thought Rudnick. He looked down at the water, and at Bateman, looking so peaceful. Rudnick craved that peace, his body and soul sagging under an immense burden of sadness and fatigue. It would be good to have it over, and a waste at the same time. Soon, he reminded himself, soon.

He looked up the stairs to the catwalk high above. It wasn't quite over. One more thing to do. He gathered the last threads of his strength and began to climb, step by step, toward the roof of the reactor.

The President stood alone in the Oval Office, his feet planted firmly over the face of the eagle on the presidential seal carpet. His hands were jammed deep into the pockets of his trousers as he stared at the red telephone on his desk.

A direct line to hell, he thought.

The arguments presented by Governors Cullen and Blake had been convincing—to the President, if not to his advisers. According to this man Kane, it was the only way out.

His conversation with Governor Cullen had been brief and to the point.

"Mr. President, either we give Kane the go-ahead or that flood is going to irradiate Portland and after that it's going to head into the Pacific Ocean. I'd hate to think what the Chinese and the Soviets would do if they woke up and found a lot of dead fish on their Pacific beaches. There's enough radioactive waste in the flood to turn the Pacific into a vat of poison for the next ten million years."

"Damn!" said the President of the United States. He crossed the room and picked up the scarlet phone. A moment later he was talking to General Hartington at Merton AFB.

The car was brought to a standstill at the intersection of Broadway and Northeast Sixteenth. The road ahead was jammed solid with people trying to reach the bridges that crossed the Willamette River two miles to the west and led to the safety of the hilly suburbs on its far side.

Somehow Bonner and the others in the car with Charlene Daly had managed to avoid any further contact with the Portland police, side-stepping across the city in a hopscotch pattern that had taken them a dozen miles from their original position. Now there was nowhere else to go.

Several of the districts through which they had recently passed were already ablaze, and flames were rising in the north and south sections of the city. The last few blocks had been empty of people, the streets vacant, occupied only by hastily abandoned cars. If there was anyone left in the area they were going to be caught in the rapidly spreading fires. There was no sign of looting; the people were in too much of a hurry.

"Now what?" asked Lachlan, putting the car in neutral and turning to Bonner.

The black man stared out of the windshield at the seething mass of humanity on the far side of the intersection. They were packed like sardines, feet shuffling, moving west on Broadway a few inches at a time.

"I guess we walk," he said after a moment.

"What about her?" asked Lachlan, jerking his thumb back toward Chuck.

"Terminate," said Hobbs, sitting beside her.

Chuck flinched at the word. Fear blossomed, constricting her chest. Dizziness swept over her and she felt sure that she was going to faint.

"I agree," said Bonner crisply. He turned in his seat and looked out of the side window. "Take her in there," he said to Hobbs, pointing to an alley between a shoe repair store and a rundown movie theater. Chuck resisted the urge to look, stiffening as she felt the end of Hobbs's gun digging into her side.

"Out of the car, bitch," said the round-faced man, nervously. Bonner turned in his seat and pulled up the lock button. He jerked the handle and the door swung open. He pushed it wider.

"Out!" he said, looking at Chuck, clearly anxious to get it over with. "Move your ass!"

Chuck stared at him, trying to work up saliva in her fear-dry mouth. She spat, managing to hit Bonner with a weak spray. He ignored it and nodded to Hobbs, who prodded harder with the gun.

"Now!" he said. Chuck did as she was told, sliding across the seat, followed closely by Hobbs, his pistol held out before him.

Chuck made her move as Hobbs was halfway out of the car. She grabbed the edge of the door with both hands, slamming it as hard as she could, catching his wrist between the door and the frame. The pistol dropped from his useless fingers and he began to scream. Chuck ducked low and ran, Hobbs's high-pitched squeals ringing in her ears. She ran back the way they had come, managing to keep the line of cars parked at the curb between her and the others.

By the time Bonner and Lachlan were out of the car, she was halfway down the block. A few seconds later she reached Seventeenth and turned the corner, heading north.

Kane watched from the small maintenance hut at the end of Portland International's runway 9 as the two bomb handlers from the Bremerton Naval Base in Seattle jockeyed the long, tapered cylinder under the gaping belly of the F1-11. Behind him at a small table, Wild Bill Canterra was leaning over a sheaf of charts plotting his course through the Cascades.

The President had initially contacted Canterra's home base at Merton, but most of the aircraft there were equipped with weapons of too high a kiloton range for Kane's purposes. The closest stockpile of small nuclear weapons was at the Bremerton Naval Air Squadron in Puget Sound. The President called Bremerton, and twenty minutes later one 20-kiloton atomic bomb, armed and set to detonate on impact, was on its way to Portland.

"How low you want to get in this thing?" asked Canterra from the table.

Kane turned away from the window and crossed the small

room. He looked down at the incomprehensible lines and squiggles on the charts. "As low as you can take it. Five hundred feet?"

"Shit!" muttered Canterra. "You ask for miracles often, Mr. Kane?"

"Can you do it?"

"Yeah. Yeah, I can do it," said Canterra, bridling. "I'll take us up over the mountains and then back along the gorge. Come at it from the east first."

"Why the long way?" asked Kane. "Wouldn't it be easier just to head straight in, from the west?"

Canterra nodded. "Sure. If you wanted to commit suicide all of a sudden. Frankly, Mr. Kane, I'm not all that familiar with high-speed runs down narrow mountain passes. That bird out there is good, but it's not a P-38. No matter which way we come in, it's going to have to be low right from the start, height and speed both. I'm not about to drop down out of the clear blue at full throttle into a pass I've never seen before. Time difference'll be minimal anyway. Five, ten minutes at most."

"All right," said Kane. "Let's get to it."

By the time the needle-nosed black jet thundered up from the runway at Portland, the flood had reached and surmounted both the McNary and the John Day dams and was rushing due west across The Dalles Reservoir, pounding toward the ragged purple line of the Cascade Mountains on the far horizon. Behind the flood lay a path of death and devastation more than eight hundred miles long.

As the dams fell and their generators dropped out of the Northwest Grid, the effects of the disaster began to spread. The wheels of the one-armed bandits in Las Vegas whirred to a halt, enraging patrons, and the trapeze artists above the gambling floor of Circus-Circus suddenly found themselves in inky darkness.

In Los Angeles a short circuit caused by the sudden drop in power caused every traffic light in the city to go green, and by the time the fault had been repaired twenty minutes later there had been accidents involving more than 1,500 motorists firm in their conviction that the right-of-way had been theirs. At approximately the same time the radar screens at L.A. International died. In the ninety-second interval between the time of the power loss and the time the emergency generators cut in there were two mid-air collisions involving seven different passenger planes. The resulting carnage on the runways forced the airport to close.

Seattle, San Francisco, Sacramento, and San Diego all suffered brownouts, and hundreds of energy-dependent industries were forced to shut down. Natural gas supplies trickled to a halt, the main pipelines having ruptured when the Grand Coulee collapsed.

Communications began to fail as line-of-sight microwave towers toppled into the flood, and all the land lines to Idaho, Washington, Oregon, and northern California became jammed as people tried to locate missing relatives in the disaster area. By four-thirty the entire West Coast of the United States was in turmoil, and a quarter of a million people were dead.

In the East it was prime time, and programming was interrupted and finally abandoned in favor of the horror stories from the West as reporters filed stories by the networks' communications satellites.

By 4:45 P.M. Pacific Daylight Time, the flood was within twenty miles of The Dalles Dam, and gaining height and speed as it battered its way through the foothills of the Cascade Mountains and its only passage through them—the keyhole slot of the Columbia Gorge.

Chapter Eighteen

JULY 4

The man in the Chris Craft watched through his binoculars as the two naked policemen made their way rapidly through the throng of nudists, flashing their I.D. cards. He swung the binoculars around, training them on the entrance to the beach from the steep pathway. At least twenty heavily armed policemen were waiting in the dappled shadows under the big cedars that lined the path. Some of them appeared to be wearing body armor.

"Bomb squad," said the man in the Chris Craft to no one in particular. He continued to watch. Within five minutes the sunbathers had been cleared away, and were standing in a tight group three hundred yards down the beach away from the gun tower. The men on the pathway moved across the sand and crept toward the tower, keeping close to the cliff, out of sight of the firing slot. They took up positions at the rear of the tower, close to the heavy metal door where they waited as two men, both of them armed with tear-gas launchers and dressed in protective fiberglass breastplates and helmets, made their way to the front of the tower. The two men walked backward toward the tideline, their weapons raised. As soon as they had a clear shot they stopped and then fired simultaneously.

The man in the Chris Craft saw the white puffs of smoke spew from the tear-gas launchers, and an instant later a faint popping noise reached him. As the benzyl bromide fumes gushed out of the firing slot, the man in the boat reached down and depressed the "Activate" switch on the transmitter beside him on the seat.

Dennis Penpraze, still seated in the gunner's chair, was by turns imploded, dismembered, and carbonized. A tenth of a second after the explosion there was nothing left of him except a melted set of white-hot keys for the truck on the bluff above the tower.

A flame eighty feet long lashed out of the firing slot, incinerating the two men with the tear-gas launchers. At the rear of the tower, three more policemen died as the concussion from the explosion blew the door off and sent it spinning through the group of waiting men. The gun tower rocked on its foundations for a moment, then settled back again.

As the thunderous roar of the blast reached the man in the Chris Craft he dropped the binoculars and the transmitter over the side of the boat, started the engines and headed slowly back toward False Creek. As he moved off he glanced at his watch again.

It was 4:51 P.M.

Rudnick stood on the top step of the stairway, breathing hard. The web of interconnecting platforms and catwalks above the floor of the fuel loading chamber was empty. He stared around blearily, searching for Snyder. Nothing.

He lifted his foot and placed it on the platform and then stopped, listening. No human sound. Just the water and the continuing hiss that seemed to be coming from somewhere close to Snyder's last position behind the coolant pipe. Rudnick shuffled along the narrow catwalk to the giant asbestos-covered pipe and listened again. The hissing wasn't coming from the larger sodium pipe, but from the small steam return conduit that ran beside it. He looked at the narrow pipe, his misted eyes finally spotting the tiny split in the coupling and the jet of superheated vapor that was rising from it. No wonder Snyder had moved, thought Rudnick. Even a yard away the steam was uncomfortably hot. But where had he gone? Rudnick looked around again, peering into the barred shadows of the catwalk as it disappeared left into the convoluted system of pipes and cables that led into the core, and right across the yawning abyss of the chamber. He couldn't see anything. He grunted. If the prick was anywhere close by he would already have let me have it, thought Rudnick.

There was only one other place. Rudnick walked slowly along the catwalk to the point where the curved wall struck up toward the roof and disappeared. He knew that the wall continued upward once outside the chamber, forming the familiar truncated dome that was the reactor's hallmark. There was an access hatch to the roof somewhere around here, leading to the dome and the ladder that twined around it to its summit. He reached the end of the catwalk between the wall and the mass of cooling machinery, and looked up. The access hatch was just above his head. A series of wide U-bolts embedded in the reactor wall led upward toward it. He put his good hand on the bottom rung and wondered if his other hand would hold out, or if in fact he had the strength to climb at all. There was only one way to find out. He braced himself. Then, as he put his other hand out, a familiar sound came from somewhere at his back. A jerking snap. Metallic. Final. The slide of a riot gun being cocked.

"Hey! Fat man!" Snyder's voice boomed out into the gigantic room, returning in the echoes. Rudnick dropped his hand from the ladder and turned.

"Over here, pig!" came the voice, mocking.

Rudnick looked down the thin line of the catwalk. The voice seemed to be coming from the far side of the chamber. He looked, but his eyes fogged and he could see nothing. He moved forward a few paces, his brow furrowed. Why hadn't the bastard fired?

Rudnick stopped halfway along the catwalk, still more than two hundred feet from the far wall. He looked again, shaking his head, his bristled jowls shaking loosely as he tried to fight off the lethargy that clawed at his brain with smooth, insistent fingers. It was almost with a sense of relief that he finally spotted Snyder. The young man stepped out from behind the large air cleaner against the wall and stood on the catwalk, legs spread wide, the riot gun held at his hip, pointing toward Rudnick.

"Thought you'd lost me, pig?" called Snyder. "Think I'd let you go that easily? No way, pig! No fucking way!"

Rudnick could hear the fear in Snyder's voice. Terror. He began to laugh, the sound welling up out of his ruined abdomen, bubbling up through the blood in his throat and rolling out into the space under the ceiling.

The laughter seemed to infuriate Snyder.

"What's so fucking funny?" There was a screeching edge to Snyder's voice.

"You are, you little shit!" Rudnick managed. He coughed, aware of a fresh outpouring of blood, not caring. "You stupid little faggot! We're both dead! We've been dead for a long time, both of us!"

"What the fuck are you talking about?" screamed Snyder, the panic ringing in his voice.

Rudnick smiled. He began to walk painfully forward, supporting himself with a hand on each guardrail. "Faggot!" he roared, the word rebounding off the walls. He kept walking, his feet banging on the grillwork. "Faggot!" he called again, laughing.

Snyder backed away, the riot gun raised threateningly in his hands. "Keep away!" he screamed.

"Faggot!" yelled Rudnick, still walking, the word purging him, a cry of defiance to the gathering shades around him.

"Shut up!" wailed Snyder. "Shut up!" He was backed up against the air duct now, his face shining with sweat and the burn.

Rudnick kept coming, each step shaking the catwalk as he crossed the void above the chamber floor.

"Faggot!" he roared once again.

Snyder raised the riot gun, sighting down the barrel, blinking the sweat from his eyes, knowing that if he killed the man who was lumbering toward him he would be impossibly alone. That knowledge was almost enough to stop him from firing.

"Faggot!" bellowed Rudnick, no more than twenty feet away.

Every detail of his thick body was clear in Snyder's sights: the corded sinews of the bullneck, the flushed, leathery jowls, the lipless mouth gasping for air, the red-flecked foam on the stubble of the chin, the blood-spattered shirt. The ultimate horror of the left hand, held up now, the three ruined fingers crooked in a talon as though invoking some ancient curse.

Rudnick stopped ten feet away. He smiled softly, feeling, inexplicably, a deep warmth, a kinship.

"You're a coward," he said gently, sadness in his voice.

Snyder's mouth worked behind the gun, the lips drawing back in a hideous grin, the skin below his eyes twitching uncontrollably.

Rudnick pulled himself upright, his spine rigid.

"FAGGOT!"

It was his epitaph. Screaming incoherently, Snyder fired. The slug from the riot gun caught Rudnick in the chest, bursting his heart and flipping him over the edge of the guardrail. He never reached the floor below.

Snyder's second shot came only a fraction of a second after the first. It missed Rudnick's body, tearing through the air above his slumping form, and slammed into the asbestos-covered sodium coolant pipe. The heavy wad of lead sliced easily through the fibrous padding and hit the pipe itself. The pipe, already weakened at its coupling, split along its welded seam. The superheated liquid gushed out of the casing and struck the hissing jet from the steam pipe, the two elements reacting to create a violent explosion.

The reactor coolant cut off instantly. Exactly one twenty-fifth of a second later, the core of the reactor, deprived of coolant, overheated, began to "run away." A quarter of a second later, its temperature raised by almost 10,000° Celsius, the core exploded.

The detonation of the huge pile lifted the entire building two feet into the air, tearing it away from its foundations. The dome of the containment vessel burst, vomiting up a pillar of flame and vapor that rose a thousand feet into the clear air. The atoms of what had once been Maximilian Rudnick and Vincent Laidlaw Snyder mingled in a brief and final embrace as seven and a half tons of plutonium erupted in a gaseous, mushrooming cloud that was a perfect, though small, imitation of a nuclear explosion.

It was 4:55 P.M.

She ran blindly on, threading her way around the abandoned cars and ducking as burning debris from the houses and buildings rained down on the streets. She never once looked behind her, afraid of what she might see.

So far she had been forced to detour twice to avoid major fires that blocked her path, and the heat was getting worse. She knew that she was running into dangerous territory, but it didn't matter. Anything was better than the men chasing her. Even getting burned to a crisp.

Her lungs ached as she pounded on, her breath coming in short, ragged gasps. Her legs were like rubber, barely able to support her weight, much less keep running. She knew that she couldn't keep it up much longer, but with every step she told herself that something would happen, that she only had to keep going a little more.

It was like running through a nightmare. All around her buildings were on fire, their roofs like torches, set ablaze by airborne sparks and red-hot cinders. Hydrants struck by fleeing cars were sending up lush fountains into the air, the water falling uselessly back to the streets. Through it all, the stoplights continued to work, blinking red, green, and yellow in the midst of the chaos. Several times she spotted bodies, huddled on the street and sidewalks, where the trampling crowds had left them.

She kept on, down Seventeenth to Shuyler and then east to Hancock. Half a dozen flaming cars at an intersection blocked her path and she changed direction again, going north on Twenty-first, then turning east again on Tillamook. She tried to listen for the sounds of her pursuers as she ran, but heard nothing except the increasing roar of the flames around her. Finally, at the corner of Tillamook and Twenty-seventh, she stopped, unable to run any longer. She turned, heart sinking, expecting to see her pursuers, closing in for the kill. But instead of Bonner and Lachlan there was a solid wall of fire, blocks wide, shooting up gigantic tongues of flame into the air, heating the asphalt of the street into a shimmering puddle of yellows and oranges. Even as she stared, her mouth and eyes wide, a building half a block away suddenly began to smoke. Then the windows blew out with a crash, glass flying in daggerlike splinters onto the road. Chuck ducked involuntarily. As she stood, gasping lungfuls of smoky air, great tongues of flame burst from the empty sockets.

The fire, pushed eastward by the steady late afternoon breeze off the Pacific fifty miles away, was coming toward her fast. She turned and began to run again, fear driving her legs like pistons, the knowledge of what would happen if she slowed forcing her on.

She looked wildly north and south as she passed the intersection of Tillamook and Thirty-first and realized that the flames were outflanking her, speeding ahead on either side, curving arms of blast-furnace intensity eager to take her into their embrace. It would be only a matter of minutes before she was completely surrounded.

A block farther on, Tillamook came to an abrupt dead end. Chuck found herself on the edge of an open field, a low institutional building at its far side. She stopped. For a moment she thought she was dreaming. Parked beside the building was a bright yellow school bus. A short-haired woman in jeans was calmly helping dozens of small children aboard. Chuck began running toward the bus.

The woman turned at the sound of her approach and moved protectively in front of her charges. Chuck came up to her and stopped once more, panting, bending down, her hands on her knees. She was on the verge of collapse. She took a few deep breaths, then stood upright again, brilliant spots dancing before her eyes. She tried to speak but the other woman reached out a hand and touched her shoulder, stopping her.

"Save your breath," she said soothingly. "The name is Drover. Molly Drover. I presume you're looking for a ride out of this hell hole."

It was 4:57 P.M.

As they jetted over the towering snow-covered cone of Mount Rainier and then banked steeply south, Kane was acutely aware of the bomb nestled in the steel womb beneath his feet. The SAC pilots carried loads like this every day, almost without thinking about it. They followed long-established flight paths in the giant B52s, flying to their fail-safe points and then home again, knowing that the chance of ever having to drop their bombs was so slim as to be almost nonexistent. To them it was nothing more than a job.

This was different. The responsibility would lie with Kane. Perhaps not in fact—the political responsibility would rest with the President, Cullen, and Blake—but in his conscience the burden would be Kane's. He prayed that his decision had been the right one. He had stated his case strongly to the two governors, and they in turn had done the same to the President. Still, Kane was plagued with doubt.

There had been no above-ground nuclear tests in more than twenty years. Before that time, the tests had been conducted with relatively unsophisticated bombs, detonated on stable landforms like the Alamogordo Range. This would be an explosion of a highly sophisticated bomb, and the site was anything but stable.

The Cascades were riddled with fault lines. Some of them had been inactive for millions of years, but many of them were quite definitely alive and kicking. If any one of those active seismic areas was close to the area of the detonation the results could be catastrophic. There was a possibility—a small possibility—that the explosion might cause a chain reaction, sending waves of earthquakes throughout the states lying along the Pacific Rim. Although atomic bombs had been suggested as a means of stopping earthquakes, they also had the potential for initiating them, and California, in particular, was long overdue for a major one.

It was a double-edged sword. If they didn't drop the bomb, and at exactly the right place, there was no doubt in Kane's mind that Portland would be irradiated and millions would die. If they did drop the bomb there was a chance that they would make an already horrendous situation worse.

As they flew high above the jagged peaks of the Cascades and then began to swing down into the east, heading over the foothills near Umatilla and the Wallula Gap, Kane dragged his mind away from conjecture. The time for carefully weighed judgments was past. He would have to follow his instincts, and his instincts told him that the only way to stem the disaster was to drop the bomb and seal the gorge forever.

A red light began to blink among the Christmas tree of instruments in front of Canterra. The pilot reached for a switch, transferring the radio call to his helmet. A moment later he hit the switch a second time, and the red light faded.

Kane switched on his intercom. "What was that?"

"Portland. The seismographs just went crazy. They just got a report from someplace in Idaho. Idaho Falls?"

"It's an ERDA installation. Nuclear test station," answered Kane.

"Yeah, well, they just picked up the tremor too, and a lot of airborne radiation indicators. Portland figures Richland blew."

"Nuclear?"

"No," said Canterra. "Not that big."

"A LOCA," said Kane, slightly relieved.

"LOCA?" asked Canterra. The pilot looked away from the forward windscreen and down over the cockpit, catching sight of something below.

"Loss of Coolant Accident," began Kane. "It's caused by—"

Canterra interrupted him. "Tell me later, Mr. Kane," he said, peering over the side of the jet, "I think I just spotted what we've been looking for. I'm going down for a look-see." He pushed the yoke slightly, tipping the rudder controls at the same time. They went into a slow, banking dive toward the river below.

They leveled off at two thousand feet a few moments later. As Kane's eyes and stomach adjusted to the gyrating horizon, he got his first look at it.

"My God!"

It had to be alive. No inanimate thing could appear so evil. The humped back stretched dark and swollen five miles at least from the rolling face, itself a terrifying vision: a never-ending tumble of shining, bilious green, with foam-tipped teeth that chewed away the land before it, the whole gigantic mass surging faster and faster as it closed on the barren volcanic foothills ahead, its hunger impossible to sate.

It was incredibly large—two miles wide and almost a hundred feet high. Its proportions were awesome even from their altitude. As Kane watched, its back hunched still farther, growing higher and higher as the narrowing valley speared ahead to the mountains. With each passing second the swell was forced upward, its face changing, rising, becoming first a smooth, crystalline hill,

then a sloping wall capped with a foaming crest, its base a mass
of broken, silt-laced spray. Finally the transformation was complete. The squeezing banks and foothills and the rapidly falling
line of the river had changed the wave from the bloated monster
of the lowlands into a fit combatant for the towering peaks that
now filled the near horizon.

When the wave struck The Dalles Dam, it was a sheer cliff of
water 9,000 feet across and 400 feet high. It rammed the 260-
foot-high upstream face of the dam at the exact moment Kane
and Canterra passed above it. The impact was so powerful that
the shock waves from it reached the F1-11, shaking the two men
in their seats. In the last instant before they roared beyond the
wave Kane saw the dam, almost in a single piece, lift and disappear into the breaking front of the wave. Then they were gone,
fleeing west through the climbing hills on either side of the river
valley. Canterra eased back on the throttle and hit the swing-
wing actuator bringing the wings forward to the extended lock
position. They dropped lower, over the placid waters pooling
back from the Bonneville Dam deep within the mountains ahead
of them.

Kane stared forward, horrified, as they screamed down on the
seemingly solid wall of mountains. He raised a hand in front of
his face, every muscle in his body spastic with terror as they
raced toward certain death. Canterra ignored his passenger and
slid the howling jet into the narrow entrance to the gorge, barely
two hundred feet above the water, and the foothills disappeared
as though behind a slamming door.

It was 5:01 P.M.

By the time the remaining children had clambered silently onto
the bus, the school and the field around it had become a block-
wide island in a sea of flame. The last escape route down Thirty-
third Street had closed as the fire took hold among the trees of
Grant Park in the north.

Chuck went up the steps into the bus, closely followed by
Molly Drover. The short-haired woman sat down in the driver's
seat, and Chuck perched on the jump seat behind her. Drover
reached out and pulled the door lever toward her. The twin
panels slammed shut, and she turned on the ignition and ham-

mered the floor starter. There was a brief stutter when the engine caught but the sound was scarcely audible above the numbing roar of the approaching fire.

While Molly Drover fought with the long shift lever, Chuck turned and looked down the bus. It was already suffocatingly hot inside the long, narrow vehicle, but the children seemed to be taking it amazingly well, staring wide-eyed out the windows, none of them uttering a sound. Chuck frowned. It seemed odd. The sight of the leaping flames and the thick black clouds of smoke that now obscured the sky was almost enough to make her cry out in panic.

"What's with these kids?" she asked, turning back to Molly.

The driver's head swiveled around as she continued her battle with the gearshift. "Deaf and dumb," she said briefly. "Day camp for them. Teachers took off a long while back, left me with the kids. Poor little things. Some cops came along and told me they'd have to walk. I told them there was no way. I waited until the boys in blue left and then I started getting them onto the bus. Guess I waited too long." She put all her weight onto the gearshift. There was a tooth-jarring crunch, and the bus lurched. "There!" exclaimed Molly.

"Now what?" asked Chuck. "Which way do we go?"

Molly looked out toward Thirty-third. "We'll try this way first. Maybe it thins out to the south." She engaged the clutch and tapped the gas. The bus rolled back and she spun the wheel, pointing the yellow snout toward the street in front of the school. She wrestled the shift lever into a forward gear and then turned to face Chuck again.

"All of the kids have got wet rags to cover their faces when we get too close to the fire. I've been driving them for a month or so and I've pretty well got the hang of the sign language. I think they know what to do. I told them that if they act really good I'll have them to their parents in no time. Just smile a lot, okay?"

"I'll try," said Chuck.

"Good," said Molly. "Let's get this show on the road." She lifted her foot off the clutch again and they began moving slowly forward. When they hit the street, Molly turned the bus south, away from the raging fires that were consuming Grant Park. The eastern wall of the inferno was less than a hundred feet to their left, the intense heat raising blisters on the side of the bus. They were being cooked alive.

They were forced to stop before they had traveled fifty yards, the still-burning wreckage of a house spread across the street in front of them.

"Now what?" yelled Chuck, trying to make herself heard over the sound of the fire.

"West!" boomed Molly. "Across the field!" She pushed down on the gas, swinging the wheel at the same time. They roared up onto the sidewalk and across it, ramming the high mesh fence that surrounded the baseball diamond, a section of it tearing free, catching on their bumper.

They bounced across the diamond, swung around the pitcher's mound and continued west over the grass. Molly smashed through the gears, trying to get up as much speed as possible. They were halfway across the field when Chuck saw the two men come out from behind a clump of low bushes. Bonner and Lachlan. She screamed.

Somehow the two men had managed to escape the flames and had followed her to the school. They stood now, 150 yards away, legs spread, pistols leveled at the approaching bus.

"Friends of yours?" yelled Molly, turning slightly.

Chuck shook her head violently.

"Good!" replied Molly. "I'd hate to stop." She aimed the bus at the two men and stomped on the gas pedal.

Chuck didn't hear the sound of the pistols firing, but the windshield suddenly starred and burst inward, showering the two women with hundreds of hexagonal fragments of safety glass.

Molly never paused. She merely leaned forward and knocked out the remaining glass. Then she whipped the steering wheel around one-handed, sending the bus into a yawning skid, and swerved back again. Bonner and Lachlan fired again from almost point-blank range. The front tires exploded and the bus almost turned turtle as it rammed down on the bare rims. Molly fought for control, gripping the big wheel with both hands. The two men, seeing that the bus wasn't going to stop, front tires or not, leaped out of the way. They were too late. Molly tugged the wheel slightly, and there was a crashing thud. Lachlan was thrown clear, his neck broken. Bonner landed in the clinging remnant of the fence, his arm tangling in the steel mesh, and was dragged along for another hundred feet before he dropped off. The bus barely rose as the rear tires passed over his body.

Chuck looked back at the children. None of them appeared to be hurt, but most of them were crying now. She stood up and grabbed the pole beside Molly's seat. The bus tore on bucking over the uneven surface of the field. They were headed for the northwest corner, directly at the fire.

"We can't go through that!" screamed Chuck. The flames were shooting several hundred feet into the air, the sky a jet-black pall of smoke.

"So suggest something!" yelled Molly. "Just get the kids' rags over their faces!"

"How am I supposed to do that, for Christ's sake?" yelled Chuck.

Molly reached into the breast pocket of her sweat-darkened shirt and hauled out a piece of rag. She handed it back to Chuck.

"Put it up to your face!" she ordered. "Show them!"

Chuck turned, still holding the pole, and pushed the cloth against her face. She saw with relief that the children understood. They began bringing out their own cloths, covering their faces.

They reeled across the last few yards of the field and dropped down onto the melting asphalt of the street, the tortured rims cutting deeply.

"Take a deep breath and get down!" roared Molly. Chuck slid to the floor and sucked in as much of the superheated air as she could.

They drove into the firestorm at over sixty miles per hour. Chuck could feel the air inside the bus being sucked out into the hurricane of fire and desperately resisted the urge to take another breath. The exposed skin of her face and hands began to crack and redden, and there was a hideous frizzling as her hair began to singe. She could feel her tongue swelling in her mouth and she began to gag. Her heart pounded like a giant drum in her ears.

She couldn't stop herself, she was going to take a breath. She'd die if she didn't. She was going to do it, she was. . . .

Consciousness fled and blackness thundered down.

It was 5:04 P.M.

The steep, tree-covered slopes of the gorge unraveled on either side of the jet as though split by the F1-11's sharply pointed nose. Kane stared out through the windscreen, trying to concentrate on the ridges and razorbacks flying past. It was almost impossible to keep his mind on the task. Even though he knew Canterra was the best there was, instant death still lurked behind each treacherous twist. At six miles per minute there was no room for error. After only a few minutes in the gorge they had had a dozen near misses, the looming banks of the river coming so close on one occasion that Kane felt sure they would be caught in the grasping fingers of the spike-topped cedars. It was only Canterra's uncanny ability to fuse himself with the plane, body and soul, that saved their lives.

His gauntleted hands held the yoke as though it were made of the most fragile crystal, feeling each vibration of the jet, acting almost without effort, his feet caressing the rudder pedals, his eyes flicking from the instruments to the gorge and back again, judging, assessing, acting, every part of him in concert with the powerful machine.

"When we get to this Castle Rock of yours you're going to have to do the honor," said Canterra, keeping his eyes straight ahead. "I need both hands at the wheel. There's a bomb release on your side, the red button on the right-hand console. The bomb-bay door release is right beside it. The blue switch. When I give you the word, hit the blue switch, and when we get over the target hit the red. I'll take it from there. You got that?"

"Got it!" answered Kane, his mouth parched, his heart beating like a trip hammer.

Not far behind the bellowing portals of the twin jet engines, the killing wave rolled on, risen now six hundred feet above the river's normal course, fueled by all Columbia's waters. It was a gigantic fist of water, traveling at eighty-eight miles per hour, fast enough to give its face the strength of tempered steel as it obliterated everything in its path. Earth, rocks, entire forests disappeared into its maw, augmented by the clinging line of the Columbia River Highway on one side and the Union Pacific tracks and roadbed on the other.

"We better find this place quick!" said Canterra urgently. "We're going to be all out of mountains pretty soon!"

Kane nodded. Canterra was right. They were almost at Bonneville and beyond that final dam the gorge began to widen as it dropped to the foothills just east of Portland.

Canterra nudged the yoke, guiding them around yet another turn in the serpentine canyon. Kane jerked forward against his safety harness and stared down the narrow valley.

"There!" he yelled.

A mile and a half up the gorge, at the end of a relatively straight stretch in the river's winding course, stood a massive isolated cliff of basalt, a butte nine hundred feet high, its southern edge almost in the river, its northern side separated from the sheer mountain beside it by a knife-thin crevice only a few hundred feet wide. At that point the gorge itself was only a thousand feet across.

"That's it!" yelled Kane.

Canterra pulled back on the yoke and they thundered up over the cliff. Kane caught a brief glimpse of the sparsely treed summit. He turned around in his contour seat, but the plateau had disappeared behind and beneath him.

"Still want to take a run at it?" asked Canterra as they moved away, heading downstream.

"Yes," said Kane, and clenched his teeth to stop them chattering.

Canterra pulled them in a long, banking turn that took them looping back to a point a mile east of Castle Rock. Then he pushed the yoke steadily forward, tapping the throttles back as they slid down into the gorge.

"Blue switch!" he called as the basalt spire hurtled toward them. Kane depressed the switch and there was a vibrating whine from beneath him as the belly of the jet split open. Canterra pushed the throttles forward again, compensating for the drag. He tilted the yoke, banking the aircraft to the right, the wing tip almost brushing the tree-covered slope of the mountain beside them. Then he twisted it sharply, tilting them up on one wing.

They entered the slot between Castle Rock and the mountain at 310 miles per hour, traveling 500 feet above the boulder-strewn floor of the gap. At the far end the space between the butte and the mountain narrowed to less than 200 feet. Canterra pitched the jet fractionally to the right and waited anxiously, one hand on the throttles, for Kane to drop the bomb. Kane sat rigid, eyes bulging, his finger poised over the red toggle, frozen with fear.

"*Hit it!*" bellowed Canterra. But they were out of the gap. It was too late.

Canterra yanked the yoke back into his lap and the F1-11 leapt almost straight up into the air, roaring past the top of the cliff with only yards to spare. As the jet reached the summit Canterra hit the rudder pedal, jerking the aircraft round to the north, still climbing to reach the safety beyond the peak above them. The steadily increasing G force of their accelerating climb drew the skin of his face back from his cheeks and jaw, his eyes rolling back in their sockets in a horrible death-mask grimace. He struggled with the controls, flipping the jet up and over the mountain peak. As he leveled off he realized what had happened.

"Sweet Jesus!" he groaned.

They would have to make the run again. He turned to Kane. The engineer was clawing at his face, shaking his head furiously. Canterra reached across and depressed Kane's microphone switch.

"My eyes!" moaned Kane. "My contacts!" He was obviously in agony. The abrupt high-speed climb had pulled the two soft lenses off Kane's pupils and driven them back into his eye sockets.

"Look!" pleaded Canterra, "I can't help you now. We're going to have to do it again."

Kane nodded behind his hands and managed a weak reply. "S'okay. Better now," he mumbled. "Do it!"

As Canterra swung the plane up and over into the gorge again he saw the wave now less than five miles away, its face a frothing horror of black water and flying spray. There was no time to approach the butte from the eastern side. He rolled the jet once more, the horizon spinning madly, and funneled the aircraft

down into the gorge half a mile west of the high dark cliff. Holding his breath he hammered the plane into the narrow slit, the
top of the cliff a hundred feet above him, its wall within thirty
feet of his wing.

When he judged that he was in roughly the position where
Kane wanted the bomb he hit the pilot-side release. This time he
felt the satisfying lurch as the load fell away.

He thundered on down the narrow alley, the huge face of the
wave now less than a mile upriver, then drove the jet upward,
cutting in full throttle as he came out at the other end of the slot
and whizzed upward, slicing barely twenty feet above the fuming crest of the wave, the windscreen suddenly filled with its
apocalyptic form. Traveling at six hundred feet per second, the
jet slid over the northern wall of the gorge and dropped down
behind it three-tenths of a second before the bomb skipped
down to the rubbled base of the basalt cliff, detonating on impact.

Kane and Canterra were facing north when the bomb went
off, but its unholy sheet of brilliance still scoured their retinas.
Its blinding flash lit up the mountains, etching them horribly
against the backdrop of the sky. The first shock wave hurtled up
out of the gorge and slammed into the fleeing jet. The heavy
aircraft tumbled wildly through the air, the pressure flaming out
the engines. The entire world seemed to be filled with the overwhelming thunder of the bomb as Canterra, still blinded by the
flash, automatically reached out and hit the eject button. The
explosive bolts beneath the escape module went off, blowing the
cockpit section of the jet up and away from the now useless
spear of the fuselage and automatically activating the rescue tran-
sponder. As the second shock wave struck, Canterra blacked out.

With a sound like the shrieking of a thousand hurricanes, the
fireball swelled blindingly up out of the narrow gap at the base
of Castle Rock, searing and melting, tearing at the foundations
of the mountain and the sheer cliff beside it. The basalt tower
throbbed and split away from the canyon floor. Then, with an
impossible roar, it leaned and toppled sideways into the gorge.

The mountain shook and began to break apart as the coiling
mass of flame and vapor rose still higher, the earth below it
cracking into jagged fissures that sent tremors shuddering

through its strata. The peak began to crumble and melt. Eight hundred million tons of ancient rock plunged down into the boiling crater created by the blast, adding a final barrier to the fortress wall that had been raised across the gorge by the fall of Castle Rock.

As the fireball drove upward to the sky above the gorge it bloated grotesquely at its base, reaching the crashing face of the wave in a blast of heat and pressure that turned the water to steam in a single instant, cutting back into the body of the wave for a thousand yards. Tornadoes of poisonous vapor seared across the landscape, scouring the mountains to the bone, leaving them lifeless rock. The remaining water, churned into a frenzy by the lashing pressure waves that tore through the air, reached the newly formed dam. Steaming, it climbed the thousand-foot barrier of white-hot rubble. Then it fell back again, defeated.

The flood's furious passage to the sea had ended. Its final battle lost.

It was 5:19 P.M., Pacific Daylight Time.

AFTERMATH: OCTOBER

EXTRACT FROM THE PROCEEDINGS
OF THE CONGRESSIONAL INVESTIGATION
INTO THE MULTIPLE COLLAPSE OF
DAMS ON THE COLUMBIA RIVER
KNOWN AS:

THE COLUMBIA DISASTER

HELD IN WASHINGTON D.C. OCT. 18–25

Congressman Hamilton J. McNeil,
Chairman

Congressional Document No. A-26-10-81

Classification: SECRET

PARTIAL TESTIMONY OF MEYER C. BURSTEIN, DEPUTY DIREC-
TOR, UNITED STATES BUREAU OF RECLAMATION:

McN: I understand that you will be giving testimony on behalf
       of the Bureau of Reclamation.
Bur: That is correct.
McN: I also understand that there has been no appointment of
       a new director for the bureau and that you are presently
       acting in that position, replacing Mr. Hodge.
Bur: That is also correct.
McN: Mr. Hodge retired recently, didn't he?
Bur: Yes.
McN: Mr. Burstein, during the past three days we have heard
       a great deal of testimony relating to the construction of
       dams on the Columbia River. Much of that information
       has been heard before. I refer specifically to the Teton
       Dam disaster hearing of 1976.
Bur: That is entirely possible. I wouldn't know. I wasn't with
       the Bureau then.
McN: Mr. Burstein, at those hearings the possibility of a multiple
       collapse of dams was brought up. No direct reference was
       made to the Columbia Power System, but the inference
       was there. The person representing the Bureau at that
       time suggested that an investigation into the possibility of
       such an event occurring was in progress. I wonder if you
       could tell the committee what the results of that investi-
       gation were.
Bur: I am not personally aware of any such investigation.
McN: You mean there was no such investigation?
Bur: I didn't say that. I said that I wasn't aware of one.
McN: I'll put it another way, Mr. Burstein. Were you at any
       time prior to the collapse of the Columbia dams aware
       that such a thing might happen?
Bur: No. The disaster was initiated by the collapse of the Mica
       Dam in British Columbia, Canada. The Bureau has no
       jurisdiction over dams in other countries.

McN: I am aware of that, Mr. Burstein, but surely the Bureau
     of Reclamation takes an interest in dams which interact
     directly with those under their jurisdiction? Are you say-
     ing that there was no liaison between the United States
     and Canada with regard to the dams?

Bur: There was operational liaison, yes.

McN: Rates of flow, storage capacity, that kind of thing?

Bur: Yes.

McN: But no direct liaison on the matter of dam safety.

Bur: No.

McN: So the Canadians were capable of building a dam that
     could cause immense destruction in the United States
     without your knowledge.

Bur: That is one way of putting it, yes.

McN: I'd like to ask you a few questions about the accident at
     Mica that started this whole thing.

Bur: Of course.

McN: In your opinion, which was the more important event, the
     sabotage of the dam, or the slide that followed it?

Bur: I don't think I can really make a distinction between the
     two.

McN: Why not? What would have happened if there had been
     no slide, for instance?

Bur: That's hard to say. Since neither event was a natural one
     it seems irrelevant anyway.

McN: You believe then that this man, uh, Penpraze, the man
     killed by the RCMP in Vancouver, and an American citi-
     zen by the way, was entirely responsible?

Bur: I would say so, yes.

McN: Evidence would lead us to believe that this man was not
     in his right mind.

Bur: I think that's obvious.

McN: Yet, single-handed, he managed to destroy the Mica Dam?

Bur: I don't like to cast aspersions, but it would appear that
     security measures at the dam weren't very satisfactory.

McN: Wouldn't Penpraze have had to be in possession of a
     great deal of knowledge about dams to do what he did?

Bur: Not necessarily. I understand he had a lot of experience
     with explosives.

McN: But you mentioned in earlier testimony that you thought there had been charges set at the point where the slide came down as well.

Bur: I think it's probable, yes.

McN: So he must have known that there was a potential for a major slide.

Bur: Possibly.

McN: Mr. Burstein, did you know that there was the possibility of a slide?

Bur: No. It was a Canadian dam, you know.

McN: I am well aware of that. You had no knowledge of a slide zone in that area?

Bur: No.

McN: Yet this supposed lunatic did. How do you explain that, Mr. Burstein?

Bur: I don't.

McN: Do you think the Canadians knew there was a slide zone there?

Bur: I'm not in a position to comment on that.

McN: But you feel that the slide could not have come down naturally, that Penpraze was responsible for the slide as well as the dam collapse?

Bur: I would think so.

McN: But is there any evidence to that effect?

Bur: There's very little evidence of any kind up there any more.

McN: You are referring to the Downie, I presume.

Bur: That's correct.

McN: I wonder if you could explain that for us.

Bur: Certainly. The Downie Slide was located just above the High Revelstoke Dam. It was one of the largest slide zones in the world. During the construction of the High Revelstoke Dam, the British Columbia Hydro engineers took great care to drain behind the slide to prevent its coming down into the High Revelstoke Reservoir. But when the flood occurred, the slide came down over a period of several weeks after the disaster, blocking the Columbia Canyon. The slide is about eight miles long and well over a thousand feet high. It blocks the canyon completely.

McN: And what effect does this have?

Bur: It's causing the Columbia to back up behind it. It has already completely covered the remains of the Mica site and the slide there, so there's no way we can assess just what happened. It would appear that the river may well back up along the original Mica Reservoir and begin flooding into the Thompson River.

McN: So it is improbable that we'll ever know just what happened?

Bur: Probably not, no.

McN: Thank you.

(TESTIMONY DELETED)

McN: Mr. Burstein, I understand that Jonathan Kane, the regional director of the Office of Environmental Safety and Inspection, will not be giving testimony at these hearings.

Bur: I wouldn't know about that.

McN: Yes, he had rather an unfortunate accident. He and his fiancée drowned while on vacation. Ironic.

Bur: Pardon me?

McN: Ironic. The drowning part of it, I mean.

Bur: Oh. Yes, I suppose so.

McN: From what I have gathered so far it would have been Mr. Kane who had the responsibility for regular inspection of the Columbia dams, with the Bureau's cooperation, of course.

Bur: Yes.

McN: And you received no communication from Mr. Kane at any time indicating his concern with the possibility of a collapse of the Mica Dam.

Bur: No, of course not. It would have been out of his jurisdiction, just as it is out of ours.

McN: But he would have reported to you?

Bur: Not directly. Through his superiors in Washington.

McN: But you would have known if he tried to contact you?

Bur: Certainly.

McN: And no such attempt was made?

Bur: Not to my knowledge.

McN: There is evidence that points to the fact that Mr. Kane visited the Mica damsite shortly before the collapse.

Bur: He would have been acting outside his authority.

McN: But you were not aware of any such visit?

Bur: No, I was not.

(TESTIMONY DELETED)

McN: To sum up, Mr. Burstein, would it be fair to say that the Bureau of Reclamation was in receipt of no information that would have led its personnel to believe that a collapse of the Mica, or any other dam on the Columbia River, was imminent?

Bur: Yes.

McN: And further that the Bureau has never at any time seen fit to implement a disaster-warning system on the Columbia River, or any other river on which the Bureau has built dams?

Bur: Yes.

McN: Even though there have been some seventy dam collapses in the United States since 1935, including the Teton in 1976, and the Georgia Dam in 1977?

Bur: Yes.

McN: Mr. Burstein, one final question. With hindsight, is there anything the Bureau of Reclamation could have done to prevent or lessen the disaster on the Columbia River? In your estimation, that is.

Bur: No. Nothing.

McN: Thank you.

PARTIAL TESTIMONY OF MR. K. D. LIVINGSTON, CHIEF AD-
MINISTRATOR, ENERGY RESEARCH AND DEVELOPMENT AD-
MINISTRATION (ERDA):

McN: Mr. Livingston, I understand the ERDA, in association with the Environmental Protection Agency, has been working on a study of the extent of ground and airborne radioactivity that came about due to the destruction of the Richland Nuclear Reservation and Radioactive Waste Storage Depository and the fast breeder reactor on the same site.

Liv: That's right.

McN: Could you give the committee a rundown on what you have found so far? I realize that the information is incomplete, but it would be valuable in any form.

Liv: We have ascertained that there are high levels of radiation in northern California, Idaho, Montana, Wyoming, and Utah. And, of course, in Washington and Oregon.

McN: I presume you are referring to airborne radiation.

Liv: Yes. The levels become increasingly low as you travel eastward. Much of the fallout from the hydrogen explosion at the fast breeder at Richland was contained in the general area of the disaster.

McN: Are these levels of radiation dangerous?

Liv: In some places, yes.

McN: Lethal?

Liv: Yes.

McN: What kind of radioactive elements were involved?

Liv: Strontium, radioiodine, cesium, plutonium.

McN: How many deaths have occurred because of this radiation, Mr. Livingston?

Liv: It's impossible to say at this point. Some of the effects will take years to show up. Put it this way, anyone who came in direct contact with the water, drank it, bathed in it, would be dead within a matter of weeks, maybe days. Things are still pretty bad out there. We'll have to wait and see. I'd say between ten and fifteen thousand actual deaths.

McN: What do you mean by actual?

Liv: The radiation is also going to cause an increased incidence of cancer, shortened life span, genetic disorders, that kind of thing.

McN: I see. How large an area will be affected?

Liv: Once again, that's hard to say. There will be some effects felt throughout the United States.

(TESTIMONY DELETED)

McN: Mr. Livingston, are there any other reactor facilities that
       are open to terrorist attacks such as the one we discussed
       in your previous testimony?

Liv: Any installation, nuclear or not, is subject to that kind
       of thing.

McN: Are there any other reactors that are located in such
       sensitive positions? On rivers?

Liv: Most reactors are on rivers.

McN: During the Teton investigation, it was shown that there
       were a fair number of nuclear installations on geologically
       unstable areas. Fault zones. Is that still the case?

Liv: Yes.

McN: And there are other waste dumps?

Liv: Yes.

McN: So this kind of thing could happen again.

Liv: I doubt that very much. These were extraordinary cir-
       cumstances.

McN: They usually are, Mr. Livingston. I would appreciate it if
       you would keep this committee informed of any new
       plans for the permanent waste repositories you made refer-
       ence to earlier, as well as what is being done about in-
       creased security precautions at your installations.

Liv: I'll see to it myself.

McN: Thank you. I'm sure the committee appreciates your in-
       terest and concern.

The junior reporter sat down in front of one of the visual display
terminals in the United Press International office and took a last
bite of his doughnut. It was late, and the long narrow room was
empty except for a few other night-wire types like himself and
the duty editor.

    The reporter arranged the copy on the metal rack beside the
VDT unit, punched the storage key and began to type, the story
appearing in glowing green letters on the screen in front of him.

COLUMBIA FINDINGS RELEASED

UPI/WASH–The Congressional Investigating Committee into the Columbia Disaster has now released its findings after almost four months of deliberation. The Committee Chairman, Hamilton J. McNeil (D-Wisc) held a press conference earlier today and discussed the conclusions reached by the Committee.

"The Columbia Disaster is without a doubt the greatest catastrophe barring war that this country has ever seen. On July 4 of this year, in a single twelve-hour period the United States lost one third of its hydroelectric capacity and three-quarters of its aluminum manufacturing capability. In all, more than 70 communities along the river, both in the United States and in Canada, were destroyed. Damage to the city of Spokane, which was affected by backwash flooding, is estimated at $175 million. Damage to Portland, Oregon, and Vancouver, Washington, as a result of fire is estimated to be in the $300 million range.

"Worst of all, the disaster took the lives of some 185,000 people and left another 200,000 homeless.

"Due to radiation in the water tables and the soil, one third of the state of Washington and one quarter of the state of Oregon have been declared by the Environmental Protection Agency, unfit for habitation.

"I think this might be the time to quash some of the rumors going around in the national press. As far as this Committee is concerned there is no evidence to support claims that there was any conspiracy involved and the rumor that the man allegedly responsible for the destruction of the Mica Dam was in any way linked to any agency of the United States Government. There has been far too much attention paid to conspiracy rumors of all kinds in this city, and I for one am getting tired of it.

"Although the Columbia Disaster was in no way an act of God the Committee has further concluded that although the Bureau of Reclamation and the Corps of Engineers had some hypothetical information relating to a multiple collapse of dams they can be in no way held responsible for the events of

July 4. The same holds true for the Energy Research and Development Administration.

"In the light of the evidence and testimony that the Committee has seen and heard over the past few months the Committee is making the following recommendations to Congress and to the President:

"One: An over-all system of alarm systems should be developed for all major dams in the United States. Two: A serious attempt should be made in the very near future to develop a potential for a long term nuclear waste storage facility that will not endanger the environment. Three: No new containment structures should be built without consideration of *all* possibilities of disaster or damage. This last recommendation would hopefully include any new nuclear facilities in the United States."

The reporter looked up and found the duty editor looking over his shoulder at the story.

"It's too goddamn long," said the editor. "Cut it in half."

Jonathan Kane sat up in bed and lit a cigarette. Beside him Charlene Daly stirred and groaned.

"What's bothering you?" she asked, sitting up and lighting a cigarette for herself. Kane shrugged in the darkened bedroom of the Georgetown house.

"I'm tired of playing dead. It's gone on for long enough," he said unhappily.

"You think they'll ever find out who was behind the whole thing?" asked Chuck, slipping in under his arm.

"Probably not," said Kane. "Look what happened to our dear friend, General Hammond. Two days after we talk to those investigators the President assigned to us he drops dead of a heart attack at the New York Mets game. Heart attack, my foot!"

"Maybe you're getting too paranoid," said Chuck. "I for one am glad to be dead. It's given my hair a chance to grow back in."

"I suppose we should be grateful. We were both lucky to get out alive." Kane paused, musing. "Especially you. If it hadn't been for those Forest Service types and their water bombers you'd have been burned to a crisp."

"Yeah," agreed Chuck. "It was kind of eleventh hour at that."
She dragged on her cigarette and peered at the glowing butt. "I
guess I'll have to knock off with the cigarettes pretty soon.
Maybe after the wedding."

"What wedding?" asked Kane, startled.

"Ours, idiot."

"We're getting married, are we?" he smiled. "When did you
decide that?"

"A month ago."

"And what does marriage have to do with smoking?"

"Cigarette smoking isn't good if you're going to have children."

"Children!" Kane laughed. "Aren't you getting a bit ahead of
yourself?"

"I don't think so," said Chuck, grinning in the darkness.

Kane shook his head. "That's one good reason not to get married. Maybe I'm sterile. All that radiation."

"You're not sterile."

"I'm not?" said Kane, turning toward her.

"Uh-huh," she said, reaching for him.

"But . . ." he began, bewildered.

"Shut up, Jon," said Chuck.

The man from Langley sat in the idling car and waited. Burstein
would be the last one. The final loose end. He looked at his
watch. Two minutes to midnight. Burstein always walked his
dog at exactly twelve, taking the spaniel across to its favorite
lilac bush across from the house in the narrow street deep within
the exclusive Maryland suburb.

Burstein should have known better, thought the man from
Langley. He should have known that we couldn't leave him
alive. There were rules to the game, and Burstein had abused
them. The man twisted the ring on his finger and waited in the
darkness.

At twelve o'clock the front door of the house opened and Burstein appeared, his inevitably gray-suited form outlined in the
light from the hall. The dog was on a leash at his heel. He stood
for a moment stroking his eyebrow with the forefinger of his

right hand. Then he walked down the short paved walk to the curb and started across the street.

It was too bad about the dog, thought the man from Langley. He liked dogs. He rammed his foot down on the accelerator and the car leapt forward.

Printed in the United States
by Baker & Taylor Publisher Services